DEAR JEROME: LETTERS FROM A COP

Published by CopWorld Press

CopWorld Press
P.O. Box 3351
Ashland, OR 97520
email: sales@copworldpress.com

Editor: Jean Jenkins
Cover & Interior Design: George Deyo

Cataloging In Publication Data is available from the publisher upon request.
ISBN: 978-1-946754-09-7

Printed and Bound in the United States of America
First Edition 10 9 8 7 6 5 4 3 2 1

Dear Jerome:
Letters from a Cop

JACK MULLEN

COPWORLD PRESS   ASHLAND, OREGON

For Jean Mullen Niemann and Bill V. Mullen who were with Billy Considine every step of the way.

INTRODUCTION

Youngstown, Ohio
Spring 2019

W HEN MY OLDER brother Jerome died some years ago we found a carton in his closet with letters I had written him. They range from 1958 when I joined the San Diego Police Department as a lad of twenty-six until I retired in 1990. I'm eighty-seven now and don't get around too well.

You see, I had run away from Youngstown after high school so I could get out of working in the steel mills where Jerome worked and where my father had been killed and where all the Considines were expected to punch a time clock. Maybe run away is a little strong. The Yankees had signed me out of high school and I spent three years in the minors before everybody agreed I'd never make it to the big leagues. Rather than go back to Youngstown and the mills, I broke my mother's heart and joined the Navy for four years, then got out and got a job delivering mail in San Diego. Anything to keep out of those steel mills. So while Jerome slaved away and supported Mom and my younger sister, Amy, I took the wild ride toward the new century.

These letters start as I joined the police department. I was single then, and they almost didn't hire me because in school I saw no reason why a future All-Star second-baseman should worry about spelling and punctuation. The police department sergeants and City College classes straightened me out but please, please bear with me and excuse the flubs in my early letters to Jerome.

These letters I wrote cover my career and how outside events affected cops and their families. I'm talking about the counter-culture of the 1960's and student revolts over Vietnam and the race riots that went along with the Civil Rights Movement and all that happened afterward. Sociologists have made much on how these events shaped our nation. A neighbor--a retired magazine editor—said Billy Considine's letters reflect the maturing of America.

You'll meet my wife (at the same time I did) and you'll get to know my cop buddies Jack Hackett, Culpepper and Frank Runyon. You'll read stuff about my jobs in patrol and vice and homicide. Much of what you will read is not pretty but a lot of it is. Many of the things that went wrong were my doing.

—*Billy Considine*

PART ONE

A Seat in the Front Row of Life

Dear Jerome: Letters from a Cop

• • •

4 January 1958 – Saturday

Dear Jerome:
Sit yourself down in your old easy chair by the Victrola and take a pull on a cold bottle of Iron City because I have news. The news is your kid brother went down to the city hall and filled out papers for the police department. That is right I am going to be a cop. They really need them bad because you cannot pick up a paper without seeing an ad to try and get you to come to work there so I guess there is not much to it except to tell them you want to sign on.

The pay will be about what I'm makeing now $395 a month but rideing around in a car all day beats wearing out shoe leather with customers yapping at you because this letter or that letter did not get delivered.

The place I did this paperwork it is the city hall on Harbor Drive looking out on the water of the bay which is the blueest I have ever seen. Any way while I am there I meet another guy doing cop paperwork, his name is Jack Hackett who is from a place in Oregon called Coos Bay he says it is full of lumberjacks and fishermen. The girl takeing our paperwork gives us the once over and says I guess a man must have blond hair and blue eyes and be cute to be a cop. She was talking about the two of us but other wise we look nothing alike he is built like the fire plug on Evanston Street, remember the one we used as 3rd base. This Jack Hackett seems like a good guy.

I am writeing this letter with my feet up they are sore as all get out from walking my route. If the post office was not giveing me credit for my 4 years Navy time I would not be doing this job. Yesterday I got bit on the ankle by the same mutt that has been after me the 6 months I have been carrying mail. Can you believe working up a sweat in January which is what I do since it is so warm out.

Truth be told I feel guilty most all of the time not being in

Youngstown with you drawing a high wage in the Ohio Works and helping Mom pay bills, then I would not have to hear her all the time saying how much she misses me and I can see her rocking on the porch saying she wishes all 3 of her babies could be in the same town. And even when you tell me working steel is not for every body I still get the guilt, but Jerome this San Diego is a good town and if you ever come out for a look at all the beaches and pretty girls and the zoo and this Balboa Park place which is big like Mill Creek Park at home you will see what I mean. When is the last time you took a vacation from Youngstown that is what I thought you can not even remember.

Your brother Billy

P.S. San Diego is big like Cleveland but easier to get around you hear people say it is just a Navy town but there are a lot of aircraft plants and the jarheads train here too. The whether is good all the time.

P.S. again. You and me and Amy have 8 uncles and 8 aunts in Youngstown so it is not like Mom has no one to cook leg of lamb for on Sunday afternoons.

Another P.S. I sent Amy a birthday card Happy 18th.

• • •

27 February, 1958 – Thursday

Dear Jerome:
Well there is more to being a cop than I figured I had to take a test there were a whole bunch of us and it took 4 hours. I was the last guy to finish and figured I'd flunked but good. There was a lot of math and I wished you were here to help me there was a load of spelling and stuff like what is the capital of Wyoming and what temp does water freeze at and crazy

questions about what things do I like and what things don't I
like and when I walked out of there I knew this Youngstown
kid was not going to make it in the police business.

I went home to my apartment which is on Fern street near
a park called Golden Hill and sets me back 75 a month and sat
there with a beer smokeing one Luckie after another thinking
I should get back to Ohio maybe you could talk to old man
Farley and get me on in your department or I would even be
a riveters helper and crawl under the ore cars. Then I got to
stewing about how if I could have hit left handed pitching I
could have made it out of the Piedmont League and on to class
A ball and to the big leagues. Of course Mom had a fit because
after 3 seasons I quit baseball and went to the Navy instead of
comeing home and she crabbed some more when I did my 4
years and stayed in San Diego so of course I lit another Luckie
and thought about that. Then I got to stewing about how if I
had stayed in the Navy I would only have 14 years left to do
and could draw a pension at age 41 and anyway the days went
by and while I was doing all the stewing I found out I had past
that test. Turns out there was even more to it--next thing I
know they had me down at the police station gym crawling
over a big wall and climbing up a rope that went all the way to
the roof and you had to touch the roof while hanging on the
rope and I did it fine because a second baseman must be quick
to make the pivot on the 6-4-3 double play and not get
mushed by the runner. I forgot to tell you a guy must be at
least 5-9 and 150 to be a cop that is easy for me because I'm
right at 6 and 180 this mail route keeps a guy in shape.

After they run us all over the gym they told some of us to
show up for what is called the civil service interview so it
should be clear sailing from now on Jerome.

Billy

P.S. The answer is Cheyenne. I put Laramie it is the only
burg I knew because I had a ship mate from there.

Another P.S. Jerome what does freezeing water have to do with being a cop.

• • •

26 March, 1958 – Wednesday

Dear Jerome:
They have me coming and going over this cop job remember I told you about the civil service interview--well it turned out to be a doozy and I do not know if doozy is spelled right I looked it up in the dictionary I bought and it is not there. I bought the dictionary because it looks like this cop job is big on spelling so now if I have any dout about a word I look it up.

But it looks like this kid will have to keep on delivering mail or come home to 34 Hampton Court because I am sure I flunked the interview--there were 3 people sitting behind a table when I walked in they all got up and shook hands very polite like and I remembered what you taught me about a good grip so I made sure they knew they were not shakeing hands with some sissy.

Only 1 of the 3 was a cop he was a lieutenant with red hair and lines all over his face who looked like he had been born a cop and been one ever since. The 2nd guy was some high school principal and the other one a retired Marine general with a voice you could hire out to warn ships in the fog. Big as the Navy is in this town you would think they might have found some admiral where an ex-sailor like me could catch a break. Talk about being nervous as a whore in the front pew at Holy Trinity. I tried not to show it and the questions did not seem to have right or wrong answers and I kept looking at them for a sign but all 3 had poker faces like the old gents we used to watch play 5 stud in the back room of Cassidys drug store.

Wait till you hear some of the questions they said what if

you were a police officer and you and your partner found a
business unlocked and you called the owner out of bed to lock
it up and while you were waiting you saw your partner snatch
a pack of gum and put it in his pocket what would you do.
And while I thought it over the boss of the high school says
this partner got you out of a tough spot the night before when
you were getting the bad end of a fight. Jerome it seemed if I
said I would tell on him it would come across like I was not
~~gratful~~ grateful and if I did not tell on him I would be saying
it was okay for a cop to steal so I said I would talk to him and
see if I could get him to put the gum back. One of them nodded so I thought I was in the clear but then the general leaned
way over and his face got all twisted and he said what if it had
not been a pack of gum what if it had been a 50 dollar wristwatch. I could see they were trying to trap me so I said real
fast if it had been a wristwatch I would never have stood for
it. As soon as I said it the cop with the red hair said so you
think stealing is okay as long as it is under 50 bucks. And before I could answer somebody asked why I had not gone back
to Youngstown when I got out of the Navy and I told them I
had been sent here the last year of my tour and liked it and
decided to stay a while. Darn if the cop did not give a big
smile and said real nice like--that happened to me too kid. So
go figure Jerome because I sure can not.

Give Mom a big hug and tell her I will be ~~phoneing~~ calling
her next week for her birthday. I suppose I will hear pretty
soon about this interview they send you a post card in the
mail along each step of the way and that reminds me I found
out the reason they are always advertising for the cop job and
they are pretty slick. They want to have 100 guys apply for
every 5 they hire so they get their pick of the litter. I really
want to get this job Jerome.

Billy

• • •

18 April, 1958 – Friday

Dear Jerome:
You better quit busting that stop sign at Myrtle and Mahoning or your kid brother will have you pinched because San Diego police officer William Patrick Considine is at your service. I will not pin the badge on until 16 May when I report to the training academy on my 26th birthday there for I will never have trouble remembering the date I swore in. It makes me feel old because you were 18 when you went to work for U.S. Steel and now you have 16 years in.

Here is what happened about the cop job I got a post card saying report to 801 W. Market Street for the chiefs interview. Since I was not expecting another interview I got jumpy because what could they want to know now.

I took the day off and got to the chiefs office half an hour before I had to because I remembered another thing you always told me be early so people know you care. So I checked in with the chiefs secretary who is a guy secretary and he nodded for me to take a seat. I had on the same blue suit I wore for the other interview which is the only one I have.

I am sitting there nervous there is just me and the secretary then the door opens and out walks this short guy he is kind of pudgy and not a lot of hair left and he says Considine and I say yes and he waves for me to follow him. I figure I am going in to see the chief but instead we walk down the hall to a room even smaller than Aunt Evelyns kitchen. There is only the 2 of us I see this box sitting on a table it has wires sticking out and he puts me in a leather easy chair and he sits in a wooden one on the other side of the table. You could tell by the way the leather was all crunched that a lot of guys had sat there and about the time Mister Pudgy is saying the word polyagraph to me I have already figured out this is one of those lie detector things. The post card said nothing at all about this Jerome.

I can not believe it was only this morning I had the polyagraph because my head is still spinning around. Any way he
tells me this test will be easy he is only going to ask me 10
questions while I am wired up to the machine and there will
be no surprises because he will ask me the same 10 before he
wires me. Jerome he told the truth about that but he never
bothered to say we would be in that room for 2 hours.

He says where were you born I tell him Youngstown Ohio
and he asks what is my favorite color I tell him it is blue he
says I guess so because of your suit and necktie and he smiles
but I did not feel like ~~smileing~~ smiling back at him. He asks
me a bunch of questions and is reading through some stuff
which must be my file because he knows a lot of things all
ready. We are jawing back and forth and every once in a while
he will write something down he says you are not married and
I say no I am not so he says do you not think that is kind of
funny a guy almost 26 years old and not hitched. I said I do
not think it is funny and he says he does not mean funny like
in ha-ha but funny strange so I said what do you mean.

He turns more pages and he says are you a guy who likes
boys more than you like girls. Jerome it hit me what he was
getting at and I thought about popping him one but took deep
breaths like a 3 and 2 pitch was coming and I says I like guys
to play sports with and have a beer with but I like girls to go
out to movies and dancing with. He asks where I go dancing
and I tell him over to this place called Tops on Hawthorne
where they have good bands and a nice dance floor and to this
place on Pacific Highway right across from city hall.

But he comes right back to this not being married stuff and
I tell him look the day after I graduate high school I am on a
train headed for LaGrange which is in Georgia to hook up with
the Yankees team in the Georgia-Alabama League then for the
next couple of seasons I am moving from one town to the next
playing ball. He says did you date girls so I told him I went out
with a lot of baseball Annies and he said he did not know what
that meant so I explained how Annies are girls who hang around

the ballpark figuring to hook up with a ballplayer who will get them a wedding ring and out of hicksville to a big league city.

He said he is satisfied with the boy and girl stuff but I was not done and I told him after I washed out of baseball I went into the Navy for 4 years and was a sea going sailor and if there were any girls on the ship they kept them hid from me and that I was no homo sexual type. He said okay okay okay lets move on.

Next thing he is asking what is the most high priced thing I ever stole. He does not say did you ever steal anything so I think about that one a while and I can not think of anything and I tell him Mister I am no thief. He says son are you telling me you never stole anything in your whole life and swear to God Jerome I think hard and can remember only 2 times I stole so I told him both of them. The first time in 1942 when I copped a comic book from the 5 and dime store and you saw it and whacked me around and then playing legion ball in 1948 I picked up a bat the shortstop from Akron dropped when he made the last out of the game and he kind of left the bat laying by the plate.

He looks up from his note paper and says you are telling me that is all you ever stole and I said Mister that is right and you can hook me up to that machine any time you want. But instead of hooking me up he asked questions about my whole life and I told him how Dad and all our uncles worked the steel mills and how Dad got killed in the mill and how my brother Jerome mans a blast furnace at the Ohio Works and Mom ~~takeing~~ taking care of you and me and Amy after Dad died and how Amy is going to college the first Considine to do it and how we are all proud of her as are all our neighbors on Hampton Court.

Then he says all of the questions I must answer either yes or no and then he tells what the 10 questions will be and one of them will be did I ever have a homo sexual deal with a man and he says when he asks if my favorite color is blue he wants me to say no it is not and when he asks if I was born in Vermont he wants me to answer yes so then he will be able to see what the machine does when I tell a lie.

Then he wires me up and tells me the machine knows I am nervous and will listen to my pulse and breathing but I did not feel nervous by then because I was telling him Gods truth. The machine makes a little humming sound and every thing is going okay until he gets to the homo question and I answer it no and he looks up at me. Now Jerome this was question 7 or 8 and he had not looked up at me one time-- he looks at me a while longer then asks the last couple of questions then he unhooks me and spreads his notes out in front of him next to this long strip of paper from the machine which I can see has lines shaped like big and little mountains.

He says son I have only one question left what were you thinking about when I asked did you ever have sex with a man. I said I guess I pictured 2 guys going at it and as soon as I said it he gave me the look Uncle Tom used to give you and me when he had the goods on us. I said look Mister when you asked me about my favorite color I thought about the sky which is blue and when you asked me about Vermont I thought of maple syrup and that is why I pictured the two homos. He had me rattled and I wondered what would come next but he gives a big smile and gets up and shakes my hand and says okay son lets go meet the chief.

My buddy from the post office is at the door we are going out for a beer so I will write tomorrow about the chiefs interview. But I made it and I am going to be a San Diego police officer.

Billy

• • •

19 April, 1958 – Saturday

Dear Jerome:
This will be a short letter your kid brother is feeling fuzzy last night I drunk 6 beers while I told my friend about my

new job. Most of the time I drink only 2 and still do not touch hard stuff who wants to end up a stew bum like Uncle Frank.

Yesterday when the polyagraph guy took me back to the chiefs outside office he had me take a seat then he went in the chiefs office and closed the door. A few minutes later the door opens and a guy in a coat and tie calls me to come in this guy is maybe 55 with grey on his head and built like a distance runner and turns out his name is Steele and he is an assistant chief.

He shakes my hand and leads me in there are 2 others there but the polyagraph guy is gone he must of slipped out the side door. The chief of police himself is standing behind his desk looking snazzy in his uniform. He shakes my hand says how do you do Considine and like wise the 3rd guy wearing a coat and tie does the same he is another assistant chief. I was too nervous to catch his name but the chief himself is Matthew Hale a fine looking guy.

Till near the very end it seemed like a piece of cake they asked me easy stuff for about 10 minutes and the chief himself asked why did I want to be a police officer. I stumbled around then finally told them I like San Diego a lot and maybe as a cop I could help people out. The assistant chief whose name I did not catch said if I think I am some kind of night on a white horse I should stay with the post office and I was thinking about that when assistant chief Steele who had let me in the door looked me up and down and asked if any body in my family is fat. I said no sir and he said what about your older brother and I said Jerome is shorter then me and thinner but Steele kept looking at me and said we do not like fat cops on our department. My belly is flat as Moms wash board and I wondered if they were flunking me but then the chief himself stood up and stuck out his hand again. I got up and shook it and he said welcome to the San Diego police department Considine and then assistant chief Steele who is worried about me being fat said you have got a problem with your ~~writeing~~ writing but there is something about you we like.

You are from a blue collar town and who knows you may make a good cop then he said after the academy is over get your ass into city college to some english classes. That is just how he said it Jerome get your ass into city college.

They let me out the side door but I could see in the secretarys office and that guy from Oregon Jack Hackett was waiting. I sure hope he makes it to.

A big hug to Mom and tell Amy I said keep up the good work.

Billy

• • •

28 April, 1958-Monday

Dear Jerome:

In 18 days the academy starts and I am scared stiff about the classroom stuff which they say there is a lot of so hold the good thought for me and ask Amy to do the same. But do not ask Mom because when I phoned on her birthday she cried and said now my boy will be in San Diego forever and why can't I be a cop in Youngstown and before I could say anything she gave the phone over to Amy so that was that. Part of me says I am ~~makeing~~ making a big mistake and should come home and the other part thinks about you telling me to listen to myself and I remember once over a beer you told me because you were so good in math you got offered a chance to work for that income tax business on Belmont Avenue after high school but everybody in town told you that the Considines and the steel mills were born for each other.

Here is the thing I must buy my own uniforms 2 pairs of pants and 2 shirts and 2 ties and a cap and a dress jacket and black shoes and a leather gun belt and holster and hand cuff case and a bullet pouch which holds 14 of them and a flash light and raincoat and rain boots. The holster is a swivel type the kind John Wayne wears and hangs low and swings like a garden gate. Jack Hackett bought his stuff at the same time because he made it too and starts the same day as me and he said what a crock paying for a slicker and boots in a town whose idea of rain is 9 inches a year. All in all it is setting me back close to 300 bucks and the hand cuffs cost 13.85 and I asked if they would take S&H green stamps because I have books of them but no soap so I had to get a loan at the federal credit union. The Navy issued us everything and tossed in a tooth brush and a razor but all the police department gives us is a gun and a badge and 20 bullets and 3 flashlight batteries. Jack Hackett is my age Jerome and worked as a logger in the Oregon forests the last 9 years and he does not worry about anything. He says do not swet the police academy Billy we will both make it fine and he says the academy will not be as bad as being a choker setter on a Oregon mountain side worrying about a boulder or a two thousand pound log shaking loose and taking his leg off.

I will write after the academy starts if I have time Jerome I wish it started tomorrow because I stew about it day and night both.

Billy

P.S. At Christmas I gave myself a little Philco TV set and if I had of known I was going to be a cop I would have used the $$ for my uniforms. The rabbit ear antenna I had to buy to sit on top of the TV cost as much as my holster.

P.S. again Jack Hackett is helping me with my english until I can get to city college. I told him I learned to type aboard ship working the disbursement office. He said the Navy typewriters must not have apostrophes.

• • •

June 15, 1958 – Sunday

Dear Jerome:

Four weeks have gone by since I started the academy I have been too busy to write because I am working or studying all the time those of us that make it will graduate the middle of August. This afternoon I took a break and lay in the sun and washed my car that blue Studebaker with the bullet nose I told you I paid a hundred $$ for. By the way gas climbed up to twenty cents a gallon here so sometimes I take the bus to work because cops can ride free even off duty.

The first day of the academy one guy showed up in white shoes. He said Sears did not have his size in the black ones so after they wrote him up we started calling him White Shoes Henderson and I have a feeling he will not last long.

There are forty-five of us in the class and we sit in alphabetical order at long tables and one of the recruits is a girl. There are only about seven or eight of them on the department this one seems nice and her test scores are always right at the top and besides that she is very easy to look at. The thing is the women cops get the same pay as us but they must have two years of college before they come on but men cops only need high school. Of course no women are allowed to work in patrol so they can never be promoted and they have to agree to that when they sign on. There are no Negroes or Mexicans in our class and I only saw one or two around the station I guess they do not go in for police work.

They took us on a tour of the police station which is a two-story building that follows the four sidewalks around the block and is like something you see in the movies about Mexico. It has a red tile roof and a bell tower and even a court yard they call a patio. They call the chief's office the corner pocket because of where it is located but I was so excited I forgot most of the tour except the jail which is on one edge of the court yard. The jail sergeant showed us around he looks like that brig sergeant named Fatso in that Army movie with Sinatra and Bert Lancaster.

I am older then most of my class mates and my ball playing time and Navy time have made me more sophisticated. But they all seem pretty smart and I think they paid attention in school while I read Mickey Spillane books and looked out the window day dreaming about playing ball with Bob Feller and Lou Boudreau.

Most of the recruits have done military time and I tell the jarheads in our class I tried getting into the Marines but when they found out I could read and write they sent me to the Navy. So this jarhead pulls a snappy one on your brother he says he tried getting in the Navy but when they found out his mother and father were married they would not take him. So you can see Jerome I have fallen in with a good bunch here.

You should see the study manual they gave us it is as big as the Cleveland phone book all full of stuff about patrol and traffic and criminal codes and vehicle codes and human relations and court procedure and what not. Jack Hackett and I are studying together he is smarter then me but I know first-aid real good so help him with that. Jack grew up in logging camps where his father worked and told me he read and studied all the time there was not much else to do. He is a good speller so I will get better too by the way they have a new baby and he does not like to leave his wife alone at night so we study over at his place. This Jack Hackett is full of life and does not let much time go by without finding something to light him up.

The lieutenant in charge of the academy came on in 1941 and there was no academy and on his first day he was told to walk beat number 3. He said he asked the sergeant what he should do out there and the sarge said do you know the difference between right and wrong and when he told the sarge he did the sarge said go walk your beat and if you see somebody doing something wrong put them in jail.

We are in the classroom all day except when we are shooting at the pistol range across town where we stick cotton in our ears to keep from going deaf. If a San Diego cop gets caught off duty without having his gun he may as well mail in his badge. You get in trouble if your gun is showing so I wear all my shirts on the outside now.

Besides the lieutenant there is a sergeant in charge of our class his name is Black and he is a top drawer guy very nice and funny but tough when he has to be. Someone told me Sgt. Black was Army infantry in WW 2 and got a chest full of medals. They do not treat us like we are in boot camp but there is no ~~dout~~ doubt who is in charge.

I have scored near the bottom on the tests we have taken so far if I do not get better I will wash out like I washed out of baseball and I cannot let that happen. Tell Mom and Amy I will be sending them a picture but to be sitting down when they look at it because I am so good looking in my uniform they will get hurt if they fall down when they swoon.

Billy

P.S. Here is how big San Diego is in square miles. You could fit in Cleveland, then Cincy, Akron, Dayton and toss Pittsburgh in for good measure. Really.

One more time P.S. Jack Hackett taught me to spell out numbers and is teaching me when to drop the E before adding ING on words. There is an awful lot to learn Jerome.

• • •

September 4, 1958 – Thursday

Dear Jerome:
Hip hip and hooray I graduated from the academy but ended near the bottom in the class standings and was feeling bum until Sgt. Black told me lots of good cops finished where I did including a captain. Jack Hackett and that girl I told you about tied for second place.

The department held a ceremony with punch and cookies and families came and I wish you and Mom and Amy could have seen the chief hand me my badge. That night we threw ourselves a party at the police pistol range across town which is a cobblestone building with a fireplace so big you could stick bunk beds in it. Only cops are allowed in so if it gets rowdy who cares it is like the taverns on Steel Street where you and the scarfers and boilermakers go and not have to worry about insulting some swell from the North side.

The party was good with music from a hi-fi and plenty of booze most of the guys had wives and girlfriends but a few of us went stag. There was one guy his name is Culpepper a black haired good looking guy and he had one of these San Diego golden beach girls with him. I guess there was a top to her dress but she was not bashful about showing her stuff and Culpepper was all over her. Some of the wives did not think she was so hot Jack Hackett's wife said the whore house must have closed down for the night. Jack Hackett's wife keeps saying she is homesick for Oregon that San Diego is too big and she will not even drive on the freeways.

By the way the guy that sat in front of me in the classroom got in a fight with his wife and the neighbors called the Chula Vista police and when they got there our hero flashes his badge and told them he did not need any help. The next day Sergeant Black told him the San Diego P.D. did not need his help either so he is gone. After we started working four hours a day with a training officer in a patrol car a couple of other recruits turned their badge in saying the work was not what they thought it would be. And White Shoes Henderson washed out too not for any one thing just a lack of judgment which Sgt. Black says you cannot teach a man.

Now I am assigned the Midwatch with Wednesdays and Thursdays off the Midwatch is 2000 to 0400 which means 8:00 p.m. to 4:00 a.m. to you civilians. Mostly it is walking a beat but once in a while you catch a sick relief and drive a patrol car for a shift or two. You walk the beats alone and have to carry a pocket full of dimes because we do not carry radios and must check in with the PBX operator once an hour by phone. There are a few call boxes left in the city but they are all on the downtown beats and I am usually three miles north of there. The reason we walk alone is while we are on our one year probation it is a test of how we work without supervision and think for ourselves. A rookie usually does at least a year on the Midwatch and then if he does some good police work he will get picked up by one of the three regular patrol squads that rotate around the clock.

But the thing is as soon as I start walking my beat I forget everything I learned in the academy or at least it feels like it and the hell of it is every citizen you run into thinks you know all there is to know. And I cannot get enrolled in junior college English classes until I get regular hours so will try to get by with help from my dictionary and from Jack Hackett who is still my teacher and says it is some mountain we have to climb but at least he laughs when he says it.

I will tell you about my walking beat the first night I did not see anybody doing anything wrong and the same is true the second night. After two nights the Midwatch sergeant says do you plan on making an arrest before you retire Considine. I said it is very quiet out there Sarge he says if it is quiet too long we will think either you are afraid of making a pinch or else you are letting people talk you out of it.

The third night out I am thinking hard about what the sarge said when I see this guy stumbling to his car at the curb he is putting his key in the door and I say good evening sir and he looks up and says hi, Lieutenant how are you tonight. I explain to him I am not a lieutenant and boy Jerome he has a full bag on. There is a coffee shop across the street I tell him I cannot let him get in his car go in that coffee shop stay for two hours with coffee you will be okay. The guy belches one or two times and goes to the coffee shop. I get thinking am I too soft like the Sarge says because some cops would have pinched him for straight drunk right at the curb. As I am thinking about it I decide to go to the corner and turn around because they teach us to keep burglars off guard by not setting a pattern and who do you think I see crossing the street heading to his car. That is right the guy with the full bag and when he sees me he grins and says hi Lieutenant so I tell him he is under arrest and he does what I say and puts his hands behind his back and I cuff him up and now I have to walk him three blocks to a pay phone to call for a patrol car to do the transport. That meant I had made a pinch and there was nothing to it and I did tell the guy you should have stayed in the coffee shop and all he did was belch again. I guess you can lead a horse to water but you cannot make him swim.

I get back on the beat after dropping him in jail and I think now the Sarge will know I am not afraid to do my duty when I see it and just then two guys in front of a rooming house are slugging it out so I run up and one guy sees me and takes off like his pants are on fire but I come up behind the other guy. He is bloody in the face and smells like a barroom floor and there is no talking to him so I say I am placing you under arrest for drunk and disorderly and the guy looks me over and says kiss my ass. He did not say it nicely Jerome he is built like that Polish guy from the Brier Hill Works so that is all you need to know about the matchup. I tell him to put his hands behind his back and he laughs and I am remembering how in defensive tactics class they taught us about spinning a guy around and I put my hand up to do that when he takes a swing at me and next thing we are rolling around on the ground. Off the sidewalk into the gutter and then back on the sidewalk and then into the gutter again and this guy is strong and I am on the bottom more then I am on the top and then a hand with a leather glove attached reaches in and gets the guy around the neck and it is the beat car he has seen us fighting and the front tire of his car is maybe a foot from my head but I never heard him pull up. When he gets the guy choked out I put the cuffs on him and the beat car says I know you would have whipped his ass, Rookie, but I needed the exercise.

Jerome, I am so out of breath I cannot talk and the guy comes to and says to the beat car I am ~~sueing~~ suing you for strangling me at which time the beat car hits him a lick in the ear with his open hand and the guy's head snapped over like ducks at a shooting gallery. The beat car says to the guy you get this every time you fight with a San Diego cop now go tell all your friends about it. We put the guy in the car and me and the beat car stand outside and the beat car lights a smoke and is looking all directions for the sergeant because San Diego cops cannot smoke in public and I say you pack a good wallop. He says being a hockey fan helps then he reaches in his glove and pulls out a puck and then I understood how he made my prisoners head dance. Hockey pocks are hard to find in San Diego but your kid brother has one now and the trick is do not let the puck be seen around the station unless you want to get suspended. Two pinches in one night the Sarge will not be getting on Officer Billy Considine again.

P.S. When I rolled in the gutter with that guy I ripped my pants and the tailor is setting me back an hours pay to mend it.

P.S. again: I am dating a girl who is a carhop Jerome her name is Reggie and she is from Oklahoma. Most of the time we go dancing or to a movie. Mom would like her because when we went to see Gigi she cried when the French guy sang the song about little girls.

Billy

P.S. Jerome, when I get one of your letters and I see the Hampton Court return address I get ~~nostelgic~~ nostalgic.

• • •

October 29, 1958 – Wednesday

Dear Jerome:

My probation is up on May 16th and I wonder if I will do enough things right to still be here on the 17th. Do not show this letter to Mom you will see why later on.

There are two guys to tell you about one is Frank Runyon who trained me when I was still in the academy and the other is Sgt. Poole who is a sergeant on the Midwatch where I am still assigned. Poole is the one I told you about who got on me for not making any arrests on my walking beat and he has gotten me two times since. The first time was when I pulled a one night stand in the ritzy part of town which is La Jolla you make the J sound like an H when you say it. People who live there like to think it is a separate city it is like country club duty to cops and not much happens but I got a call to see a lady about a disturbance. It turns out her neighbor's cat has been after her birds but the thing is as soon as I step on her porch she yells about wanting the La Jolla police department not the San Diego police department. I explained to her it is one city one department but she will have none of it and is standing there with a martini in one hand and a cigarette holder in the other demanding La Jolla cops and finally I say lady this is the San Diego police department we serve the Negroes down in southeast and the Mexicans down in Logan Heights and the people of La Jolla now how can I serve you?

She almost swallowed her olive and called in a complaint and Sgt. Poole counseled me and said yes what I said is correct but until I get my probation in it is better to squeeze the truth when necessary.

Poole got me good when I stopped a guy on my walking beat for what we call a field interrogation and took him to a phone and called in and sure enough they had a warrant out on him for grand theft. After I got him booked I was back on my sidewalk and here comes Sgt. Poole and Jerome he is a wide shouldered guy who looks like one of those Marlboro cowboys in their new ad and he smokes cigars and looks pretty gruff and when he pulled up he told me to get in his car and I figured he would say good going on that pinch Considine. But instead he said did you search that prisoner and I said yes and he said did you search him good and I said Sarge I am a rookie I search people real good. He said well the guy had a pen knife taped to the inside of his belt and the jailor found it when he searched him so sign this it is a two day suspension because that is the law of the jungle. So I signed it and then Poole got out of his car and showed me how to run my fingers around the inside of a belt to look for contraband. He said a good man is like tea Considine because his real strength appears when he gets in hot water so shut your yap and work your day off.

Jerome on some suspensions you can work one day off without pay for every two days of suspension. That way the department gets extra manpower and the officer does not get hit in the wallet but if it is serious enough there is no such deal you must do your suspension without pay.

By the way I am no longer dating Reggie from Oklahoma one night we parked in front of her apartment and things were getting pretty serious if you know what I mean so we went inside. The next morning she is fixing me bacon and eggs and I am walking around this little living room and I say to her who is that whitehat on the table. She says what and I said who is the sailor in the picture. Reggie says that is a cousin from Tulsa and I said he must be a special cousin because there is another of him in the hall. The bacon is sizzling and I reached over and turned the burner off and sat her down at the table and in a couple of minutes I had copped her out. She is what cops call a WestPac widow because her husband is serving in the fleet somewhere and at first I was sore but she started crying and telling me how lonely she has been and she thinks he is playing around overseas so I ended up just wishing her good luck and walking out of their there. So that is that for Reggie the car hop.

Now about Frank Runyon who trained me I do not think I told you all of our patrol cars are one man except for a cou-

ple downtown and a few in the Negro and Mexican part of
town. The department saves manpower that way and tells us
we are really safer because a one man unit is less likely to get
sloppy over safety precautions thinking they can ~~relie~~ rely on
a partner which Runyon says is pure horseshit.

Runyon works a one-man car and I learned more with him
in forty hours then I have the whole five months I have been
on the department. Frank is maybe five years older then me
and has been on about ten years and I heard he had gotten
kicked off the Vice Squad and bounced back to Patrol and now
is going through a divorce. I never saw him smile once Jerome
he is not friendly with the citizens but stops short of any one
being able to complain. At first I thought he would wash me
out all by himself because I would be driving down the alleys
and side streets and Runyon would yell out goddamnit slow
down I cannot see anything and neither can you. I will tell you
this if there is something to see Frank Runyon will see it.

Another thing is the department wants two tickets a day
and if I did happen to spot one while driving I would lose
him in traffic and Runyon would shake his head and say you
better learn how to drive this son of a bitch. He taught me
when doing a field interrogation to not ask for a guy's ID until
I had asked his name and a few other questions even though
most cops always ask for ID right away and suspects are used
to that. Runyon said if a guy tells you he has been in town
only a week and you have not asked for ID the guy figures
you are a soft touch so starts laying a story on you. Then when
you make him break out his ID you find rent receipts and stuff
showing he has been here for eight weeks and is a felony liar
and maybe a burglar so you have yourself a pinch.

I already find drivers dropping names on you trying to get
out of a ticket like they will say officer do you know Assistant
Chief Steele he is a friend of mine or do you know Captain
Jones I play golf with him. We do not wear name tags like
some departments so what Runyon does when the driver is
finished asking is say to them do you know officer Frank

Runyon and the driver will scratch his head and say no I do not believe I know him. Then Runyon will start writing and say well that is to too bad because Frank Runyon is the only cop who can get you out of this ticket because that is me.

In the academy they taught us about getting our feet in the right position when talking to ~~some one~~ someone in case he tries to cop a Sunday punch on you but Runyon stands the guy in front of the car facing the grill and puts himself on one side of the hood by the fender so they are only a few feet away from each other but there is a lot of metal separating them.

With Runyon we never once went in a restaurant or made a coffee stop because Runyon always brought a thermos and a lunch pail to work. He said Considine while we are sitting at some lunch counter a burglar could be walking away with a sack full of our beat.

One night we stopped a guy who told us he had been in town three days from Phoenix but then we found pawn tickets in his wallet dated ten days before and all of a sudden Runyon walked across the street and stared at a palm tree like he was thinking of buying it. I kept talking to the guy and finally Runyon came back and said has he been placed under arrest, Considine? I said no and Runyon said why not? So I put the guy under arrest for suspicion of burglary because the pawn tickets were for ladies jewelry and radios. After we got the guy booked Runyon looked at me and said you had better learn to make decisions because if you do not your classmates who do are going to take your f......job away from you.

The last night I was assigned to him Runyon said Considine the last two weeks you have changed how you treat people. I said I had not noticed but he came right back and said you are not being as nice to them. I remember unwrapping my ~~baloney~~ bologna sandwich and wondering what to say and then Runyon said do not try and be like me, Considine because you have something going for you in how you size things up and how you get along with people and that is most of what this police job is all about. He said what I want you to learn from me is how to recognize a burglar when one sits on the hood of your car and how to stay out of the morgue. Boy Jerome if I could be half the cop Frank Runyon is I would be a happy guy.

So you can see I am not doing all that well but my two best buddies Jack Hackett and Culpepper are cinches to make their probation unless they fall out of an airplane.

Billy

P.S. Working in a car one night I got a call to a mobile home park and found two old timers dead inside they were a man and a woman both in their eighties who had been married for sixty years. A neighbor had seen the newspaper on the porch all day and their door was locked but when I peeked through the blinds I could see legs on the floor so I broke a window and went in. They both had plastic bags tied over their heads and their hands tied behind them and they had both written suicide notes saying she had cancer and was dying and he could not stand the thought of living without his Adelaide. Next to the notes were checks they had written for the milk-man and newsboy and telephone company and the bills were clipped to the checks making things all nice and neat.

I went outside and radioed for homicide and waited in the rain and by then their kids who had been phoned by the neighbor had arrived the kids being fifty or sixty years old and they stood crying and hugging each other on the curb. When homicide showed up I briefed the sergeant and his team which like all detectives wear hats making them the only men in San Diego that do. The sergeant is a grey-haired guy named Otto he is growing a stomach and I hear he takes a drink. I told them I had been careful to walk around the edges of the room and did not touch anything and I described the position of the light switches and window shades and told him it looked like a mur-der-suicide instead of a double suicide. That maybe they had each tied their own plastic sacks over their heads but you could tell by the knots on the wrists he must have tied hers then tied his own. The sergeant said to wait outside and half an hour later he came back and said it is a double suicide. I started to tell him about the wrist knots again but he cut me off and stood there looking over my shoulder at the old couple's children who were still crying and he said real softly, listen carefully to me Considine, they each tied their own knots is that clear? I told him it was and he said go make my report and put it on his desk. Just after I cranked up the engine he stepped over to my car and said you did a good job, Son.

I wish he would tell that to Sgt. Poole

• • •

January 9, 1959 – Friday

Dear Jerome:

I have been way too busy to write because this job takes all my time. When they pull me off Midwatch onto a regular squad for one or two or three night stands in a car it means I must learn the streets of a beat I have never been on. Believe me there is nothing like getting a Code-3 call which is red lights and siren and getting lost and ending up on a dead end street having a bunch of people running out of their houses staring at you then starting to laugh.

The thing is between catching sleep and going to court and studying this penal code and that traffic code and even a municipal code your kid brother does not have time for much else. In four months if I am lucky my probation will be up but I am not relaxing yet because they have been known to dump guys the night before their year is up. When I do get spare time and try to catch a game or hit the beach I get nailed by either Jack Hackett or Culpepper and we sit down to work on report writing since I still have not been able to get signed up at the community college because work hours are not regular enough. Culpepper says I am improving but told me while he understands how I get balled up on apostrophes and that some punctuation can be

tricky he thinks I am just lazy about not using question marks
and Jack Hackett is after me to use my dictionary even more. I
guess it works okay because they told me how to look up the
word cannot and I saw it is joined together and not in two lumps
like I used to write it. Culpepper told me the same went for anyone and somebody so now my nose is in Websters half the time
and if I bitch they close their book and look at each other and
say let's the two of us go get a beer. If Considine does not give a
rat's ass about making his probation why should we?

And that is not all of it Jerome the report sergeant said my
sentences are so long he fell asleep reading one. Most of the cops
think this report sergeant is a fuss budget but I like him the other
day he called me over and handed me back a report and points
to a paragraph and says Considine this is redundant do it over. I
sneak over to the big dictionary they keep in the squad room to
check on this redundant word and sure enough I see what he
means. I had written how this guy knocks out his ex-girlfriend's
windshield with a tire iron then later I have said it again in a different way. The sarge said Considine go buy the MacMillan
Handbook of English get the 3rd edition it will help you out
and pay a lot of attention to punctuation. The book set me back
$3.25 but I am reading every day about sentence structure and
paragraphs. The sarge said I really need to work on paragraphs.

I hardly have time to read the newspaper or watch any news
and just today I am behind the Greyhound at 1st and Broadway
catching a smoke with one of the drivers who does the Salt Lake
City run. He starts talking to me about the governor of Arkansas
shutting down all the Little Rock high schools so he will not
have to let Negroes in like the court told him he must. I did not
know what in hell he was talking about but he said this Arkansas
mess has been going on for three months. But see that is what I
mean I do not even know what is going on outside my beat
much less outside of San Diego. I will try to remember what the
Youngstown cop told you about not letting police work make a
numb skull out of me.

Remember how some of the guys at the mill would

moonlight at one job or another for the extra buck well we are not allowed to do that here because the chief said cops have enough to do on the job and taking care of a family.

Tell Mom her boy is fine and not to pay any attention to those shoot 'em ups on TV. That is all a bunch of Hollywood stuff.

I got to run now Jerome take care of yourself.

Billy

• • •

March 16, 1959 – Monday

Dear Jerome:

In exactly two months my probation year will be up we get a raise if we make it. The Studebaker is drinking oil faster than the gas station can order it I had planned to wait for the raise before I dumped it but am now the owner of a 1953 Chevy four-door white over blue. The used car salesman thought he was slick and started way up with the price but by the time I got through with him and his buddy the sales manager, they took a good trimming and I drove down El Cajon Boulevard with a smooth running vehicle and a little $$ left in my pocket.

I am feeling easier when I pull car duty but even making a car stop there is much to do while pulling the guy over. Like flicking on the rear flasher and then the overhead flasher and then writing down the license number and turning your radio to outside speaker so you can hear it when you are out-side but not so loud the neighbors bitch and all of the time watching for movement by the driver and any occupants of his car who may be stashing something. We jot down the li-cense number in case we get shot the cover units have some-thing to go on and best you dummy up about that to Mom.

I told you there are three regular squads going around the clock and I already know the one I would like to get picked

up on. The Captain is named DeFreese and his squad is the
best because of how he runs it. About Frank Runyon the guy
who taught me so much I hear he will never be going back
to detectives again because once a cop digs himself a hole the
department's memory gets longer and longer.

The other night I worked a car and on the beat next to
me they assigned Culpepper so between us we had nine
square miles of city and I bet the citizens would not have slept
good knowing two rookies were taking care of them. I asked
Culpepper how is the blonde bombshell he took to the graduation party and he laughed and said he dumped her he is
taking out a elementary school teacher she likes to get naked
then put his gun belt on and parade around the living room.
Culpepper is some lady killer but none is rubbing off on me.

I am working on what is left of a six pack Jerome so if you
are not tired of reading I am not tired of writing. 415 is the
radio code for a family disturbance and me and Jack Hackett
and Culpepper are surprised because we get so many calls
that are 415. In the academy Sgt. Black told us the police cannot fix up in ten minutes what it took two people ten years
to mess up so what we do is get them to shut up and not
bother neighbors so we can get back on our beat and hope
we have solved it until at least the end of shift. Frank Runyon
said most always it is the man who is the ass.... and boy is he
right. I feel sorry for the wife a lot of times the guy has blood-
ied up her face and the kids are crying and hiding under a
table but the thing is the department policy is very strict
meaning do not put the guy in jail because we know his wife
will not show up in the morning to sign a complaint and he
will be let out of jail and a whole bunch of officer's time and
paperwork goes down the toilet. The wife just wants him out
of the house for the night she knows payday has to keep coming so usually we end up being a referee and taking one of
them to a friend's house until things cool off. A wife beater
hates even odds, so doesn't get tough with a cop if he gets
mouthy we lure him out into the front yard then pinch him

for drunk in public view. Why in hell does a woman not leave the bum so she can keep her face from looking like a hamburger patty? Answer me that one Jerome.

Me and Jack Hackett have been having beers after work if the bars are open--they close at 2 a.m. and it turns out we were almost not classmates because an arrest up in Oregon kept him from coming on the department a year earlier. The pinch went like this. At four in the morning Jack Hackett was leaning against a tree in a small town and a new cop who grew up in Portland walked up and said who are you and what are you doing here? Jack Hackett looks at the cop and said I am a hoot owl waiting for a crummy. The cop looked him over and saw the blue jeans cut off at the knees and big ragged red suspenders so the cop said what I think you are is a wise ass vagrant waiting for a booking number. Then he grabbed Jack Hackett to put the handcuffs on and Jack Hackett knowing he had done nothing wrong gave the cop a wallop. Jerome one day for fun Jack Hackett and I put the gloves on in the police gym that being the first and last time for me that is how good he wallops.

The district attorney for the little town said they cannot file a criminal charge because a guy cannot resist an arrest that is unlawful. The new cop from the big city did not know Jack Hackett was waiting for an old bus which the loggers call a crummy which takes him to work. It picks him up every morning at that time to take him eight miles back in the woods to work the tall trees and they trim their jeans so when they get to the logging area and put on their cork boots with the big spikes the jeans will not get caught in choker cables or chain saws. Loggers working that early shift are sure enough called Hoot Owls but it took San Diego P.D. background investigators quite some time to be sure that was all there was to the arrest. The delay is why Jack Hackett ended up in my academy class. Lucky for me.

I asked him how he ended up at city hall filling out the cop application he said he wanted out of Oregon wether weather and was looking for steady $$ and benefits for his wife and kid he said he has had lots of jobs but nothing this good he would not give up being a cop for anything. Culpepper on the other hand was a San Diego sunshine baby who's whose father is a retired San Diego police captain. After he lifted a few vodkas one night Culpepper said a couple of things that made me and Jack Hackett think being a cop was more his father's idea than Culpepper's.

In your last letter you said Amy is knocking them dead at Youngstown State and doing a double major in criminal justice and history. Is she telling the dean how to run things yet? What will she do when she graduates next year?

Billy

P.S. About those two areas Negroes gather. If they show up in any other part of San Diego you can bet a bundle they will be stopped by a patrol car and checked out. That is the unwritten policy but I have a little trouble with it.

P.P.S. Sgt. Poole gave me a letter to sign where some family wrote to the chief saying I did a good job finding their lost kid. Sgt. Poole said you may make your probation yet Considine, I hear you are a good cover officer and I can overlook some of a man's shortcomings if he is good cover. I said thank you sergeant but Poole said do not think I am a pushover you are not there yet.

• • •

May 17, 1959 – Sunday

Dear Jerome:
I am sitting by my kitchen window and can see the Sunday morning people heading for a church down the avenue. I just got home because Jack Hackett and I have been at a gin mill

called Bernie's which is on the waterfront near the police station the place opens at 6: a.m. and since by the time we do reports we never get off duty until 5:30 we just wait. Jack Hackett says knocking back a few whiskeys relaxes him before going home and now, after a shift, I am always ready for a few cold ones and a couple of shots.

Here is what happened. Probation was due to be up yesterday we had lost fifteen from our class since day one which works out to 33% then the night before last Sgt. Poole drove out to a walking man's beat and axed him so last night I did not want to see Poole at all. I took my beat and walked the alleys avoiding the sidewalks and ducking in the shadows and I am rattling the doors of a warehouse and up cruises a black and white. I hope it is the beat car but of course Poole is driving it. He says get in the car and I do and I swear I can hear my heart pounding and he pulls out a folder it is my personnel file because I can read the name on it backwards. Sgt. Poole says well Considine, and I said before you tell me I have something to say I think I am getting a dirty deal I know I do not write the best reports but I am working hard at improving and have never missed one minutes work in this whole year not one minute and I cover good and volunteer for calls and the only grease I got in came from doing police work.

Sgt. Poole says are you finished and I said yes and he said good you have not been around long enough to be making speeches. Congratulations, you have passed your probation and he shook my hand. Then he reaches in my folder and takes out a copy of a ticket I had written and said we got another complaint on you do you remember writing this lady for failing to stop for pedestrians and he handed me the ticket. I said I did remember she almost wiped out a family crossing Eagle northbound at Washington they were all eating ice cream cones. I told him it was a good ticket.

Sgt. Poole said the lady agrees she deserved the ticket but she is mad because you wrote down her weight at 165 and she has lost 30 pounds since that got printed on her driver's license. Then he laughed and said if I see you at Bernie's I will buy you a drink Considine.

So it is over Jerome. Me and Jack Hackett and Culpepper we all made it. I do not know what is in the store for me now I hope I get picked up by a regular squad so I get permanent hours for three months at a crack and can register at City College. But First-Class Patrolman William Patrick Considine is ready for whatever the old world throws at him.

Billy

P.S. Amy told me in her letter that Mom wants me to make probation but then said if I do not at least maybe my boy will come home. Does it ever stop Jerome?

• • •

October 8, 1959 – Thursday

Dear Jerome:
Tell Amy I could not wait for regular hours so enrolled at City College taking English B—Techniques of Reading and English 1A—Reading and Composition. The teacher says it all ties in to writing better reports by the way they give you twelve units of junior college credit for graduating from the police academy so you can see I am on my way to being a Roads scholar.

Jerome people think cops see dead people all the time but I only saw a couple until yesterday when I worked downtown and as soon as I left the station here comes a call to the Santa Fe Depot on Kettner and Broadway. An old gent had gone into the toilet stall and shot himself and since I had a long wait for the coroner there was just me and this dead guy slumped all over the john and I wondered why he had done it. When the coroner went through his pockets guess what? He was a retired railroader. The depot is old and Spanish style, a fine looking place and we figured it must have been a special place to him.

I leave the Santa Fe and twenty minutes later get a call to the Golden West Hotel at 4th and G where a lot of pensioners live for the cheap rent. A guy had died in the lobby sitting there watching TV and the way it works is folding chairs are lined up in rows like at the movies and the old folks sit there and kill time. This old fella dies and all they do is put a sheet over him and call the cops and everybody else including the people sitting to his right and left just keep watching As the World Turns. I guess they are so used to death they can sit right next to it and not be afraid. It is a good thing they had a sheet over him or I would not have known which was the dead one. Frank Runyon said prick them all with a pin the dead person is the one who does not jump. ~~So I am in the~~

So I am in the lobby of the Golden West waiting for the coroner again and a retired machinist comes up and says if it was not for his social security check he and most of the others at the Golden West could not eat. He says because it was the democrats who pushed it through in 1935 they could put his nuts in a vice he still would not vote Republican.

Another thing how come every time a mother or father with their kids see me they say to the kid you had better be good or I will have that policeman get after you. Then the kid looks at me like I have a red eye in my forehead so now he will grow up afraid of a cop but will love the goddamn fireman who is everybody's pal.

I have never told you how the department is laid out around the city. Me and all the guys on the Midwatch work out of the central station on Market Street but there are two sub stations--one a little bitsy place in La Jolla called Northern Division and the other right on the Mexican border in San Ysidro called Southern Division. Last year San Diego went to great trouble to annex San Ysidro and if you got a gander at the place you would know someone pulled a fast one on our city council.

But the two sub stations are nothing like central headquarters on Market Street. We have a coffee shop and next to it is a shoe shine stand and a trustee named Johnny Montoya gives the best shine in town for two bits. Then when Johnny's time is up everybody misses him but he goes on a toot for a week until a downtown car picks him up and then our shoes look good again.

Another thing Jerome this police department is clean. There is no monkey business here or I would know about it by now. The old timers tell me we used to have some cops who could keep a grand jury busy full-time but when Chief Hale took over in 1946 he knew the bad cops and dumped them. ~~This will surprise~~

This will surprise you there is not even any numbers in this squeaky clean town. Jack Hackett said he never heard of such a thing as numbers in Oregon and thought I was kidding when I told him how in Youngstown you could go to the gas station or Blair's market and buy a 3 digit number for a dime then when the newspaper printed the stock market info on top of the front page you won $$ if the last 3 numbers matched yours.

Another thing you cannot buy your way out of a ticket. When I worked with Frank Runyon we stopped a guy and when he handed us his license there was a five dollar bill stuck to it. Runyon said how long have you been here from Chicago? The guy says about six months and how do you know I am from Chicago? Runyon told him never mind just put the money back in your wallet we do not do that here and flashing money to a San Diego cop will end you up in the clink for attempted bribery.

My love life is not going too well Jerome. I have been on a lot of dates including a girl I met at the city college she had been the homecoming queen at Hoover high school so of course was something to look at but her idea of music is rocking around the clock with this Bill Haley guy. She had never heard of Duke Ellington and thought Benny Goodman is the guy who sells clothes on late night TV.

I almost forgot to tell you about Jack Hackett. He pulled a one day stand in a beat car in Linda Vista which is Unit 61 and on the beat is this eatery called The Barbecue Pit. He is partial to barbecue and sees the beef and chicken going round and round in the big window so in he goes and the place is crowded. He is waiting in line with his tray at the ready and reaching for a slab of ribs when he hears a crash and glass breaking and at first he thought there had been an explosion but then he realized a car had driven through the front window. People are screaming but nobody is hurt and Jack Hackett says to himself now I have to take an accident report instead of eat ribs and he looks closer and the car that came through the window is painted black and white. Yep, it is Jack Hackett's car he had parked it outside on a little slope and when the safety committee got through with him he had to work three of his days off. His wife got sore and told him he is gone all of the time anyway why not just bring a cot down to the station and phone their kid on her birthday.

So maybe it is good to be single as I have enough to do without worrying about a wife. Take care of yourself Jerome and root the Browns home for me.

Billy

P.S. I see Ike is getting weak in the head he says the government is too busy to help the steel workers get a raise yet Congress has plenty of time to hold hearings on the TV quiz shows that were rigged.

• • •

May 9, 1960 – Monday

Dear Jerome:
Two months ago I got picked up by Captain DeFreese's squad when his crew started twelve weeks of night shift. The

Captain has fourteen years on and was a Navy corpsman attached to the Marines in the Pacific though he does not talk
about it. He is a big guy and his hair is parted almost in the
middle like those movie stars when we were kids. On the first
night of the shift the Captain talked to us at roll call and said
he had paid the detective division squad room a visit that afternoon to remind them Defreese's squad is starting night
shift so be ready to get off their dead asses there will be plenty
of arrest reports for them to process and less burglaries to investigate. That is just how Defreese said it.

In the roll call room we sit in chairs and DeFreese stood
up front and held on to the lecture stand with both hands
and his voice is like a radio announcers. He told us to get
the streets cleaned up they had gone to shit since his squad
left night shift six months ago and to bring him all the pimps
and hookers and burglars and grifters and ~~gypsys~~ gypsies and
we will make the jail doors slam. A circus was playing in Mission Valley and DeFreese said the chief's office told the pro-
moter the carny workers cannot leave the grounds so if we
run into one lock them up. The Captain said if we think
someone belongs in jail but are not sure why bring them to
him it is a big penal code. By the time he finished his speech
and yelled for us to take our beats the guys almost ran
through the wall like Rockne telling Notre Dame to win
one for the Gipper.

I got assigned Unit 51 which covers Old Town and the
Pacific and Rosecrans area but will tell you about that in another letter. I waited until I had brought Captain DeFreese a
few solid felony pinches then told him he should pick up Jack
Hackett and Culpepper that they are good cops who would
bust their ass for him and last week he did now it is old home
week for the three academy buddies. You hear on TV about
cops having a sixth sense and while I do not know about the
fancy language I know guys like me and Jack Hackett and
Culpepper have something we did not get issued in the academy. Part of it is experience and part is having worked with

the Frank Runyons of the department but a big part is being
willing to get off our cans to make car stops and talk to pedestrians and see what we can shake loose. I know this much, a
guy cannot be a standout detective unless he was first a good
street cop.

School is going okay the teacher would make a good report sergeant she lets you get away with nothing. She had ~~all~~
~~ready~~ already retired from teaching for five years and when I
asked her why she came back she said when you are old and
alone it is good to feel useful again. She said one of your
problems Mister Considine is you never use contractions and
after she told me what that meant I told her I do not know
where the apostrophes go and also I get confused on some of
the plurals. After class she wrote out a formula for me so we
will see. She is not happy with my paragraphs or my sentences
she said neither will ever suffer from malnutrition. Jerome the
book I told you I bought, MacMillans 3rd, says a new paragraph starts with a new thought or point but they do not tell
you how you know you are finished with your thought.

The city manager went to Washington DC for some meetings about cops and community relations and listened to a
psychologist talk and ended up hiring him to come to San
Diego to teach classes for us. DeFreese said we do not need
expensive training it is simple just be nice to the law-abiding
people and throw the assholes in jail. ~~Anyway this lecturer~~

Anyway this lecturer turned out okay he came across more
truck driver than professor. He said what happens is cops get
thinking that some girl with a hard body in the secretary pool
or slinging hash at a drive-in is more sympathetic then the cop's
wife who is only home raising the kids and washing and cooking and cleaning and is dead tired when the cop comes home
smelling like a brewery two hours after he got off duty. It made
me think of a guy on our squad name of Hathaway who thinks
he can put the make on every girl he runs into but the fact is
he would win a gold medal for dandruff because it looks like
every gull in Ocean Beach has crapped on his shoulder.

I see Ike got embarrassed when the Reds shot down that Powers guy in a spy plane and if Kennedy wants to be President he will jump all over that. It tickled me what he told those Catholic haters in W.Virginia if they did not think he should be president because of his religion then he should not have been in the Navy or the Senate either.

I got thinking about what happened a couple of months ago when the colored students would not get up from the lunch counter at Woolworths down in North Carolina. Here the Pope just put the first ever Negro in the College of Cardinals but if there was a Woolworths in Rome this new guy could not go in and have a sandwich.

When I played in the Piedmont League in 1952 all the teams were from Virginia and there was stuff going on I did not like with the white and colored drinking fountains and two bathrooms and all.When I was a kid Mom heard me say the N word and she boxed my ears then sat me down and said yes the word gets used in Youngstown but it will not be used by her children she talked about when our grandparents came over from Ireland people made it rough for them. So I promised Mom I would quit saying the word.

The Negroes in San Diego are not a problem. I told you a lot of them drink and loiter in lower downtown and ~~further~~ farther to the southeast crowds of them are always around 30th and Imperial and National Avenue and Oceanview Boulevard but that is more then two miles from city hall so nobody cares.The ones on the street raise hell and we get called but the rest are home because they are working stiffs and just want peace and quiet.

There are maybe five Negro officers in patrol and they all work down in Negro town and the one or two Negro detectives only work Negro crimes. My opinion is citizens do not care if a Negro cop works in white territory but the department brass and city hall will not allow it. I feel sorry when a Negro officer in the locker room hears the N word coming from the next row I guess if I was a standup guy I would brace the cop who said it.

A Negro officer named Eddie Thomas told me he went on vacation to his hometown in Mississippi and visited some relatives then walked toward his aunt's house a few blocks away when a cop pulled up and said where do you live, Boy? Eddie told him he was from San Diego visiting relatives and the cop said be off the sidewalks by dark, Boy. So Eddie told him he was a San Diego police officer and showed him his badge and the cop looked at it and said that is a smart looking badge but be off the street by dark. If that is how those rednecks treat a fellow cop think how they must hassle an ordinary Negro.

I swore I would date no more college kids but tried one more time and all she wanted to talk about was the ~~effect~~ affect of secondary level education on kids in Panama. She was full of some paper she had written so that ended up just the one date. I meet a lot of girls on radio calls but the department looks at you funny if you hustle them and even though I made probation I still feel like I just got here and need to mind my P's and Q's as Mom would say.

So I will close by telling you of a girlfriend who is now an ex-girlfriend she is a relative of my landlady and is new in town from Phoenix which she says is the biggest city in Arizona. We went out maybe six or seven times and she is a very nice girl Jerome and the truth is I was getting stuck on her. Then coming home from a dance she said she wanted to talk to me and she said she liked me a lot, that that was the trouble she liked me too much. Turns out she did not want to be getting serious with a cop she said in listening to me the job would get in the way of things and then she started crying. It was like she wanted to know if I would give up police work to be with her. It was hard to walk away but I am over her so all the other girls in San Diego are lucky again though your kid brother is not getting any younger and you know what that says for you.

Speaking of girls, you wrote that Amy is trying to get into law school when she graduates next month so I wrote her a letter and as Mom would say, Amy got madder ~~then~~ than a wet hen. My letter must not have been out of her mailbox five minutes before Amy grabbed a pen and wrote me a letter. Jerome, the first sentence only had two words. She went on to say she is not a girl she is a fully grown woman and now that I am a cop I wear my wienie on my hip. Whatever she means by that I do not know. It could be she is sore over a crack I made in my letter about a girl going to law school. I may have said something about being a school teacher or a nurse instead.

Remember when Amy was ten years old and Ray Bolger came out with that song and whenever she got mad at me I would sing it to her to try and make things right. Once in love with Amy, always in love with Amy. And when I sang it sometimes she would either smile just a tiny bit or else get even madder. Please tell her that all day today I have been going around singing Once you're kissed by Amy, tear up your list, it's Amy…

I have to go Jerome.

Billy

• • •

July 1, 1960 – Friday

Dear Jerome:
Unit 51 responding with a big 10-4 to Youngstown. I told you Captain DeFreese assigned me beat 51 and there is plenty of activity if a cop knows where to look. Picture the area from Calvary Cemetery to Lake Newport and you will know the size of my beat it is three miles from downtown and the south part of it is called Five Points because five streets come together. Jack Hackett works the beat next to me so we cover each other a lot and trade notes about crime on our beat because it can slop over.

Samoans hang out at these Five Points gin mills Jerome,

they are barrel chested and some of them look like they were captured instead of born but they are good guys sober. I arrived at a fight call and was glad to see Jack Hackett pull up right behind me. I figured we were in for it but the biggest Samoan looked Jack over and said you're a little shit so Jack Hackett said I will come back when I am bigger and turned and headed for his car. Then the Samoan started laughing and it turned out okay.

More about my beat there are some ritzy homes in what is called Mission Hills near Presidio Park, then there is Old Town where San Diego got started and has a bunch of good Mexican restaurants and shops, then a little west of that Pacific Highway cuts through and a lot of L.A. cars drive it on their way to Tijuana which is the Mexican border town.

There are a bunch of run down motels where transients stay like the Twin Palms and the Blue Bell and the Easy-Rest. I make a routine of talking to the clerk and checking the registers and if I get a gut feeling I knock on the door of the room. Casual talking can lead to a search if you do it right and yesterday I made a good pinch in room 9 at the Easy-Rest. There were two guys and I found guns in the drawer, it turned out they were wanted from Colorado for stick-ups of grocery stores. They didn't put up a fuss Jerome, we get more guff from drunks and traffic violators and after I got them cuffed I treated them good because Frank Runyon said leave a man some dignity no matter what.

I stop any guy who looks like he isn't working forty hours a week even strolling down the sidewalk at high noon. If it turns out to be a crook type then that's good and if the guy is legit at least I know who he is and will expect to see him again and wave to him next time.

DeFreese got a beef on me because a guy I stopped for blowing a stop sign told me cops are lousy, they have ticket quotas and I told him he is right and ten more will win me the toaster. DeFreese cooled the guy off when he ran down to the station and yelled, but later DeFreese said Considine a good cop knows how to smart off and get away with it and I see you are still learning.

But there is a quota even though the brass hates the word and says we should always call it an average but at the end of a ninety day patrol shift a cop better have 180 tickets or the sergeant will rack him up. That makes a 2.0 ticket average and if that is not a quota, then as Uncle Denny would say I will kiss your ass on the fifty yard line at half time.

Even though I've only been on two years they gave me a rookie to train, a real mallet head who could do nothing right. I sat in the coffee shop telling Culpepper about him and Frank Runyon must have heard me from the next table because Frank hollered out that Considine would know a mallet head when he sees one.

I told you Jack Hackett works Unit 1 which is the beat next to mine and since we are both one-man cars we came up with a good gimmick. Smith Street cuts into Pacific Highway at an angle and parking on Smith gives you a real good view of the L.A. assholes heading to the border. So Jack parks behind me, leaves his engine running and jumps in my car. We shoot the breeze but all the time staring at cars on Pacific and when we see one that gives either of us the feeling Jack runs to his car and we make the stop together. People in the car think we are stopping them for a traffic violation but all we care about is are they wrong numbers and maybe wanted or have guns or loot in the car. Most of them we end up cutting loose but we make some good felony pinches and De-Freese is all smiles when we bring them down.

Amy sent me my favorite oatmeal cookies so thanks Jerome for whatever you did to put out the fire. I am tickled about her full scholarship to Case Western Reserve, it is a good university and Cleveland is only seventy miles from home. She will make a good lawyer and I see her as a prosecutor because Amy Considine will claw their balls off and make crooks wish she was teaching school.

Ike came to town to pimp for Nixon and the whole department got called in to work the parade. Jerome you know the last election was my first and even though the whole ship voted for Ike I was loyal to the steel mill unions and went with the guy from Illinois whose head looks like an egg. I thought about that when Ike passed 3rd and Broadway waving to everyone though I had my back to him looking at the crowd as that is what we are trained to do.

Culpepper did something special. It was daytime and he got an accident call in Point Loma where two cars collided while one was making a left turn into a residential driveway. Culpepper was the first cop on the scene and found three dead and four hurt in a station wagon. The other car had injured people too but here is the thing Jerome. The station wagon was arriving at a big family reunion including two sets of grandparents and aunts and uncles and what all. The driver of the station wagon had made an airport pickup and was probably excited and looking at the house instead of the car coming from the opposite direction.

Culpepper told me relatives poured out of the house yelling and crying and running in circles. He was still the only cop there and sized things up knowing he would have to give first-aid and help the fire department and ambulance when they arrived and block the street but at the moment everybody was screaming and in his way. Culpepper saw a guy come out of the family reunion house wearing a priest's collar so Culpepper ran to him and said Father, I think it's time to pray and Culpepper pointed to the front lawn. The priest caught on and made everybody kneel on the grass so Culpepper ran back to one of the cars and a lady in the front seat was bleeding and hysterical. Culpepper realized the small kids in the back seat were critical so while he worked over them and she kept screaming Culpepper kept saying to the lady, I'm the only one here and I am helping your children…I'm the only one here and I am helping your children. and he said it over and over and louder and louder until the lady finally calmed down.

Jerome, where do you find the Culpeppers of this world?

It's late and I'm tired but there is something else to tell you. The officer who relieves me on Unit 51 had been finding a lot of stolen cars parked on the beat but the engines were cold which means the damn things were there during my shift. I couldn't figure it out because I check the hot-sheet real good and after three cars had been found DeFreese called me in and said, Considine when I picked you for the squad I thought you were an alert felony cop, now I see you are driving past stolen cars on your beat. What's going on? Are you watching the girls instead of taking care of business?

It was embarrassing and driving me crazy until one day I caught Jack Hackett and another cop rolling a car from Jack's beat onto mine. I ran the plate and sure enough it was a stolen they had recovered on their beat and they got red in the face and mumbled and all the time DeFreese has been in on the gag. Jack Hackett bought me a few whiskeys as a peace offering but I told him revenge would be sweet.

Jerome, I would do this job even if they didn't pay me. Frank Runyon says cops have a seat in the front row of life.

It's the 4th of July weekend but fireworks are against the law here so set some off in the back yard for me and tell the neighbors hello from San Diego.

Billy

P.S. I see the Yanks are winning again after taking last season off because they felt sorry for the White Sox.

P.P.S. Sorry Mom didn't like the Mexican pottery from Old Town. Maybe one of these days I'll do something right.

PART TWO

Janet Williams

• • •

September 27, 1960 – Tuesday

Dear Jerome:
It's hard to concentrate because Jack Hackett who is sleeping on my couch has been snoring like Aunt Bridget since he passed out at midnight. He was in no shape to drive home. His wife took their kid to Oregon for a visit she was supposed to be gone two weeks but has been gone for four. Jack is sore about it and came over here with a bottle of Old Crow.

Jerome. Have you ever heard of the Hells Angels? They are a motorcycle gang who got started in Oakland up next to San Fran and they are bad characters. Sometimes they storm into small towns where law enforcement is a long ways off then tear up the place knocking people around and abusing the ladies.

The other day the intelligence detail got word the Angels were heading down the coast to Mexico so that would mean Highway 101 through San Diego. DeFreese called in guys on their day off and we set up a road block. There must have been a hundred bikers and our orders were run warrant checks on every biker and check their bike registrations, because we know they usually don't carry paperwork and they switch bikes with each other just for drill. DeFreese said if paperwork matchups were not clean he wanted the rider in jail for suspicion of auto theft and the bikes impounded.

Well, we booked eighty Angels and impounded sixty bikes. Some went to jail for contempt of cop which is a Frank Runyon arrest charge. DeFreese told the leftovers they were not allowed to drive in San Diego wearing their colors, they should find another route or he'd find something to put them in the clink for. The next day Chief Hale said to DeFreese who gave you the authority to set up a road block and DeFreese told him you did when you made me a captain.

Tell Mom to remember this trick in case she gets married

again. I got a call on Goldfinch Place some guy had shoved his wife around because she flushed his teeth down the toilet. Her eye had already started to turn purple but she laughed like hell and pointed at him and said he likes to go to Gene's Tavern on Washington Street and charm those widow barflies. She said they won't think he's such a dandy without his choppers.

In July, I decided to go to the Del Mar Fair, Del Mar being a beach town that borders San Diego and they hold a fair every year right next to a race track where Bing Crosby and the Hollywood types like to come and get their $$ down. I went with a cop from Iowa who is a live stock freak and he was all giddy watching them weigh bulls in the exhibit building.

There must have been a hundred types of food on the Midway along with the rides and booths and carny barkers and while my buddy was gone I saw a place selling cotton candy. I remembered I hadn't had any since you took me to Idora Park in 1940. I was about the third customer from the window and that's when it happened. A voice in line behind me said I almost didn't recognize you without your ticket book. I turned around to look and she says Sunset Boulevard and Arden Way, 40 in a 25 zone. Jerome, three quarters of a million people live in San Diego and I can't get cotton candy without running into someone I wrote a ticket to. I told her it was 44 in a 25, I gave you a break writing 40.

We didn't say anything else so I paid for my candy and it had to be ninety degrees so I looked for an empty table under the umbrellas. This same girl is standing a few feet away juggling a plate of barbecue and a soda pop and we both see this table open up at the same time. I didn't want to sit with her but we looked at each other and shrugged our shoulders at the same time and took a seat. It turned out her girlfriend was at the other end of the midway at the flower show. This girl is a librarian and we talked for a while but she never said anything else about the ticket.

A couple of days later I went to the main library in the 800 block of E Street and~~their~~ there she sat behind what they call the reference desk. I told her if I said I was in the neighborhood it would be a lie, do you get a coffee break on this job?

We walked to a place down the street and it turns out she is a college girl. She got her degree in history but then had to go to graduate school at the University of California at Berkeley that is across the bay from San Francisco for what is called a master of library sciences which she got last year.

Being on the reference desk is what she likes, otherwise she would be stuck in a back room doing research and not showing people how to find what they are looking for. We agreed we are lucky because we have important jobs that we like and get to help people.

It must be getting pretty in Youngstown now with October coming up. Everything always looks the same in San Diego.

Billy

P.S. Jerome if you didn't see the light-heavyweight from Kentucky winning the gold in Rome you really missed something. His name is Cassius Marcellus Clay and he is smooth as silk.

P.P.S Saturday I saw a guy walking in the traffic lane on Pacific Highway and when I pulled up and got out he took a swing at me. He was an Indian and after I got him cuffed I said what have you got against me and he said, you killed the buffalo.

• • •

October 4, 1960 – Tuesday

Dear Jerome:
Since I wrote you last week I have been feeling terrible about what I said to that librarian about our doing work that

is important. After I mailed it I got thinking, maybe you thought I took a slap at the work you do.

I told Jack Hackett and Culpepper about it at Bernie's and they said Jerome probably didn't take it that way. But they know nothing about steel and thought I was bullshitting when I said every mill in the Mahoning Valley is more than a mile long and for a stretch of twenty-five miles along the river it is like 4th of July because the mills shoot fire in the sky day and night.

Don't get sore but I told them what you sacrificed for the family. How you had been in love with Joannie but kept putting off giving her a ring afraid your paycheck wouldn't stretch for Mom and Amy and me and a wife. That by the time Mom found a job where her arthritis wouldn't kill her Joannie had broken it off and found another guy.

Culpepper slugged down his vodka and said Billy you are showing your guilt about running away from Youngstown and maybe he is right because all these years I have been telling myself it's only because the Yankees gave me a contract that I left. But the truth is maybe I would have gone anyway. Dad went to work when he was fourteen and the mill killed him when he was thirty eight. Uncle Liam told me Dad was dead before the ambulance got there he was all crushed inside. Cripes, he never even got to see Amy. Liam told me about him and Dad being in the riots of 1916 when the workers had to burn down East Youngstown in order to get a union and not have to work twelve hours a day seven days a week. And for what?

I told Jack Hackett and Culpepper how our grandfathers worked the mills, that I'd seen pictures of them next to the little stone blast furnaces before the Bessemer converters came along. I said Jerome and all the guys have pride in what they do, and how when you leave work you're full of sweat and cinder dirt but you have given the American people steel for bridges and ships and tanks and cars.

Bernie's gave us a round on the house and I was feeling no pain so I told everybody steel meant more to Youngstown then just coke and ore and limestone. I told the whole bar what you had tacked up on the wall of your room, those words written by that poet Carl somebody when he said smoke and blood is the mix of steel.

I honestly hope I did not offend you because I love you like a brother. Ha Ha.

Billy

• • •

November 24, 1960 – Thursday

Dear Jerome:

I suppose you had Thanksgiving at Aunt Anna's like always and I'm sure Uncle Jerry drank his Irish, then ran to the front porch and yelled to the whole neighborhood a Scarfer is the toughest job in the mill and the best mill in the valley is the Campbell Works. Jerome, this is not a happy day for me, but I didn't want you to read this until after turkey day, here is what happened. DON'T SHOW THIS TO MOM she will worry herself sick.

Our squad is on afternoons which means I work 3:30 p.m. to 11:30 p.m. About ten days ago I got off work and went home and the next morning, it's a Wednesday, I'm just waking up at nine. The phone rings and they want me down to the captain of detective's office, I figured it's about a drunk pinch I made a few days before because the next day they found out the guy is wanted for murder in Louisiana.

I got down there and a detective and a detective sergeant took me into a room, the detective I had seen around a couple of times, I didn't know the sergeant. They said Considine, last night you got a call to Gannon Street over in Navy housing, tell us about it. I told them I got the call about 2000 (that is 8: p.m.) and a lady wanted to report some money stolen, about fifty bucks. The sergeant says you didn't make a crime report and I told him no, I made a memo instead because there was no forced entry and her husband had left on night duty and I thought maybe he had the money and didn't tell her he took it.

Then the detective left but came back a little later, he had gotten the memo from records, it had been late getting sent over to detectives. I'm thinking why did they make me come downtown just because they couldn't find a report, and if they didn't have the report how did they even know there was one?

The sergeant says how long were you in the house and I told him about fifteen minutes. Now I know something is fishy because detectives don't care how long patrol guys take on a call so I said what is this all about?

They acted like I hadn't asked them and the detective takes my right hand and he says how did your knuckles get swollen? What happened Jerome, I had put a drunk in the car and pushed his head to keep it from hitting the door jam and he spun around and my hand hit the door. I told them and the sergeant says then I'm sure you wrote up an injury report and I said no, I work for Captain DeFreese and he says only candy asses write up anything less than losing an arm or leg. One of them says are you right-handed or left-handed and I said right-handed and the sergeant smiled and said, you had to be right-handed to play second base. How he knew I had played ball I do not know.

I asked if I could smoke and they said why, are you nervous and I said I would like a smoke so I lit up a Luckie and they lit up too. I said when are you going to tell me what this is all about and they said tell us what this woman looked like. So I said she was maybe thirty and kind of hard looking and half drunk. They said what was she wearing and I said a house coat. They said was anybody else in the house and I told them no. There was just the two of us and she kept saying did I want coffee and I kept saying no.

They had me down at the station until dinner time because the woman told them I raped her and punched her face and told her I would kill her if she screamed and would kill her if she told anybody. I couldn't believe what I was hearing, but I knew they weren't joking and they said would you take a polygraph and I said hell yes, lead me to it. So I took one but they would tell me nothing about the result.

They said what kind of blood type are you Considine, and I said I'm type "B." They already knew that from my personnel jacket. They said well, the doctor is right now swabbing this lady's vagina they will get sperm and they will be able to tell if it is yours, so it would be better for you to just come clean now. That's when I got good and sore because I'm a cop and they're treating me like a criminal and I said, take all the blood you want from me because this is all bullshit, I never touched that lady and I'm telling you the truth about everything. They said there is evidence of this lady being hit with a fist on her left cheek and a right-handed man would have done that. I told them there might be another right-handed man in San Diego.

So they took my blood and interrogated me some more, then they drove me to my place and wanted all the clothes I had been wearing the night before. I gave them everything. Uniform and underwear and socks then they took me back downtown. Then the worse of all happened, they put me in what is called a live lineup. The lineup room is right next to the jail and stinks from a million bodies that have stood there and you hear cell doors slamming in the distance and they had me on the stage with five prisoners about my age and size. The lady must have been looking through the glass, I couldn't see anybody on the other side. I'm a cop who has done nothing wrong and I'm standing there next to the kind of people I put in jail.

Then they interrogated me again and said she has identified me and I said of course she has, I'm the son of a bitch who went to her house and took the report. The sergeant said getting mad at us is not going to help, Son.

By then it had to be eight or nine p.m. and they said consider this your work day and we see you're off the next two days, Thursday and Friday. I said what will happen now? They said the investigation is continuing, go home and relax. Fat chance of doing that.

Jack Hackett and Culpepper came over after work and I told them about it, even though the detectives said say nothing to nobody. I wanted to see Captain DeFreese but he is gone for a week in the mountains with a bunch of cops to fish and play poker. DeFreese told Culpepper all he fishes for is full houses. I want to look DeFreese in the eye and tell him I'm innocent.

I told you Jack Hackett finished near the top of our academy class, he is one smart guy, Jerome, he said 12 percent of the population has my blood type, type "B." He said when they swab the vagina they get epithelial cells (I have no idea if that is spelled right) and must separate out the sperm cells. Then they may be able to tell the blood type of the rapist by testing the sperm.

After my first day off, the morning paper which is the Union had a story that a cop is being investigated for rape, though they had no details. But the afternoon paper said a source named the suspect as Officer William Patrick Considine. Friday was my second day off, so Saturday they had me work a desk in the Auto Theft Bureau compiling statistics. In the coffee shop a girl from records came up to me and said Billy, I know you didn't do this thing. This is a girl I have hardly said ten words to but it sure made me feel good.

Frank Runyon said if you did it, get a lawyer. I told him I didn't do it and he said I don't think you did either and walked away.

The Sunday paper came out with a big story, the lady got a lawyer and he says citizens are supposed to be able to trust their police, not be brutally savaged by them. It made me sick to my stomach. The lawyer said he expects the police department to cover for me, he told the paper he understands I have been suspended in the past and he is demanding the state attorney general conduct an investigation so his client will receive justice. He said he is going to file a lawsuit.

So the next day which was Monday, the F.B.I. came into

the case because Navy housing is involved, even though we patrol it. But before the Feebies showed up, the detective and detective sergeant who I had started with sat me down and said Considine, it looks very bad. The sperm is type "B" which is your type and in case you're wondering, her husband is blood type "O". They said we have given you chances before to come clean, we are going to give you just one more. Tell us how it went down, we will do the best we can for you with the D.A. and the judge.

Jerome I went into the bathroom and threw up. Then I got the dry heaves leaning over the bowl and got all sweaty and honest to God I thought I would pass out on the floor of the crapper.

The F.B.I. guy showed up and I'll tell you something right now. Cops make fun of the Feebies and say there are three things in the world that are ~~over rated~~ overrated. Home cooking, home screwing and the F.B.I. But this agent is a good guy and seemed very fair, his name is Flynn and he had been in the Cleveland office once, so we spent the first few minutes talking about the Browns and the Indians.

When we got down to business he said he had interviewed the woman and her husband, he said the lady swears she never offered me coffee, she said I had asked her what time her husband would be home and when she told me not until daylight I tried to kiss her. She told the agent she pushed me away but I grabbed her again and punched her two times in the face, then took my gun belt off and did it to her on the bed.

So I went through the whole story with him, then he left me in the room with the door open and a little later I could see him talking to our two detectives and a guy from the lab. I got scared stiff and figured they were going to lock me up. The lab guy left and they kept talking and then the lab guy returned and came into the room with the agent. The lab guy said get some saliva working in your mouth, and I said what for and the agent said just do it. So I did and the lab guy put a soft piece of paper in my mouth and told me to get it wet. I did and he took the paper and left. The agent said we have more testing to do. He shook hands with me and I went back to my Auto Theft job.

The next day was Tuesday and the paper said the District Attorney is reviewing the case and the lady's lawyer screamed for me to be charged with rape and battery. I worked yesterday, now today is Thanksgiving which falls on my day off. Jerome, if they put me in jail all I can do is swear to you and Mom and Amy I didn't do this thing. I did nothing at all wrong in that house.

Jack Hackett says if I don't come to his house for dinner this afternoon he will come over and drag me there, his wife puts a cranberry stuffing in the turkey like they do in Oregon and also she makes good cranberry bread which he says is the only reason he married her.

I was going to tell you about something else in this letter, something that is a happy thing but I'm not up to it. Tomorrow is my day off too so will write you about it then.

Trust in me,

Billy

• • •

November 25, 1960 – Friday

Dear Jerome:
If I had put this letter in with the other yesterday I could have saved four cents postage. Those Oregon girls know how to cook and it was the first real meal I've eaten since this rape investigation thing started. After dinner Jack Hackett's wife did dishes while he and I got into the bourbon which made it a little chilly in the kitchen so we ended up down at Bernie's where all the sailors were crying in their beer because they couldn't be in Altoona or Sandusky or El Paso for turkey day.

Jerome, a couple of months ago I told you about a girl I

met at the Del Mar Fair back in July but I've said nothing else because I feel silly writing about all these girls who end up false alarms. But the thing is I have been seeing her a lot. Her name is Janet Williams and she is four years younger ~~then~~ than me, remember I told you she works at the library.

The second time I showed up at the library to go on coffee break with her she was helping some customer at the desk and they were talking in French. It made me remember the day we met at the fair and sat at the table, me with my cotton candy, and a Mexican guy came running by waving his arms and it turned out he lost his little boy in the crowd. Janet started talking Spanish to him and got him lined up with security.

So when we left the library and walked to the coffee shop I said how many languages do you speak, a dozen? She said no, four. Turns out she knows German too. Janet says language comes easy to her but Jerome it's like pulling teeth to get her to say ~~some thing~~ something good about herself.

After we got our coffee she took a sip and said, after the fair I didn't expect to see you again. I asked why and she just looked down at her cup, but I think it's because Janet doesn't have looks that turn heads, as if that matters to me.

We started going out and the girl knows her music. They have a trio at the LaFayette Hotel, a piano and clarinet and drum and we had our first dance to Body & Soul.

Janet is different from any girl I have ever known and I can't believe she walked into my life. I should say drove into my life. You can tell Mom she is not Irish but is very nice anyway. After we had been going out a couple of months she said Billy maybe we are moving too fast, I would like to take a break. That idea sounded terrible to me and I tried to talk her out of it but then I said okay and we agreed to go five days and not see or talk to each other. Three days went by and she telephoned me I said how are you Janet? She said miserable and I said me too and she said why don't you come over, so I hung up and had my car started before the phone line went dead.

We talk on the phone every morning before she goes to work even if I'm half asleep. A couple of times she said you're supposed to be up for school and I told her I had worked overtime and she said get yourself out of bed and get to class. So there is no chance of hooky playing with Janet in the picture.

She rents a duplex in Pacific Beach and as soon as I turn onto her street my troubles start to go away. The other night I taught her to play cribbage so of course she is beating me already. We watched the first debate at her place and I said Kennedy stepped all over Nixon but Janet is from Whittier which is Nixon country near L.A. so we canceled each other's vote. Mom must have been all excited getting her Irish-Catholic president.

There is another thing, Jerome, before this mess happened at work the other day I started to read a novel. Janet picked it out for me, it's called The Last Hurrah and it's about a guy who is mayor running for re-election. She said reading novels takes people places they have never been and swears it will make me spell better because according to Janet I have a very good memory. I told her if I had remembered what pitches lefties had been throwing to get me out I would be getting my mail in Yankee Stadium now. Janet said well then how would we have gotten together and I told her I would have found her no matter what.

So I'm pinching myself that this college girl is spending time with a guy just now learning about prepositions and conjunctions. I had to drag out of her that she was an honors student and got offered a big job being what is called a single-subject librarian for a museum in New York City. But she turned it down because she wanted to work in a public library and help people find study stuff and such.

I know I'm going on about Janet but I can't stop thinking about her. We go for picnics and swims in Mission Bay at the Crown Point Shores and take the pedestrian ferry to Coronado and go for Chinese at an upstairs joint in the 1000 block of 3rd downtown where the bartender makes great martinis and loads them up when he knows you're a cop. And get this, your brother has seen a Shakespeare at the Old Globe Theater in Balboa Park. Janet explained what it would be about so I followed it pretty good. I snuck a few looks around and if there were any other cops in the audience they were hiding under the seat.

The thing is Janet never gave a hoot about baseball but I took her to a game when Sacramento came to town and by the seventh inning she wanted me to teach her my score keeping system. And when it was 3-3 in the bottom of the ninth, bases loaded nobody out, she noticed the outfield was playing in and wanted to know why.

What I'm saying is, she is the only girl I have ever been with where I didn't have trouble knowing what to say. Janet kids about our being opposites, her having brown hair and brown eyes and me blond and blue. She has freckles on her nose and cheeks like Amy.

One night at Crown Point the stars were shining in her eyes and I told her she was beautiful and that our song should be Just the Way You Look Tonight.

Janet is spending Thanksgiving in Whittier with her folks and we talk every day but I didn't tell her on the phone about this mess at work. Do you think I should have, Jerome? Anyway I can't wait to see her because when she is gone nothing seems right.

I didn't think I could sit still to write this letter. Maybe today I will hear from the department, I don't know if I can stand going the weekend without some kind of word.

Billy

• • •

November 26 1960 – Saturday

Dear Jerome:

This is crazy. It's five in the morning and this is the third letter I have written you in twenty-four hours. At noon yesterday (Friday), I walked to the corner and mailed the other two letters and the phone rang when I came in the door. I hoped it was Janet but it was the detective sergeant and he said come to the station right away.

I threw on slacks and a sport shirt and walked into their office and both of the detectives and F.B.I. Agent Flynn was there. The sergeant says it's all over, Considine. I said what do you mean and they said do you know what a secretor is? I said I have no idea. (All I have been studying is school work and no promotion stuff at all.)

Then they went into a long complicated story about 80 percent of the population being a secretor but the bottom line is I am not one and am cleared of the charge. I was confused and the detective sergeant said Considine, we have scientific proof that the semen from the lady's vagina is not yours. Agent Flynn said that is why the lab guy stuck the piece of paper in my mouth, they test my saliva on the paper which tells them if I am or am not a secretor.

Then they gave me the whole story, because after the lab cleared me Flynn and the detectives did re-interviews with the lady and her husband and hit them with the evidence. Turns out the lady has been sleeping with a neighbor who is another white hat and she and the boyfriend got into a fight and he grabbed her fifty bucks and went drinking. She had to find some way to explain to her husband where the $$ went so she called the police to report a theft and Officer Considine knocks on her door.

After I left, her boyfriend came over, he is shit-faced and wants some loving but she is still mad and says no dice so he belts her and throws her on the bed and does it to her anyway. She had always made him use protection because her husband is sterile but that night he doesn't use any. Now she's worried because of her messed up face and the fifty bucks and maybe getting pregnant.

While she's stewing about it her husband comes home at

7: a.m. and she says a cop did this to me. He goes ape shit and calls Shore Patrol who call the police.

The lady tells the detectives I was stuck up for not having coffee with her so she didn't feel bad about framing me.

After the detectives finished explaining it they shook my hand and cut me loose, so I ran to Bernie's like a tiger was chasing me and was still there when Jack Hackett got off at eleven and we closed the place. But before Jack got there I realized the F.B.I. guy had got things going my way so I called to say thanks and told him my goose would have been cooked if I had been one of those eighty percent. He said maybe someday blood and semen will be as exacting as fingerprints are now. Fat chance, huh?

While we were still at Bernie's drinking boilermakers the barkeep yelled at me waving the phone so I grabbed it and it's Captain DeFreese. How he knew I would be at Bernie's I do not know. He said Considine, I take a week off to go fishing and you fuck up my squad. Then he started laughing and said when you come back to work, let's have coffee after lineup.

At closing time Bernie's threw us out so we went down on 4th Avenue for Huevos Rancheros meaning eggs and tortillas and beans and salsa but I was so keyed up when I got home I started writing this letter. I report back to patrol today and they will get the word out to the troops that I am innocent but how the rest of the city will find out I do not know. I don't expect those horseshit newspapers to clear my name.

You probably don't remember this, Jerome but when I was sixteen you told me there are times a person can't do anything about what others think, the important thing is to be straight with yourself. I'm holding on to that thought.

After work tomorrow I will tell Janet all about what has happened. I sure wish you and Mom and Amy could meet her.

Billy

• • •

December 10, 1960 – Saturday

Dear Jerome:

My Christmas present to you is a sister-in-law. That is right, Janet and I got married a week ago yesterday. I am writing Mom a separate letter so she can't yell about having to hear everything from you. There was so much stuff to sort out we ended up getting in the car and going to Las Vegas. Jack Hackett says Janet is a wonderful girl but I'm crazy to get married and Culpepper is worried I haven't known her long enough. All Frank Runyon said was do it once and do it right.

A jeweler in the Robinson Building downtown sold me a nice ring and when we got to Vegas and found city hall a little guy with white hair and a red sweater vest did the ceremony. We didn't bring anybody along to stand up for us but Vegas took care of that, they take care of everything, Jerome. One chapel had signs outside saying we perform marriages that last forever so we laughed about that, but Janet grabbed my hand and said ours is going to.

The thing is, the sweater vest guy did it very seriously not making us feel part of a mass production even though couples sat on the benches outside his office waiting their turn. It was the best day of my life and every one since has been even better.

We had a week plus the weekend so stayed a couple of days at the Grand Canyon which is all it is cracked up to be then headed south and came home through giant cactus, then past the Salton Sea which is back in California. As for the Salton Sea they should issue clothes pins for your nose.

The motels along the way set us back about ten bucks a night but they were extra nice and Janet made me carry her over the ~~threshhold~~ threshold at every one. And when we hummed along those roads she would put her head back and say Janet Williams Considine over and over and over again.

All the stuff we needed to sort out is about religion. Janet's a Baptist and a month ago we drove up to Whittier so I could meet her folks. They were nice enough to me, but I knew Janet had told them I am Catholic and a couple of times it seemed they were hoping the whole thing would just go away. We said nothing about getting married but her father kept saying young people should move very slowly making big decisions about life.

I told Janet the story of how Mom's mother and father came from County Sligo and were Catholic and Dad's mother and father came from County Tyrone which is Protestant, and how when Mom and Dad started keeping company in 1923 Dad told her all he wanted was to marry her and they shouldn't let religion get in the way. And how you and me and Amy got raised Catholic and what a good marriage Mom and Dad had. So in my letter to Mom I will tell her I'm just doing the same thing Dad did but in reverse, and our kids can be raised Baptists which is fine with me as long as I have Janet. How can Mom kick about that? We are going to hold off having kids for a while and save some dough.

I'll phone Mom right after she gets my letter and rely on you to steady the ship. When Mom meets Janet she will fall for her KERPLUNK like I did.

Love from old married man Billy.

P.S. Janet made up a strict schedule and goes over English and grammar homework with me. When Jack Hackett was my study buddy we'd pour a drink after half an hour but Janet Williams Considine is all business.

• • •

March 4, 1961 – Saturday

Dear Uncle Jerome:
Yes I said UNCLE because Janet's in what Mom calls a fam-

ily way and the Doc says little Considine will arrive in September. We were very surprised and Janet said the baby had better not come before September or her folks will be sure we ran off to Vegas because we had to. It's a good feeling and if it's a boy we will name him after Dad but then the second boy will be Jerome Patrick. We are going to have seventeen kids.

The thing is we are buying a brand new house and signed up for it before the Doc gave us the news. But Janet put the pencil to the paper and said we'll make it okay $$ wise. She can work for a few more months and then she will quit for good. In two months I'll get bumped to first-class patrolman which will kick my pay to about 575 a month, our house payments will be 99 a month which is high but includes principal and interest and insurance and taxes. We got it under my G.I. bill and only had to put a dollar down. It cost $12,999.00 and is called a tract house because they put a bunch up at the same time and I wish you and Mom could see it. It's being built now, the way it works you pick it out from a model, our street will be Dellwood which is part of a complex called the Royal Highlands so all the streets have names from Scotland.

We are very excited, a built-in refrigerator and stove come with it, Janet picked a coppertone color, it has three bedrooms and a bath. The yard isn't as big as Hampton Court's but they throw in an 8 by 10 patio. It turns out Culpepper is a concrete man so when they come to pour he will have laid out more forms meaning we will have an extra big hunk of patio. Culpepper will take no money for it, he just wants the first Porterhouse grilled on what he calls his masterpiece.

Cops don't come under social security so Jack Hackett figured up if we retired after twenty-five years at age fifty-one we will knock down about three-hundred a month in our old age which will be fine if the house is paid off.

Speaking of Jack Hackett, I went into Bernie's the other day and the bartender said he figured I had left town. Jerome, I go straight home after work now. Culpepper likes his booze but doesn't hang out at Bernie's since he's usually off romancing.

Anyway while we were having a couple of drinks Jack Hackett told a story about seeing a girl on the side, he had never said a word to me about her. He told the guys at the table that the first night he got under the sheets with her he kind of snoozed after they finished and felt something nice happening to his wienie. He still had his eyes closed and said to her, I like it when you do that. She said I'm not doing anything. Turns out her cat had got under the covers and was licking him. Jack said he fell out of love with the girl a month before he fell out of love with the cat. So I guess he doesn't feel the same about his wife that I feel about Janet.

With a baby coming and getting a new house and going to school and court I'll probably not be writing as many letters. There's always something going on at work and the other day it was Culpepper's turn. He looked in a liquor store window and saw a guy putting a gun on the clerk and saw the clerk handing over money, so Culpepper put it out on the radio, then he got out of his patrol car and crouched behind the fender. When the suspect walked out Culpepper had his gun out and yelled at the guy to freeze. The suspect looked at Culpepper then started running like hell. Who can outrun Culpepper I do not know, and two blocks later the suspect is on the ground and cuffed.

The liquor store clerk is happy and Culpepper's proud of his pinch and took him down to Capt. DeFreese with a booking slip all made out for DeFreese to sign. DeFreese listened to how it went down and signed the slip and as Culpepper's about to walk the suspect over to jail, DeFreese said, give me your gun. Culpepper says what, and DeFreese says give me your gun. Culpepper does and DeFreese puts it in his desk drawer and says, now you can go book your prisoner and return to your beat. Culpepper says but Captain you have my gun. DeFreese says yes, you don't need it. DeFreese says you must be a civil libertarian and would rather put your life on the line than shoot someone. If during the chase that son of a bitch had gone to his waistband and wheeled around, I'd have a dead cop on my hands. Culpepper just stood there so DeFreese said book the guy and get back to work, you can stuff rocks in your holster to keep it from swinging.

Culpepper told me he only had two hours left on shift so he parked behind some trash dumpsters in an industrial complex and hid out there. He said he was scared stiff he'd get a radio call and decided next time he'll put five warning shots in the middle of the crook's back.

Remember I told you I'd get back at Jack Hackett for pushing those stolen cars onto my beat. Well I took care of that last week. I drove through downtown on the way to my beat and the smells from the Greek deli drove me nuts. I decided to pick up a sandwich and parked in a loading zone in front of a hat shop next to the Greek's. I'd heard the hat shop guy is a chiseler who takes two bucks from people to park in the public loading zone for twenty minutes. So I get my sandwich and I'm opening my car door and there the guy is on the sidewalk looking like a bulldog waiting for the mailman. He says that place is for my customers, not for public servants to park while they screw off on duty.

I said to him, well we all have our troubles and he says I demand your name. The engine is running now and I stick my head out the window and as I'm pulling away I said, my name is Jack Hackett and don't forget it, you miserable schmeckle.

I knew Jack was off that day, but I didn't know that bulldog-face gives free hats to Assistant Chief Steele. But it worked out fine because Jack got on and off the chief's carpet in about two minutes and nobody is any the wiser except Jack Hackett and when I told him he laughed so hard you should have been able to hear him in Youngstown.

On beat 51, I hide out in Old Town to eat the lunch Janet packs or to work on my file box where I keep names of all the hoodlums on my beat and their associates and cars, all of it cross-indexed. One day I'm parked by this little cemetery on San Diego Avenue and here comes a kid, he leans on my door and says what's your name? I said Officer Considine, what's yours, and he says Hector Morales. He says what's your

first name and I told him it's Billy. He says well Billy, we'll be
seeing a lot of each other. Jerome, he's ten years old!

He's going to special classes to learn English and believe
me he's learning it good. Turns out he's from way deep in
Mexico and came to San Diego a week before school started.
So a neighbor taught him to say, my name is Hector Morales,
I'm from Mexico so I speak Spanish but I'm learning to speak
English. Hector lives with his folks in a rundown auto court
in the 3800 block of California Street in Five Points. He's a
good kid and still calls me Billy but he can be a real pain in
the ass. It seems like every time I'd go off to hide Hector
would pop up. So I tried to out fox him when I needed to do
paperwork but the next thing I know he's leaning on my door.

I made the mistake of telling Janet that Hector has a birthday coming up, so she went out and bought him a ball glove,
so I suppose now there will be no getting away and I'll end
up playing catch while burglars and stickup men are having
a field day on the other end of my beat.

Now I really must go. Tell Amy to keep studying hard that
I'm counting on her becoming the district attorney of Mahoning County.

Billy

• • •

September 1, 1961 – Friday

Dear Jerome:
In your letter you said you've been marking the calendar so
you know the baby's due any day now. Even though we moved
into our new house last week, the expectant father stayed up
half the night with a paint brush because the expectant mother
wants the baby's room beige instead of the shade of white the
painters put on. If it makes Janet happy I'll paint the house purple because we're having a heat wave and she's big and miserable and moves like a Sherman tank so I just follow orders.

The house is all we hoped it would be and am putting pictures in with this letter. That's Janet standing next to Philodendron bushes I planted. As I planted she tried to get out of a lawn chair to show me how far apart they should be, all the time I'm laughing at her and she's doubling up her fist which turned out okay because she can't run very fast. In the back yard picture, Jack Hackett is on the left and Culpepper is the guy wearing shorts.

This is some world Little Considine will be getting born into. Commander Shepard goes 116 miles into space and Kennedy says soon we'll be walking on the moon like Buck Rogers. I think the job must be making him weak in the head.

Your kid brother is pulling down "B's" and one "A" in school, so now maybe I can take some time to study for sergeant, though I'm continuing with grammar courses. One night at school the teacher took me aside and told me to quit worrying about how 'that' introduces a restrictive clause and 'which' introduces a non-restrictive clause. He said concentrate on my punctuation and paragraphs and worry about the other later.

And even though Janet is still being brutal in my study sessions with her, she will not edit my letters, saying it is time for me to fly on my own.

Janet's last day of work was June 23rd and she hasn't smoked since she got pregnant though her girlfriends think she's silly, telling her it makes no difference to the baby. When she sees me reaching for a Luckie she points to the door, so out I go to puff away on the patio. Jack Hackett says I am p.... whipped.

Jack Hackett's wife and kid are off to Oregon again, this time for a month. Truth be known, Jerome, I think he's glad to see her go. His wife's still having trouble getting used to San Diego but Janet says it's Bernie's Tavern she's having trouble getting used to.

A loud mouth cop got me riled in the coffee shop the other day when he said getting their asses kicked served those white freedom fighters right, that they had no business getting on buses and sticking their noses in Alabama's business. So I yelled out what's so bad about wanting to let Negroes into public places and he said do that and next thing we'll be marrying them. He really got to me, because when I was playing ball and we were on the road in places like Lanett, Alabama or Newport News, Virginia, our colored players couldn't go in and eat with us when our bus stopped at a diner. We'd bring out sandwiches but our shortstop wouldn't eat them. He said that's how Jackie Robinson handled it playing in the south and he said he's no better than Jackie. Hell, Negroes and whites get along okay in San Diego, why not Alabama?

Which reminds me, I talked to a cop who had worked the L.A. Coliseum the night Kennedy got nominated there last year. Now get this! The rednecks from the Mississippi delegation heckled Sammy Davis Jr. when he got up to sing the national anthem. If they have the nerve to treat a famous entertainer like that, think how vicious they'd be in their own backyard. I'm sure glad we have no Negro problems in San Diego.

Guess what? My little pal Hector Morales has been made a school crossing guard. He goes to the elementary school on Congress Street and I had put in a word for Hector with a guy I know in the traffic division which runs the program. So now Hector's hot stuff standing there in his red sweater and gold cap. All crossing guards salute when a cop drives by and at first Hector did it with his left hand. I had to tell him to use the hand closest to the church on the corner.

Jack Hackett and I really pulled one off, Jerome. At morning watch lineup the sarge read off a description of two suspects who broke into the house of a Safeway manager the night before and kidnapped him. One crook took him to the market to open the safe while the other terrorized the guy's wife and kids at gunpoint.

So we break lineup at 3:30 a.m., inspect our cars and head for our beats. I drive out the same way every day and I'm going up India Street and when I get to the corner of Kalmia, I see Jack Hackett standing outside his car with his lights off waving me down. So I cut my lights and pull in behind him and I see someone sitting in the back of Jack's car.

There's a dry cleaners on the northwest corner called City Dye Works, and Jack says he cruised by and saw a pair of legs moving between the rows of clothes hanging up. He pulled to the curb and there's a guy sitting on the bus bench who Jack figures must be the burglar's lookout because no buses run up India that time of morning. So he cuffed the guy up and put him in the back seat.

We made a quick plan. Jack goes around the rear and I take the front door. The back door had been kicked in and when the suspect hears Jack he makes a run out the front door right into my arms. He goes down real easy and we keep the two separated and they have no ID and give us Joe Blow kinds of names and Jack and I look at each other and can't believe it. These two are the shit birds they read off at lineup. Age, hair, size, right down to their clothing including a shirt with a tear under the right arm pit. Armed kidnappers kicking in doors of dry cleaners and falling into our lap five minutes after we break roll call! I had a manager in Georgia who said he'd rather be lucky than good.

Jack puts the inside guy in my car and talks to him while I get in the other car and take on the lookout. Frank Runyon taught me that you do better if you don't hard ass people, so I start slow and easy, getting this guy to talk about how he grew up in the hill country of Texas and how he got abused and had to run away from home and all that bullshit. The guy gets real impressed when he finds out I was a pro ballplayer. I might have told him I played a season or two in the American League and he wants to know why I'm a cop and I tell him so I can help people like him who get in trouble.

Next thing he's copping out to the Safeway manager job, plus three jobs in Yuma which is in Arizona, and telling me where they stashed the guns and money from the night before.

Capt. DeFreese writes us up department commendations, Jack Hackett for alertness and knowledge of his beat, and me for interrogative ability. Janet put mine and the newspaper clippings in a big envelope, she says someday she'll put a scrap book together.

Speaking of DeFreese, I brought in a guy who had no ID
and had burglar tools in a knapsack and the guy's telling us how
innocent he is and DeFreese says to the guy, you haven't got a
stitch of ID, we don't know who you are, you could be John
Dillinger. The guy says who's that? DeFreese looks at me shaking his head and says where has the time gone, Considine?

Jerome, I'm going to cut this off because Janet is timing
pains and wants me to help her. I'll be back in a couple of
minutes because we've been through these false alarms before.

• • •

September 6, 1961 – Wednesday

Dear Jerome:
Everything is still fine and I enjoyed talking to you and
Mom on the phone Saturday morning after Little Considine
said hello to the world. I didn't have time for all the info
Mom wanted, so here goes.

It was some adventure. I switched off between sitting with
Janet in what's called a labor room and the father's waiting
room which has chairs and couches and a bunch of guys reading the Sporting News and Police Gazette and seeing who
could blow the best smoke rings.

Janet was really hurting and I sat there holding her hand.
A pain would come and she'd moan and after a few hours
she started saying, I can't take another one, I can't take another
one. And because I felt so sorry for her and felt so helpless all
I could think of to say was, you made it through the last one,
you can make it through the next one. It made sense to me,
but she got madder then hell and that's when I'd go blow
smoke rings for a while.

Just before noon Saturday the waiting room phone rang
and the guy nearest picked it up and he said, Considine, is
there a Considine here? I said that's me, and I just sat there. I
said do you know who it is and another guy said President

Kennedy, take the goddamn phone. When I did say hello a nurse said, why don't you come down and see your wife and baby, Mr. Considine?

I ran down the hall and there's Janet being wheeled on a gurney and she looked so beautiful and I leaned down and asked if she was okay. She said I'm fine, then she nodded to the baby and said, his name is James Patrick Considine.

He's beautiful, and I ran out and got a copy of the newspaper so Janet can put the day's headlines in his scrapbook which she started six months ago. Then I sat with Janet until she went to sleep, then I went to Bernie's and passed out cigars and bought the house a drink. The Doc said he'd keep Janet in the hospital for the routine three days, so yesterday I picked her and Jimmie up and took them home.

I guess that new color in his room is the right one because when I ask Jimmie how he likes it he smiles at me. He's beautiful, Jerome. I never thought anything this nice would ever happen to me.

Billy

• • •

July 7, 1962 – Saturday

Dear Jerome:
Cutting right to the important stuff. Your nephew is the toast of Dellwood Street. He stands up holding on which I think is very good for ten months old, and eats like a guy on the soup line. We take him to Balboa Park almost every week, there's what is called a children's zoo and kids can walk around with the animals and pet them. When we go to the movies we take him to a theater on El Cajon Blvd that has a crying room, though Jimmie hardly makes a peep.

There's a six-year-old who lives down the block and he's a real pain in the ass. His name is David and anytime some kid's ball or bike is missing everyone knows where to look.

Janet named the kid David Crook. Anyway, one day just before payday I'm taking Jimmie in his stroller over to the market on Ashford Street to turn in some bottles and use the
money to buy smokes. There's David Crook standing in front
of his house and he says can't that kid walk yet? I said he's
only ten months old. Then he looks at Jimmie and says he
sure has a big head. I stopped the stroller and looked at Jimmie and at first I didn't think it looked too big. I told David
Crook he was no leading man himself.

We have a two-car garage attached to the house and we
keep the washer-dryer there. When I got back Janet was putting another load of diapers in and I said, do you think Jimmie
has a big head? Janet looked at me funny so I told her what
David Crook said. She started laughing and said children Jimmie's age have to grow into their heads. But then I guess a
mother would side with her kid, wouldn't she?

Janet and I are on the same side on the California election
coming up and wonder if it's making any news in Ohio. Who
ever thought Nixon would be running for governor, but he's
leading this guy Pat Brown in the polls. Brown is a governor
nobody seems to get mad at, but cops don't like him because
he's against the death penalty. Nixon is a shoo-in.

As for work, things have never been better. Captain De-
Freese finally assigned me and Jack Hackett to a two-man car.
Ours is Unit #3 downtown, a great place for cops like me
and Jack Hackett. It's sure different than Unit 51, with horns
honking and people on the sidewalks day and night and never
dark. The downtown units average maybe seven or eight
pinches a night because there's so much going on. The sailor
bars have been here forever with salty names like The Buc-
caneer, Barbet, China Doll, Singapore, Porthole and such.
Cops don't take sailors to jail for drunk or fighting unless
they're real assholes. Instead we take them to shore patrol who
gets them back to their ship and the sailor doesn't get in the
grease over it.

If we do a good job downtown maybe in a couple of years

we'll get transferred to vice or juvenile. That's usually the next step if a guy's going to work his way out of uniform, but right now I'm so glad to be downtown I don't even think about what might be down the line.

Jack Hackett is a helluva partner and we know each other's moves so well that it only takes a look to know what the other will do or what he's thinking. He still bugs me to go to Bernie's after work every day but I only go now and then.

The tough thing about leaving Unit 51 was saying good-bye to Hector Morales. Hector is eleven now and he cried when I told him I'd be moving downtown. He said I'll never see you again, so I told him I'd come up and play catch with him. He's some kid, Jerome. He said someday, Billy, I'm going to be somebody important. Turns out Hector had seen a guy in a suit and tie studying the bridge over Washington Street at Pacific Highway so of course Hector went up and bent the guy's ear. The guy was an architect looking over the structure and they must have had a long talk because Hector told me some day he would go to college and build bridges or tall buildings and make his mother and father proud. I said I'm proud of you now, Hector, and he put his arms around me and said you're the best friend I have, Billy.

There's one more thing to tell you because I can't get it off my mind. It happened my last day on Unit 51. Janet keeps telling me I should tell her things that bother me, but I don't because I don't want to upset her. Frank Runyon told me if he had it to do over he would talk to his wife about the job, but I just can't do it and Jack Hackett says that's why cops tell each other stories.

Anyway, I get a call to Bradman Drive over in Navy housing and there's a woman who won't let us in but says she has a gun and will kill herself. Sergeant Poole (remember my old midwatch sergeant--the Marlborough Man) shows up and we stand clear of the door and try to talk her into coming outside. She will have none of it, and a neighbor tells us her old man is probably drinking at The Hole, which is a sailor gin mill two blocks away. Poole tells me to go get him, so I do and his belly is full of beer and he isn't making sense and he keeps saying, why would she want to kill herself?

He's a chief, a roly-poly guy and his uniform is all rumpled and I'm back with him in five minutes and we tell his wife he's there so she tells us okay, have him get out on the lawn, she wants to talk to him. Poole and I figure that's no good she may shoot him, so we tell her we'll have him stand behind the police car and talk to her. The neighbors have come outside and can hear everything everybody's saying.

The chief starts saying something and she yells out, take off your hat when you speak to a lady, you son of a bitch. So he does. Then she tells him, say you'll come home after work every day. He says it, then she says, tell me you won't ever blow your paycheck again. So he says that, too. She says, promise you'll never call me a fucking bitch again. He starts to say that and she yells, louder, louder, LOUDER!

By now he's yelling it as loud as she is, then she says to him, get down on your knees. He looks at me and I motion for him to do it, so he does, and she calls out, now I want you to say I really do love you, and I never loved anybody like I love you. The chief says it and I can see he's crying, then she calls out, okay, you can get up now.

Me and Poole figure it's over and we move toward the door to talk to her again. That's when she blew her head off, Jerome.

I went to Bernie's after work and wondered if maybe a long time ago the Navy chief and our dead lady had it as nice as me and Janet have it.

Billy

• • •

December 23, 1962 – Sunday

Dear Jerome:

Six years in San Diego now and it's still hard getting used
to Christmas. The store windows are gussied up and lights
hang all over town, but yet I worked up a sweat in the yard
this morning, and then took Jimmie to a few innings of a
semipro game this afternoon. His head swings back and forth
when the pitcher and catcher toss them, then he looks up at
me like there's something fishy going on.

Mom and Amy will be home by the time you read this.
We tried to talk them into staying but you know Mom and
being home for Christmas. When they arrived and got off the
train, Mom grabbed Jimmie so Janet and I didn't see him for
five days. We had a good time, took them to the beach and to
a mountain town called Julian for apple cider and pie, and to
the zoo, then drove them to L.A. and let them see Hollywood
& Vine. I told Mom it was a zoo where they don't charge ad-
mission. Mom wanted to go knock on Gregory Peck's door
but I wrestled with her on the sidewalk and won the argument by promising to show her Garbo's footprints.

A bunch of prosecutors gave Amy the eye when I took her to
the D.A.'s office. They fell all over themselves talking law school
to her and giving her a courthouse tour. Being Amy, she had a
million questions and a guy answered one by saying--the guilty
are easy to convict, the innocent take a little longer. She didn't
find it all that funny, and asked where the women prosecutors
were. I hadn't thought about it but I don't think there are any.

On the way down in the elevator I asked Amy if you had
to turn in your sense of humor when you start law school.
That did it, and she didn't speak to me until the next day
when Jimmie mooned everybody and broke the place up.

Jerome, there's a bar on "F" Street downtown called the
Sports Palace and it's next to the Hollywood Theater. The
Hollywood is a burlesque house and a broken down come-
dian named Eddie Ware tosses around dirty jokes while the
girls strip and hump the curtain. Cops aren't supposed to be
in downtown bars off duty. So one day I duck in there off

duty, not to drink but to take my time looking at the wall full of Ruth and Dempsey and Bing Crosby and I hear this voice yell out, Considine, what the hell are you doing? It's Captain DeFreese and he's in a booth by himself over in a corner. He says sit your ass down.

We drank whiskey for three hours, Jerome. DeFreese ran away from North Dakota at age sixteen, rode the rails to Seattle and did odd jobs. He swept floors in a pharmacy until two years later when the Japs bombed Pearl Harbor, so he joined up the next day. Typical Navy, they made him a corpsman when they found out he'd worked in a pharmacy and that's how he happened to go through the South Pacific with the Marines.

He wouldn't let me pay for a drink and said, tonight it's Lloyd and Billy having a good time, tomorrow it will be captain and patrolman again. DeFreese is a born leader.

Frank Runyon got his leg banged up pretty bad. He had a car pulled over for speeding when a drunk driver headed for him. Runyon tried to dive out of the way which probably saved his life, but the car clipped him. I went to the hospital but they said Frank wanted no visitors.

This working downtown is a different world than the outlying beats. We rarely get burglarized but we pinch some burglars. They live in the shithouse hotels on our beat and catch buses or walk to the residential areas. We nail them on the sidewalks when we stop to check them out and we also watch the pawn shops to see who and what's coming in and going out. Downtown is full of low class whores and pimps and hustlers.

I almost forgot to tell you about the aircraft carriers. There are four of them based here and the hustlers work overtime when they come into port because each ship carries about 5,000 sailors. Knowing there will be lots of fights, Jack Hackett and I wear our oldest uniforms when the carriers hit town. Their names are The Constellation, The Oriskany, The Bon Homme Richard and The Ticonderoga. From the G Street pier you can look across the water and see them tied up, each one longer than a football field.

Broadway is the main street and it's full of clip joints selling dime jewelry and stuff to the whitehats. Sales guys with pimply faces and shiny suits stand in the doorway alcove and try to lure them in. If that isn't working they bring in the girls with big tits and tight asses to flirt with them. Next thing the poor sailor knows he's having his picture taken and buying ten dollar frames for Daisy Mae back in Nashville. These kids are so lonely they don't even mind getting fleeced.

There are a lot of bums downtown, at night most of them are in the mission or curling up in cardboard by the railroad tracks or on some loading dock south of "J" Street. None of them are young and almost none are women. Just a bunch of winos with a few nut cases mixed in. Sometimes they're the hardest to manage. Not nutty enough to be locked up but too goofy to be walking around on their own. Jack Hackett and I feel sorry for them. Janet packs an extra sandwich because she knows sometimes I give half my lunch away and sometimes we mooch a burger for them.

Jack Hackett is some piece of work. The night before last we see some sailor weaving all over the sidewalk in the 1000 block of 3rd. Jack pulls over, we get out and Jack says, put your hands behind your back, Seaman Stain. The kid says, what for? Jack says for about a minute until we can get you cuffed up and to Shore Patrol where it's warm and safe.

Well, the sailor starts dancing like this Cassius Clay and he's throwing punches in the air and it's obvious he's been in the ring, maybe a welterweight. He makes up a melody and he's singing, Come on cops, show your face. Let's see you take me where its warm and safe.

Now a crowd's gathering and this goofy whitehat starts doing a tap dance, still throwing punches, still singing, and people begin clapping and throwing money.

Jack Hackett and I are laughing so hard it was the first time we didn't know what the other would do. I call over to Jack who's all doubled over and I said, well, wise guy, this one's yours, what do you want to do? Jack reaches in his pocket, pulls out some change, tosses it at the kid's feet and says, let's get the hell out of here.

Jack Hackett and I do the same thing with hotel registers downtown that I did with motels on Unit 51. Usually, we're not looking for anything in particular but come up with a lot of runaways and people who are wanted. There are more girl runaways than boys and some of them end up being hookers. We check the Greyhound Depot about three times a shift because a lot of them hit town that way. Some sweet-talking pimp who's good at picking them out of a crowd springs for a hamburger and gives them a place to sleep, then pretty soon he's making $$ off them. So some sixteen-year-old who had no thought of being a whore when she left Lake Mishigoogoo is turning tricks and getting her face punched to keep her in line. When one of them finally works 5th and Island where the Negroes hang out it's the end of the line for her and the white pimp goes shopping at the Greyhound again.

Culpepper is working Unit 21 which is basically an all-Negro beat, and he's in love with some American Airlines stew who's based in L.A. so as soon as his work week is finished he heads north. He keeps promising to drop some of those little airplane whiskey bottles on us but we haven't seen any. Mom fell in love with Culpepper and wanted to put him in her suitcase.

The days go by fast. Janet keeps asking have I gone up to see Hector Morales yet and I keep meaning to but something always comes up. Maybe after January 1.

We're still doing okay with Janet not working. We got kicked to $616 a month and put the extra into a college account for you-know-who. I asked Janet if she missed the library and she smiled that wonderful smile and said, Billy, a mother can't count on having her baby more than eighteen years. I don't want to miss a single minute.

Speaking of our baby, when I get home on the night shift it's about 4 a.m. and I tiptoe in and grab a beer and sit in the dark at the kitchen table. When I finish and head for bed I stop in Jimmie's room to check him out. I look at him and kneel down next to his bunk and whisper and tell him what a big world it is out there and tell him about all of the things he can do.

Do you think those kids who get off Greyhound buses had parents talk to them while they were sleeping?

Billy

• • •

June 26, 1963 – Wednesday

Dear Jerome:

My spirits got lifted hearing about all the steel money floating around Youngstown. I'm glad times are good and you're able to do additions to the house. And Amy's finally getting her own bathroom, though how often she'll be there to use it when she becomes a big shot lawyer I do not know. We've always had the best looking house on Hampton Court because of the way you work the yard.

I got my five year service award and not long afterward took the sergeant's exam for the first time--a gasser. About three hundred of us sat at tables in a big room in the Conference Building in Balboa Park. They put an empty seat in between everybody so you couldn't see the paper of the guy next to you.

It took me the whole four hours, and the rub is, you get penalized a point and a half for each wrong answer whereas you get credited with a point for each right one. So if you guess instead of leaving it blank you're rolling the dice. Since only the top forty scores will pass, my hopes aren't high. For the next test in 1965 I will have studied more.

And guess what? Jimmie saw the president. He and a hundred thousand others. JFK gave the commencement address at San Diego State and all days off had been canceled because they motorcaded him from the airport out to the campus. I got as-signed the corner of Fairmount and El Cajon so Janet decided to take Jimmie. She got a good spot at my corner and had him dressed in red, white and blue and when the first secret service cars and press cars got near, the crowd really roared. I didn't get to see Kennedy because when he passed I faced the crowd like we're taught, but Janet said he's even more handsome than on TV. It's impossible to cover every roof top with cops and secret service so I was glad when he got past my corner.

Well, Jack Hackett and I had our first beef. A few of us from the squad had a table at Bernie's and Jack showed up with some tootsie. Knockers hanging out and giving every-body the pleased-to-meetcha routine. Jack was already stinko when they got there and started tossing down doubles. He'd never brought a girl around before.

A couple of nights later I said, Jack, you have a drinking problem. He said it's no problem at all, just bend the elbow and bring the glass to your lips and if you're referring to the other night at Bernie's, Considine, I don't need a lecture on morality.

That got me hot so I told him I didn't care about his girl-friend but I'm tired of him coming to work smelling like a peppermint factory. Jack got out of the car and took a leak on the railroad siding and when he came back he said, I suppose you've already told DeFreese about this since you and him are drinking buddies. So I blew up and called him a couple of names and told him if he thought I'm the kind of guy who would snitch to DeFreese he should get a new partner. It all happened last night and I hope it cools down over our days off, because Jack Hackett and I have come a long way together.

He is something. There's this operation called a vasectomy where they can make a guy shoot blanks the rest of his life and a lot of cops get them. I have no problem going against the church on this but want to wait until Janet and I have more kids.

Anyway, Jack Hackett wants to get one real bad but his wife won't go for it and no doctor will do it unless the Mrs. signs an okay. There's a doctor up on Maple Street next to the park who gives cops a pretty good price break, so Jack stashes some $$ from a couple of paychecks and one night we're parked behind Johnnie's which is a greasy spoon on Broadway where you can smell the liver and onions a block away. A waitress who we know comes out and says to Jack, what did you want to see me about? Jack says how would you like to be my wife for an hour? She says your cop buddies ask me that all the time, and Jack says, no, no, not that, I'm asking you to come up to Maple Street with me and sign something so I can get clipped.

And that's how Jack got it done. His wife still doesn't know and for three nights afterwards he felt very tender and moved ~~gingerley~~ gingerly so I let him stay in the car on fight calls. Is that being a good partner, or what?

A couple of nights later we're trying to talk a guy out of jumping from a ledge on the sixth floor of the Trust & Savings Building. He's a coat and tie guy, an insurance salesman working out of an office down the hall. We'd been talking to him for over an hour, saying everything we could think of. Telling him there's help out there, and lying about how other people we talked down told us later they were glad they didn't jump.

But he's not impressed and edging closer to the ledge and something tells me he's going to do it, and I'm desperate, so I think maybe I can jolt him. So I said, look buddy, come on inside, my partner and I were due off an hour ago, and there's something important I have to take care of this morning.

He turned and looked at me, Jerome, and said, well pardon me to hell, I didn't check your schedule before I came up here. There's something I have to take care of too.

Then he jumped. I'll never forget the look in his eyes. Times like this I wonder if I should have stayed in the Navy.

Billy

P.S. The government says the 80th U.S. soldier has died in Vietnam. What's going on over there anyway?

November 22, 1963 – Friday

Dear Jerome:
It's 11:45 p.m. and in three hours and twenty-five minutes I have to be at roll call, but I can't get to sleep. Janet finally closed her eyes a few minutes ago and I'm at the kitchen table, still unable to believe our president is dead.

Our squad is on morning watch (3:30 a.m. to 11:30 a.m.) and Jack Hackett and I usually head for the station from the beat about 11 a.m., but this morning we had a potful of reports so decided to go in at quarter of. I had to take a leak so bad I couldn't even wait to drive the seven blocks to Market Street, so we pulled into the Standard station at Pacific and Ash. I took care of my business and headed for the car when the attendant says, did you hear about Kennedy? I figure he has some cornball joke so I said make it fast, I'm heading in.

The kid has his hand wrapped around a gas hose and he says the president has been shot, I just heard it on the radio. I'm still thinking it's a gag so I said what's the punch line? But he says I'm not kidding, and by the look on his face Jerome, I believed him. He said it happened in Dallas but he had no details.

I got in the car and told Jack Hackett and we zipped to the station and when we pull into the police garage I know right away it's for real, because we see about forty cops gathered around the vehicle sign-out board listening to a radio. By now it's about 10:50 a.m., two hours earlier than Dallas.

We go into the squad room and grab a typewriter and one of the cops has a transistor radio, so we're listening while we write reports, but the info is all jumbled and nobody seems to know much. Everything is unreal. Twenty cops clicking away at stupid typewriters while the president's in some hospital. My report had to do with a ten thousand dollar grand theft that didn't seem important anymore. The cop with the transistor finishes and leaves with his radio, so all we know is that the wounds are serious.

Then it happened. The squad room is right next to the press room where they have a teletype machine, and this old reporter for the Union, his name is Pliny Castanien, he opens the door to the squad room and we all look up and Pliny stands there for a few seconds looking at us. Then he says real softly, he said, well boys...he's gone.

I finished my report and don't even remember changing clothes. When I got home it was a little after noon and Janet was sitting in a chair in the living room listening to the radio. She got up and we hugged each other and started crying. Then I said, isn't it on TV? Janet said, oh my God, I must be in shock. She said she'd been folding clothes and listening to a music station when they had cut in with the news, so she'd been sitting there staring at the radio for two hours.

Just before the news broke Jimmie had been taken to the park for some neighbor kid's birthday party. So Janet and I did what everybody else did, watched TV all day. I could hardly eat anything and wasn't able to go to sleep.

You read about Lincoln and McKinley in the history books, but who would have believed some crazy son of a bitch would take Kennedy from us, then kill a Dallas cop for good measure. I've got to shake this off and go to work.

• • •

November 24, 1963 – Sunday 11:45 p.m.

What's happening to our world, Jerome? Have only forty-eight hours gone by since I wrote the first part of this letter? I'm at the kitchen table again, and the streets of San Diego are dead. The few customers in the super markets stand at the checkout counters with tears in their eyes. People are hugging total strangers. I stood next to our police car on Union Street and some lady came up and threw her arms around me.

Then at 9:30 this morning I'm out of smokes, so I go into Rose's Liquor on "F" St. I'm paying the clerk and he says, imagine that, getting shot in Dallas right at the police station. I thought where has this clown been for two days? I said he didn't get shot in front of the police station, it happened in a motorcade. The guy gives me my Luckies and says, I'm not talking about Kennedy, I'm talking about Oswald. I said what about him? He said some guy jumped out of the crowd and shot Oswald when they were taking him from the police station to the county jail.

I walked out of the store and Jack Hackett said what's the matter? He told me later I kept shaking my head saying what's the world coming to?

There's hardly any radio calls coming in because nobody has anything important enough to report. No fight calls. The city is shut down out of respect for President Kennedy. The whole country! Except that greedy bastard Pete Rozelle who had the NFL play football today. Frank Runyon said guys who wear suits are always ruled by $$.

I go to work in a couple of hours, then I'm off for two days. It's strange, sitting with Janet watching TV and even though we see the same thing over and over we can't stop watching. We think the world really has stopped, but there's Jimmie running around playing and laughing like nothing's happened. Once he looked up at us and said, Mommy and Daddy cry. Janet said three months ago Martin Luther King went to Washington and told 200,000 people about his dream, which gave her real hope for a new beginning. And now this, which has zero to do with race.

We'll all have to get over it. I just don't know how.

Billy

• • •

May 25, 1964 – Monday

Dear Jerome:

Today I got badgered in court by a defense attorney trying to make me say I lied about getting permission to search the trunk of a car. When that didn't work, he accused me of planting two wristwatches under the seat. The jury found him guilty but when I got home and grabbed a shot of Old Crow and a beer Janet hands me a letter from Amy.

She's going to start work for some outfit in Cleveland and all they do is defend crooks. Here's Amy graduating number two in her class, a smart, smart girl who can charm a grizzly bear and is good looking to boot and who juries will love, and she's throwing it all away.

You probably heard by now that I didn't wait to write her, but phoned as soon as I finished reading the letter. As usual, Amy flew off the handle and we got into it. When I hung up, Janet said it's too bad we don't live closer to Youngstown, it would be easier for you to run your sister's life. How Janet comes off saying that I do not know.

A guy from our squad got transferred to Vice last week and I'm glad for him because he's a good street cop. Then DeFreese called me in. He said Considine, it was between you and the other guy for Vice, and I recommended him but I want you to know it was a close call. He told me our written reports made the difference, that mine were almost where they should be and to keep working hard. I got so pumped that when I walked out of the captain's office I phoned Janet, something I never do because it's not good to be connected to home when you're working.

The big news at work is that Chief Hale retired after thirty-two years as a cop and Asst. Chief Steele got appointed to replace Hale. Steele should be okay because he worked a long time for Hale and knows his way around.

Not much else is new. Frank Runyon's leg is almost better but they still have him working light duty in what's called the business office. One guy called and told Frank the department hasn't kept the streets safe so he sent his daughter to church in a taxi and wants the city to pick up the tab.

JACK MULLEN   89

A lieutenant grabbed me in the patio and said, I hear Jack
Hackett is on the sauce but good. I said where did you hear
that? He said I listen to locker room talk. So I told him he'd
better check his source, that Jack takes a drink like most of us
but there's no problem.

The truth is, Jack's a mess. His wife told him to choose between
the job and her and when he said he wanted a little time to think,
she started packing before he finished the sentence. So they found
somebody to take over payments on their house in Allied Gar-
dens, making no dough on the sale, and now Jack is sharing a
dingy little apartment with a divorced burglary detective.

Jack's sending most of his $$ to his wife and daughter in Ore-
gon so instead of going to Bernie's, he picks up a jug and goes
home, saying to anyone who'll listen that it makes no difference,
a drink is a drink.

He's sober when he comes to work but he doesn't have the
fire in his belly anymore. I have to coax him to get off his ass and
make good felony stops. One day he called the wrong guy an
asshole, a working stiff who didn't have it coming. I stepped in
to smooth things over and had Jack sit in the car, then told the
guy Jack is going through rough times. We talked some more,
then the guy shrugged and said what the hell, everybody's en-
titled to a bad day.

The next day Jack got mad at a hooker he's been trying to
cultivate as an informant. That was the first I knew about it,
and when we cleared, I told him Frank Runyon said getting
too connected with hookers is risky. Jack said Considine, you
may think Runyon is Jesus Christ, but I don't. I almost took
a swing at him.

Jerome, the local Muslims have what they call a mosque
on Unit 21's beat and they wear dark blue suits and advertise
themselves as religious and non-violent. Trust me, Jerome,
they're an unfriendly bunch when it comes to whitey.

When he trained me, Frank Runyon said that on this job,
on every contact, I should put myself in the shoes of the other
person. He said the trick is to see how fast you can tell if

they're a good citizen or a shithead. Last week we had coffee and Frank said right now Negroes are thumbing their noses at government and cops are part of government. He said they' got tired of the backs of buses and segregated schools with crap facilities and all that. He said every Negro in San Diego has either been jerked around on the street by SDPD or knows someone who has.

I told Frank Negroes have it good in San Diego compared to the south, and Frank said, oh yeah, ask a San Diego Negro what it's like to go into a clothing store or jewelry store and have the manager assign an employee to follow them around. Frank said they don't do it to white customers and someday it's all going to blow up in our face.

Billy

P.S. The Republicans must be drinking silly water because Considine-Hackett would have a better chance than Gold-water-Miller.

P.P.S. I wasn't going to say anything about this, but Janet said go ahead. It looks like we can't have any more kids. It's something about fibroid tumors and Janet may have to have a hysterectomy. She said we can always adopt a brother or sister for Jimmie. The important thing is the doctor says Janet's in no danger.

• • •

December 30, 1964 – Wednesday

Dear Jerome:
I won't be phoning New Year's Eve because some high school pal of Jack Hackett's sent him Rose Bowl tickets and he doesn't want to go. He says Michigan will trim Oregon State good unless Pasadena falls into the sea. So Friday at

about 4 a.m. the Considine family will line up on Colorado Boulevard for the parade and Jimmie will be on my shoulders so look for us on TV.

But don't look for a guy smoking a Luckie because Janet and I quit. She saw the surgeon general's report, then started pounding on me. I'm not having too bad a time so far, but picked up five pounds. The owner of Rose's Liquor told me since the report was published his cig sales are down 30% but pipe tobacco, beer and liquor all went up. He's a little guy who chews with his mouth open and mumbled that Americans love their vices and the only business better than his is selling girls. ~~Speaking of girls~~

Speaking of girls, guess what? Your kid brother delivered one in the back seat of a police car. A lady on a bus bench flagged us down at 5th and Broadway. She needed to get to County Hospital but didn't have cab fare and didn't think she could wait any longer. I'd been driving but Jack Hackett broke into a sweat and knocked me over so he could get behind the wheel. It went just like they taught us in the academy, and Jacqueline Considine Robinson was born at 2:15 a.m. going through the intersection of 1st and Washington. The mother said she already had one named Billy. Jack Hackett said he'd rather swallow razor blades then play doctor.

Jack has been sniping at me because I told him he should get his ass to an A.A. meeting. He said, they should rename you Father Considine because I heard you've been telling Culpepper he should settle down and get married, I don't know how you have time to do police work and be Dear Abby too. So there's no talking to Jack Hackett and I'm giving up.

In your last letter you asked about Hector Morales. I still haven't had a chance to get to my old beat and see him but will try next week. I've been busy putting up a swing set for Jimmie and hauling in wood chips to go under it. He picked up a hammer and banged his thumb and Janet who was at a neighbor's three doors away heard him crying. So she got sore at me for not watching him and I told her it's hard to put up a see-saw and watch a three year old at the same time. While we argued poor Jimmie's thumb got big as a marshmallow so we took him to the ER and used our new dependent's benefit plan for the first time. The police officer's association is going into the insurance business and for $17.55 a month I get Janet and Jimmie covered. Anyway, nothing was broken and we stopped at A&W on the way home and he drank a Papa-size root beer float so all was well with the world again.

The other reason I didn't go see Hector was because I caught a suspension and had to work two days off. You can guess how happy Janet was about that. All patrol and traffic cops wear helmets now instead of the soft uniform caps, because the city got fed up with medical costs on cops getting bopped in the head with rocks and bottles. So they issued helmets and it's an automatic two days off if you're caught with the chin strap unsnapped. I was first.

Janet has had highs and lows since having her hysterectomy and we still can't thank Mom enough for coming out to take care of Jimmie so I wouldn't have to take vacation time. Mom said getting over the physical part is one thing, getting over the part about not being able to have more babies is tougher.

As for school, I'm doing pretty good. A counselor said I should work toward what's called an associate of arts degree in criminal justice so I'm taking history and math courses as well as the police stuff. Without Janet's help I couldn't handle the schedule.

Well, Jerome, the party's over. Five blockheads on the Supreme Court say we have to advise crooks of their constitutional rights before we question them. It's called the Escobedo Decision. Chicago cops took Escobedo to the station because the dumb shit teamed up with some guy and killed Escobedo's brother-in-law. Escobedo's lawyer showed up while the cops were questioning him but the cops played hide-and-seek with the lawyer, moving Escobedo from place to place.

Now before we talk to a crook we have to give them what is called "their rights." The D.A. gave us little cards and we must read from them, telling them they have a right to remain silent, anything they say can be used in court against them and they have the right to a lawyer.

I understand the Feds have been stuck with these rights for a long time but so much for us ever getting confessions again. The vote on the court was five to four, but as you used to tell me, close only counts in horseshoes and hand grenades.

I hope 1965 is all you want it to be. Since Amy will be home for New Years Eve, plant a big one on her for me and tell Mom I love her.

Billy

P.S. After I delivered the baby I got thinking about the mother of those six kids and all the people we run into on this job who will never know how nice it is to own their own home and put up a swing set. They didn't get the breaks I got, growing up around people like you and Mom, then getting a craving for cotton candy and bumping into Janet.

PART THREE

You're Ruined for Life, Kid

• • •

July 10, 1965 – Saturday

Dear Jerome:
Last night at roll call the sergeant said, effective tomorrow Officer Waldron is assigned to Juvenile, Captain DeFreese is promoted to inspector and Officer Considine is transferred to the Pussy Posse. That's just how the sarge said it.

So tonight I report to the Vice Squad which meant Janet ran to the May Company basement and picked up two suits for me at thirty-three bucks apiece. They're not fancy, but vice is night work with no brass around the station. Then we hustled downtown to buy me a fedora. Janet says the hat makes me look like a cross between Dick Tracy and Cary Grant. Jack Hackett said Deputy Dog is more like it.

I'm glad to get out of uniform but the downside is none of the troops want to partner with Jack Hackett, so he has to leave Unit 3 and work a one-man car out in the college district. I tried to get Culpepper to team with him, but Culpepper says for Jack's sake its better he has to go it alone and have no one to lean on. How Jack will manage that I do not know. Hold a good thought for him, Jerome.

Vice Squad Officer Billy

P.S. In current events I had to get up and tell the class what I'd been hearing as a cop from the man on the street. The answer is a huge buzz about the civil rights movement.

P.P.S. There's no pay raise going to vice-still making 713 a month. On our department detectives make the same salary as patrol cops and that's how it should be.

• • •

October 18, 1965 – Monday

> *Dear Jerome:*
> Well, Amy must be thumping her chest. In Mom's letter she put in the newspaper clipping about how Amy got that burglar off because she found two witnesses who said they were with him at the critical time. The article didn't say where, but I suppose in the Christian Science reading room.
>
> Speaking of burglars, Culpepper got transferred to detectives, is working burglary and just made a big case. A suspect the squad room named Society Sam had been hitting ritzy homes in La Jolla, Pt. Loma and Kensington. When Culpepper found out the victims had always been attending some well publicized social event while the burglary went down, he figured maybe the crook read the society page to get names of people who wouldn't be home. He convinced his boss to give him stakeout manpower and sure enough, the second night out the guy broke into a house on Neptune Place and two cops were in the living room to welcome him. Way to go, Culpepper.
>
> As for your kid brother, it turns out I didn't need those May Company basement suits until just the other night. For three months I've been undercover in one capacity or another. There are eighteen cops in Vice, fourteen night guys who wear coats and ties and the rest on days working bookmakers and assorted stuff.
>
> By the way, now that LBJ has doubled the draft and we're bombing North Vietnam pretty regularly, some of the younger cops who are reservists are hoping this mess gets cleaned up fast. One of them, a guy on my old patrol squad, told me he'd rather roll around in gutters he's familiar with than go six thousand miles away to do it in jungles.
>
> Since I'm off today I went to Old Town to see Hector Morales, but his family has moved. One neighbor said she thought they went back to Mexico and another said there'd been talk of moving down to Logan Heights. Now I wish I'd come earlier.

Jerome, this Vice lieutenant is something. His name is Soderholm and he's a big guy, maybe 6-3 but turning soft in the middle. A scar runs all the way down the right side of his face and Frank Runyon said he's one psycho son of a bitch. The window behind Soderholm's desk is glazed so you can't see in. Soderholm told the city he needed it that way so people couldn't see who was in his office on sensitive stuff, but some guys think it's so nobody can look in when Soderholm's "interviewing" girls for cabaret cards because the lieutenant has to okay licenses for barmaids and Go-Go dancers. Some cops think Soderholm takes a look at the pictures attached to their application, then selects certain ones to come to his office where he finds out how bad they want to get licensed. So I don't know.

The vice sergeant sat me down and said, Considine, think of the Vice Squad as a big ocean, and all of the guys on the squad have a boat, but since you're the newest guy, you have the smallest boat, so don't make any waves. Then he puffed on his cigar and said, do you get the picture, Considine? I didn't really, but I'm keeping my eyes open and my mouth shut.

The day in July that I reported I figured I'd be going to nights, but Soderholm called me in and said he'd have me working undercover. For a short while is how he put it. I'd never talked to him before and he seemed friendly enough. He said you drink, don't you, and when I said yes he said good, because you'll be going into some bars for me.

Soderholm gave me ten bucks, the keys to a beat up undercover car and the names of four joints. My job. Go in, have a couple, and at the end of the day write him a report on everything I saw. I worked nine in the morning to five, so by noon I'd be pretty full of beer and would switch to bourbon and water. It was costing me more than a sawbuck a day so I made it up out of household money and then put it on my expense report. Soderholm looked at it and said you like to drink, huh Considine? I said, Lieutenant, if a customer's at the bar at nine in the morning and nurses his drinks, any bartender worth his salt smells something fishy. Soderholm grunted and coughed up the money.

Gambling is what they wanted me to get a line on, but all I ever saw was a customer running horse bets for other customers if he happened to be going to Caliente or Del Mar that day (Caliente is a track in Tijuana).

Janet got sick and tired of me coming home blitzed every night and falling asleep over my mashed potatoes.

After that Soderholm put me in the sailor bars downtown to see if the barmaids were mingling with the customers which is a big no-no under a city municipal code. Remember, Jerome, when the Browns or Indians played a big game and you could walk down Belmont or Mahoning or Market and every place you passed would have a radio blaring so you never missed a play. I thought of that, because every joint I walk into has the juke box blaring and either Petula Clark is singing Downtown or Nancy Sinatra is telling how she's going to walk over you with her boots.

Here's one for you. I told you the downtown Negroes hang out in the 500 block of 5th Ave and that one of the places is called the Zebra Club. Soderholm sits me down and tells me there's a whore the night guys have been unable to nail and he wants me to go in there and see if she hits on me. He gives me a sailor uniform to roll up and carry under my arm (it's supposed to be a government violation for a cop to actually wear it).

That's all well and good, except guess what day I walk into the Zebra? August 14th, Saturday. The Watts riot in L.A. is going full blast and your pale-faced brother is in this Negro joint with just a chicken shit sailor suit for company. I forgot to tell you, when you're undercover you can't carry a badge or a gun because these girls feel you up if they're at all suspicious.

The Zebra is wall-to-wall people, and I'm the only white guy in there. A little TV was mounted over the bar and of course the news from L.A. was on. Jerome, they were showing the tanks and National Guardsmen going through Watts and

L.A. cops beating the shit out of looters. It's real drunk in the Zebra and the customers are screaming at the TV set to get them honkies, kill them blue-eyed devils. All of a sudden I'm wishing I'm back working Unit 3 with Jack Hackett, but I bellied up to the bar and said, bartender, give me a bottle of Budweiser. And every time they yelled kill Whitey, I called for another one. The whore never hit on me, so after four beers I walked out and hit another place.

The last thing to tell you is that ten days ago Soderholm called me in and said, Considine, I'm putting you in the St. James Hotel for three nights, spend all of your time at the bar in the Melody Room (it's right off the lobby of the hotel) and have sandwiches delivered for your dinner. He gave me the mug shot of some big out of town bookie they had a warrant on who was supposed to show up.

But the rub is, we're sitting in Soderholm's office and he tells the sergeant, call the St. James and get the rates. The sarge does and hangs up and says, three bucks without a bath, five with. Soderholm says Considine can use the shower down the hall and we can save money.

A Santa Ana came in and it turned out to be the hottest October on record for the date. The suspect never did show, and all I did was get drunk and eat Philly steak sandwiches from a joint called Caruso's two blocks over. That ended my undercover career and I don't know who's happier, Janet or my liver.

It felt good to get on nights which I started last Friday. We do mostly bar checks, looking for minors being served, waitresses mingling with customers, dancers without a license and stuff like that. With the coats and ties and hats we're not trying to fool anybody because the bars know the Vice Squad is all over the place and means business.

We're also supposed to spot-check liquor stores, that is sit on a place and when a borderline customer walks out, check them out to see if they're twenty-one. And we're expected to nail a street whore from time to time and crash dice games and check for joints that serve after hours. So there's a lot to do and the shift goes real fast. We work 7:30 p.m. to 4:00 a.m.

They partnered me up with a guy named R.Q. Hutchinson and he is some piece of work, Jerome. He'd been in patrol when I was a rookie so I'd seen him around. R.Q. is as big as Soderholm but hard as a rock, and has a reputation as one tough guy. But I can tell you after working two nights with him, he doesn't push people around. He said, Considine, I want to win a gold medal for loving, not for fighting, and from what I've seen he'll at least get a silver.

R.Q. is from Rochester and his family worked for Kodak like ours worked the mills. Like me, he came to San Diego in the Navy, then decided to stay because of the weather. Anytime it's under seventy degrees, R.Q. sounds like Uncle Liam, complaining to anyone who'll listen that it's colder~~then~~ than a well digger's ass.

My first night with him, we pull into the parking lot of the Turtle Inn which is on the corner of 43rd and National in the Negro part of town. I knew the Turtle Inn from patrol and it's as rowdy as the Zebra Club only three times bigger. Because of the Watts riots I'm looking around pretty good when we get out of the car and when we open the door of the club, R.Q. stands in the doorway and yells out, are there any nigg...in here?

I'm standing there looking at maybe one hundred black faces and thinking my revolver holds six rounds should I save the last one to use on myself. I thought, well, Jerome has read his last letter from me and I hope they bury me at second base on the high school diamond and put up a plaque saying, here lies Billy Considine, the Pete Rose of Youngstown.

About that time, someone pulls the juke box plug and it gets deathly quiet and I hear a loud voice from the crowd call out, no sir, Mister R.Q., just us colored gentlemen are in here. R.Q. wipes his forehead like he's really relieved and yells back, okay, then I guess it's safe for my partner and I to come in.

I guess I must have still been in shock. We go in and end

up checking a few IDs and talking to the bartender, and R.Q. shakes a few hands and is as polite to everybody as if the Queen had invited us for tea.

R.Q. is single and not much of a boozer, though when he's off duty he likes a Jap place called Miyako's at Pacific and Hawthorne. He says Soderholm has told him to stay out of there because one of the assistant chiefs likes to drink there and doesn't want any low level cops around. But I don't think R.Q. Hutchinson is a guy who takes advice real well.

Take care of Mom and tell the neighbors I send them my best.

Billy

P.S. The Yankees will be calling for me any day. Sixth place!!!

P.P.S. We didn't have any trouble here during the Watts riots. On the second day, Chief Steele ordered patrol to march down the middle of Oceanview, National and Imperial Avenues and close down all the bars just to let them know who's boss and keep them from getting any ideas.

• • •

April 18, 1966 – Monday

Dear Jerome:

I've been on night vice six months and have a better handle on things. Lieutenant Soderholm reports directly to Chief Steele which irritates the captain and other brass in between but I guess it's because vice stuff is sensitive.

Since the night crew has Sundays and Mondays off, we throw a party every Sunday and rotate houses, just vice cops and their wives, no lieutenant or sergeant. Janet's drinking more at the parties then I've ever seen her, probably out of self-defense. At one party some loud mouth talked about how Soderholm makes us take the Go-Go dancers backstage and measure the size of the pasties they're wearing over their nipples to make sure the pasties aren't smaller than the municipal code allows. Janet didn't say anything but I saw the look on her face, and on the way home she gave me hell for not telling her about it. I said I didn't want you to be upset over nothing but she fired right back and said Billy, you lied by omission.

It was almost light out when we got home and I walked the baby sitter to her house, thinking Janet would have cooled off when I got back. But Jimmie was up and hungry and she was getting him ready for school and was still sore. So I took Jimmie to kindergarten and when I got back she was in a fine state. She said I don't think you love me anymore. I said Janet, what are you talking about? She said you hardly ever tell me that you do. She said you have a single partner and spend your shift around young girls with big tits and small brains. Jerome, wouldn't you figure Janet knows by now how much I love her? The next day I brought some flowers home but it didn't do much good.

Soderholm wants us to bust more gambling games because he needs statistics for his budget request, so R.Q. and I get a tip about a dice game. We're going up and down this street trying to find the right house and a car comes toward us weaving so bad they almost hit us. Even though we're in coats and ties we can't ignore it, so we put out a call for patrol and somehow get the guy stopped--in the middle of the street.

Just when you think you've been on this job long enough to see it all. Turns out the driver is blind! It's the passenger's car, but the passenger is drunk so he's directing his blind buddy how to steer. Both of them scream at us to give them a break because they're only a block from home. The patrol car that covered us turns out to be Jack Hackett and Jack is laughing so hard he can't talk.

R.Q. keeps a bag of dog food in the office, so when we hit a game he always has a pocketful. The people who run games usually have a big watchdog and when we sneak up on them, R.Q. is able to make friends with the mutt real fast. Another time we staked out in some bushes looking through a window watching some Chinese guys play and a German Shepherd took a leak on my leg three times in ten minutes.

When a bar sets a pattern of giving patrol a bad time, Soderholm calls the owner in and tells him patrol has been getting a lot of calls to his bar and having to fight their way out. Soderholm tells the guy to clean up his mess, and that usually takes care of it. But if the guy bows his neck, Soderholm pats him on the shoulder and says never mind, that's what we cops are paid to do.

The next night all eighteen guys on the squad meet around the corner from the problem bar, and we send the smallest guy in by himself. He checks a few IDs and gets catcalls but keeps track of the wise asses, which is usually everybody. Then the door opens and the rest of us barge in, with Soderholm leading the way. By then patrol has backed the paddy wagon up to the door and the party starts.

One night R.Q. and I are sneaking down the hall in the Metropole Hotel listening for bed springs creaking, because in the Metropole, anytime bed springs are creaking it's a whore deal. We end up knocking on the door of a room at the end of the hall and a drunk sailor wants to know what we want. We jerk him into the hall and he tells us he paid five bucks for his companion. We flick the light on and you should have seen her. R.Q. says, that woman is older than my grandmother and my grandmother's seventy-five. The sailor looks at her and says, she's older than anyone I know. Then he threw up.

We have her dress herself under the blankets and get her I.D. out of her purse. Her date of birth is 3-27-1884. Do the math and you'll know why, after we booked her, R.Q. and I went into an eatery called Vesuvio's and sat there having coffee laughing ourselves sick.

Soderholm sat R.Q. down last week and said this is your final warning, stay out of Miyako's. I told R.Q. that baseball managers won't let players drink in the hotel bar when they're on the road, because the managers don't want to put up with guff from some utility player with a snootfull who thinks he should be starting. I told him to find another place.

That's it from here,

Billy

• • •

April 20, 1966 – Wednesday

Jerome, I feel awful. R.Q. got bounced back to patrol. He went into Miyako's for a drink on our night off Monday and word got back to the chief's office. When we came in to work last night Soderholm was in the office and told R.Q. to clean out his locker and report to patrol. R.Q. said piss on you, Lieutenant, and walked out. So now he's an ex-cop.

P.S. Karate classes are popping up all over San Diego. One of the guys on the squad named Crowley is a southerner and we were talking about all the screaming and shenanigans that go with this Karate, and Crowley said, back home in hill country, the boy doing the yelling is the one getting hurt.

P.P.S. Crowley's father came out for a visit and said if a Tennessee mountain boy is being paid $700 a month to be a cop, something is terribly wrong.

• • •

August 18, 1966 – Thursday

Dear Jerome:
Here's some news. I'm working days with Sat and Sun off. On July 1 they transferred me to burglary and Janet was so

thankful to be out of vice she led me to the car and to the Cotton Patch for a steak. The next day she bought me a couple of sports coats decent enough to wear to work when the sun is out. How Janet manages our money so well I do not know.

Here's how I got motivated to study for sergeant. Janet sat me down with a pad and pencil and showed me how much more a month we'd get as a sergeant. That number wasn't so impressive, but then she did the math on retirement pensions, calculating what a sergeant would get over the years compared to a patrolman. That did it.

Anyway, these hours are nice and over the last two weekends we've been to Balboa Park and caught movies at the Midway and College Drive-Ins. Jimmie runs from the time we get to the park until we leave and at the movies he zonks out before the previews are over, unless it's a James Bond, in which case he tries to stay awake while Janet frets about him seeing Bond's girlfriends wearing outfits the size of dinner napkins.

As for burglary, I'm learning the routines and Culpepper is helping me. There's a sergeant for each of the five districts and mine is ancient. He dips snuff, has a photographic memory, sorts paper at his desk, all the time squirting juice into his private waste basket. Private because the janitors won't even look at it so the sarge takes the basket outside himself and fertilizes the Hibiscus bushes on the Pacific Highway side of the station.

I handle residential and commercial burglaries plus process people arrested by patrol. The Escobedo ruling I cried to you about didn't turn out to be doomsday but it still hurts. The problem is, a crook waives his rights, confess, then gets to court and swears you never advised them. So now we have them sign a form.

Last night Chief Steele went on TV to tell the city how clean our department is. You probably saw in the national news where another blue ribbon commission is investigating corruption on the New York P.D. Our local media doesn't like to let a day go by without being a pain in the ass, so when

the N.Y. story broke they climbed all over Steele asking about
our department. Steele came across pretty good on camera
because he admitted that prior to 1947 we'd had some problems, and then he told how Chief Hale and he had cleaned
house and professionalized us.

It's my turn to read to Jimmie so I'll finish this letter
tomorrow.

• • •

August 20 – Saturday

Well, I couldn't finish the letter last night because Culpepper
surprised everybody by getting himself in the grease. A first for him.
He got assigned a residential job out on Winona Avenue where the
back door had been pried and the old widow lady who lives there
discovered it when she came home from the quilt shop. The burglar
had ransacked hell out of her place, but worse yet had strangled her
poodle, who the old gal says yaps when anybody comes calling.

Culpepper said the poor old lady is feeble and uses a
walker and was more upset about her dog than the burglary.
She starts crying because she'd arranged in her will for her
sister to take the dog but now the dog's dead and she doesn't
have money for a decent burial.

Culpepper is feeling so sorry for her he tells a whopper.
Says he has a friend who works at a pet cemetery and
Culpepper is sure his friend can arrange a nice burial for the
mutt, but he can't tell her where the cemetery is, because if
word gets out Culpepper's friend will get in dutch and maybe
even fired for doing this on the cuff.

Culpepper says the lady thanked him twenty times, then
Culpepper wrapped the poodle in a pillow case and drove
off. Jerome, one mile southeast of her house is the Chollas
city garbage dump, so Culpepper buzzes by there and tosses
the dog on top of a pile.

Near quitting time the chief's office phones burglary. A lady has just called the chief to thank that sweet Detective Culpepper, but she forgot something important. Muffin was wearing his rhinestone collar and she'd like to have it back as a keepsake before the services are held. She tells the chief's office she raved about Culpepper to her nephew who happens to be a weekend anchor on Channel 8.

Culpepper grabs me, we head for my house, grab two shovels, explain things to Janet, buy a case of beer at the market on Ashford Street and head for the dump.

At midnight we're still digging but by now Muffin has to be under a ton of garbage and Culpepper and I smell like Hogan's goat. We polished off the last two beers and called it quits.

When hell broke loose Culpepper got written up--four days off for conduct unbecoming an officer, so he'll work the next two weekends and his airline sweetie in L.A. will have to go without.

My best to everybody,

Detective Billy Considine (Professional digger)

• • •

December 7, 1966 – Wednesday

Dear Jerome:
Look at the date on this letter. Twenty-five years ago today was a Sunday and you had taken two dimes out of your savings jar and were getting ready to take me to the Uptown Theater at Market and Indianola. Then the Japs started dropping bombs.

Everybody had their radio on and I asked you what a Pearl Harbor was and you said it's a place way across the ocean. Then you put your arms around me because I was afraid and you said, don't be scared, Billy, they can't get us here in Ohio and everything's going to be okay. You were only 17, Jerome. You've been some brother to me.

Janet told me she wrote Mom about my transfer from burglary to robbery. Burglars come in when nobody's around but robbers stick a gun under somebody's nose and take what they want. A sergeant is in charge of robbery and there are five detectives. At thirty-four your kid brother is the baby. Since I've been on the department I've noticed that the robbery guys have a way about them walking down the hall or across the patio. Not exactly saying we're the big cheeses, but they look like detectives who know exactly what they're doing.

Sergeant Stanley is my boss and he said, Considine, you were only in burglary long enough to find your way to the can, but I have an opening and Inspector DeFreese says you have the stuff it takes to work this detail. He said I see your report writing went from horseshit to acceptable and you've got a couple of suspensions. I didn't say anything to that, then the sarge said, the suspensions don't bother me because I'm suspicious of cops with squeaky clean files because if they never get in trouble they're not doing much police work to begin with.

The sarge is a tall, good looking guy with grey hair who's been on since 1941. I forgot to tell you, about six months ago the chief said detectives didn't have to wear hats anymore, and most of us dumped them. But Sergeant Stanley still wears his and he's a real clotheshorse. Word around the squad room is he's forgotten more about robbery than the rest of us will ever know. He told me solving stickups is about four things. Names, faces, M.O. and getting off our asses.

He told me never make a case on an eyewitness if that's all you've got, because there's a hundred reasons why they can pick the wrong guy out of a lineup and a hundred more why they might not knock off the right guy.

I'm learning a lot from these robbery detectives. Yesterday a suspect's girlfriend answered the door and we pushed by her and found our guy laying on a bed bare-ass naked. We cuffed him up then dressed him. We found the ski mask under the mattress and the gun plus the paper bag the $$ had been put in which matched the coding of the bags the liquor store uses.

Some old uniform cop with gravy stains on his tie had gone in with us and he says, looks like the elites in robbery are running scared, afraid to let their suspects put their drawers on. My partner got right up in his face and said, listen, nobody's going to use a hidden gun to cancel my ticket just because I let him pull his shit-stained skivvies on.

Half of the detectives who call robbery and homicide the lighter-than-air squad are kidding, and the other half are jealous.

There's a lot of talk in the squad room about the Negroes. About how this Black Muslim leader Elijah-something says whites are afraid to fight and real Muslims have no fear. Then Cassius Clay says he's going to get out of the draft because he's a Muslim minister. He's ministering like I'm doing those heart transplants down in Houston.

How do you figure Martin Luther King preaching peaceful protesting but they riot in Watts again.

I told Janet, King bad mouths the president saying he should pull the troops out of Vietnam while Johnson is stepping up the bombing trying to get it over with. I told her LBJ's Great Society may be fading a little around the edges, but he's still the president and if he says we need to be in Vietnam then we need to be there. Janet looked up from her book and said robbery cops should worry more about things they can control, like solving bank stickups.

I'm glad you're thinking about going for a higher spot in the union like Uncle Mike did. He helped the workers more and quit coming home from the blast furnace every night wrung out like a dish rag. With your smarts and the way you get along with people, you're just what the local needs. There. I get to give you advice for once!

You said you'd been in Cleveland for an Indian's game in July and almost got caught in the riot. I'm glad you're okay, but be sure when you're there or in Pittsburgh for a union meeting, you know beforehand what street you want to travel on. You probably saw where they had to call out 2,000 national guardsmen in San Francisco to put down a riot. I guess

Frank Runyon's predictions are accurate, but we haven't had any rioting here and are keeping our fingers crossed.

The war stuff is getting to be a pain in the ass. Jack Hackett still works patrol in the college area and he says some students are wearing black arm bands to mourn the dead. I saw Jack yesterday and he said there's even talk of students and faculty going on a forty-eight hour fast to protest our being in Vietnam.

Speaking of Jack Hackett, he cleared all the booze out of his apartment and went three days without a drink. On what would have been day number five I saw him and said, how's it going, Jack? He looked pretty rough, Jerome, and said the day before he'd been at the liquor store when it opened at 6 a.m. He said he still thinks he can quit if he really wants.

He wanted company so I went to Bernie's with him and forgot I was supposed to be home at seven for a tour of Jimmie's kindergarten class. Janet had another bite of my ass.

We're going to the Chicken Pie Shop in Hillcrest to eat, so I have to sign off. Xmas presents will be coming in the mail. Tell Mom her boy loves her.

Billy

P.S. It looks like the Medicare thing that's starting up is going to be good for old goats like you. Ha-Ha.

P.P.S. Here's one for you. About thirty mothers had picketed a store downtown holding signs about how terrible the store is to sell military type toys. An old WW II patrol sergeant ended up in the grease because a TV cameraman caught him shouting to the picketers they should be home baking pies or knitting.

P.P.P.S. Janet asked if I learned anything by the patrol sergeant getting in dutch over the baking pies crack. When I said what do you mean, she said you've answered my question. Let me know if you figure that one out, Jerome.

• • •

March 4, 1967 – Saturday

Dear Jerome:
Only crazy California can put a movie actor in the governor's seat. Well, at least Reagan is a law and order guy and we
need one of those. There's more dope on the street than ever.

Jack Hackett said the student power movement is driving
him nuts. He can't go to the hot dog stand at College and
Montezuma without catching crap. The other day he placed
his order and a kid opened up on him. Jack said she looked
like the girl next door but talked like the ship's parrot. I see
Bobby Kennedy's bitching about bombing North Vietnam,
too. That kind of crap just eggs on the students and makes it
harder for Jack Hackett to buy a hot dog.

Janet says to put a hug and kiss in the envelope from her
and to tell you and Mom she's excited about our trip to
Youngstown for Easter. I've been telling Jimmie about the
Isaly dairy stores with their deli and soda parlors, and he
agrees that while I'm having one of those baked ham sandwiches and sour pickles he'll be on the dairy side knocking
back their special chocolate ice cream.

Janet's always on the go doing a hundred things and keeping the place nice, but says her golden time is when she gets
to go one-on-one with Jimmie. When I want to take her out
to dinner she usually says no, let's stick a few bucks in the college fund instead. Even when we do eat out she's thinking
about the $$ and says let's go home for dessert.

That son of a bitch Earl Warren and his Supreme Court
cronies are at it again. Last summer they ruled on what's now
known as the Miranda Decision. I told you a few years ago
about the Escobedo Decision where we had to advise crooks
of their rights. If we thought that was bad, get a load of this.

Phoenix P.D. nailed this Ernie Miranda for rape and kid-
napping and got a confession. Miranda had signed a form say-

ing his statement was being made voluntarily and he understood his rights and understood that the statement could be
used against him. But since Miranda didn't have money falling
out of his pockets, Warren's boys say Phoenix should have advised Miranda that if he couldn't afford an attorney, a free one
would be appointed for him before questioning.

It was another 5-4 decision, and just like Escobedo, it was
Warren, Douglas, Brennan, Black and Goldberg vs. Harlan,
Stewart, Clark and the old football player, Whizzer White.
Everybody knows Douglas is loony tunes, but get this. Warren
said the room in which Miranda was questioned was cut off
from the outside world. He said it was a police dominated at-
mosphere. Well, no shit! Does he want us to question the guy
at 4th & Broadway? Ike must be shaking his head wondering
why he ever appointed him.

Robbery detectives interrogate guys who would lie to
their diary. Some are cagey and some so dumb they'd play
Russian roulette with a pistol instead of a revolver. Here's a
different one. A sad one.

The other day at noon the American Airlines office in the
U.S. Grant Hotel gets hit by a suspect described as fifty-something years old with a revolver. Last seen walking south on
4th from the front of the hotel.

Downtown patrol cops follow his trail to a flea bag hotel
and grab him while he's sitting on the edge of his bed finish-
ing off a pint of vodka.

It's my case, and this guy isn't fifty-something, he just
turned seventy. When I walk in the interrogation room and
look at him, I think he must be a twin brother of that boilermaker from the Ohio Works who lives on the street next
to the cemetery. The one with the head full of white hair
who looks like everybody's grandfather.

This guy's name is Valentine McAuliffe so you know what
day his birthday falls on. He's older than Mom, and I found
myself calling him Mister McAuliffe. If anybody tries to tell
you this institutionalized-man-syndrome is a lot of crap, tell

them about Valentine McAuliffe. All he wanted was a ticket back to prison. They'd sprung him five days before the robbery and he couldn't make it on the outside. Told me, Sonny, I've spent most of my life in one joint or another, and at San Quentin I had respect from inmates and from officers and I worked the warden's yard and his wife said nobody had ever tended flower beds like me.

I said, Mister McAuliffe, that's why you did everything but leave bread crumbs for patrol to follow. He smiled a little and said, I used a toy gun because I didn't want any accidents and I know a toy gun is still first degree, and they send first degree guys back to the joint and not to a lousy halfway house.

From now on, I will think of the old boy every Feb 14th.

When I started this letter, I swore I wouldn't say anything about a very dumb thing your brother did. And got away with! You're the only person I've told beside Janet and I'd like to keep it that way. Here's what happened.

I worked a case where an old man out on 38th Street answered the door one night and a guy on the porch tells him he's got a Western Union for him but needs a pencil to write the receipt. This old gent lives alone and he steps inside to get a pencil and as soon as he does three of them bull their way in. They rough him up, cover him with a bedspread, tie him up, and ransack his house looking for his gold coin collection. When they can't find it they stomp on his chest and break some ribs till he coughs up where it's hidden.

Without boring you with details, I did the best police work I've ever done and ended up identifying the three suspects. They were all L.A. assholes, so I went up there and worked with robbery-homicide detectives from LAPD and we pinched one of them at his apartment, and missed the other two by minutes. So I booked the one and got warrants on the other two. Two days later we knew they'd skipped, so I went back to San Diego.

Three weeks ago Miami P.D. teletypes and says they've got the two of them locked up in the Dade County jail. Miami had busted them for slapping some barmaid around and when they ran them through records up pops my warrants. Both of them sign extradition waivers, so Sergeant Stanley and I jump on a National Airlines flight. I told you the sarge still wears the fedora hat, but I didn't tell you he wears it everywhere. Inside, outside, when he eats. How in hell he shampoos his hair I do not know.

We did some drinking on the plane, got to Miami and kept on bending the elbow. Thirty-six hours later we get these guys out of jail, Miami P.D. takes us to the airport and away we go. Coming back with prisoners you fly first-class, because there's only two seats across, and if you flew coach some citizen would be sitting in the same row as you and your prisoner, and the city lawyers and the airline lawyers say nix on that.

Jerome, not only do they give you an actual meal menu in first class, but drinks are on the house and the sarge and I relaxed with Beefeaters on the rocks while the prisoners drank straight 7-Up.

We'd left an unmarked cage car in the airport lot at Lindbergh Field, so we load these guys in and I'm driving out of the airport and as I'm starting to get in the left lane for downtown, the sarge says take me home, damn it. The right lane takes you toward Ocean Beach where Sgt. Stanley lives, and I remembered he and his wife planned to leave for a week's camping early the next morning.

I'd had enough Beefeaters so I took the right lane, figuring I'd drop him at the house, then take my two prisoners to the station and book them. They're both cuffed up, not saying shit.

The sarge's driveway goes right up next to his front door and it's just getting dark. He says, come on in, I want to talk to you. I said, Sarge, let me book these guys first and I'll come back. He says, bullshit, bring them inside.

That was about quarter after five. At midnight, we're still there, me standing in a doorway between the kitchen and a game room, watching these two robbery suspects shooting pool, in front of a big brick fireplace, and never without a fresh glass of Beefeaters in my hand. The sarge and his wife are seated at the kitchen table a few feet from me and I'd hate to tell you how much gin the three of us put down. I only gave my prisoners soda pop because I was only dumb, not brain dead.

The sarge's wife finally phoned for Chicken Delight to be delivered. So we fed the suspects and I guess the three of us must have gnawed on the chicken, all the while keeping a good grip on our glasses.

You can imagine the shape I'm in at midnight, but we cuff them back up, put them in the car, I say goodbye to the sarge and Mrs. Stanley, then I drive to the station. Before I went into the patrol captain's office to have the booking slip signed, I had a patrol officer watch my prisoners while I went into the john and threw water on my face and made sure my tie was straight and I didn't have an olive growing out of my ear. I crammed five pieces of spearmint gum in my mouth and fortunately the captain was working a cross word puzzle when I walked in and he hardly looked up, just signed the booking slip.

I walked the two prisoners across the patio to the jail, handed them to the jailor and went home. Janet knew what time the plane got in and of course I hadn't bothered to phone her. She took one look at me and said, I don't even want to know. I said, you're right, you don't.

The next day I told her, and she said the same thing you must be saying now, Jerome. And she said it real loud. Billy Considine is a dumb shit!

But it's been over three weeks and we've heard nothing so we've skated. I've written it off as being dumb and lucky at the same time. I can't believe what we did.

Take care of yourself, Jerome, and I'll see if I can't do a better job of doing the same.

Billy

• • •

July 31, 1967 – Monday

   Dear Jerome:
   What a great trip to Youngstown! In her letter, Mom said she's over being upset about me and Amy and said she's thankful we didn't get into it until we were leaving for the airport. No matter what Amy claims, when I called Ernie Miranda what I did I wasn't slamming Mexicans everywhere.
   Remember my telling you about the pudgy guy who gave me the polygraph exam when I applied to be a cop. I've never talked to him since but yesterday I stopped him in the hall and told him he'd really rattled me when he said the needle jumped on those questions about being a homosexual. He laughed and said he does that to every applicant and ends up getting amazing confessions. We grabbed a cup of coffee and he told me some stories.
   One applicant said he felt sorry for a paraplegic friend and jacked him off. Another guy copped out to banging his neighbor's Collie because he fell in love with the Lassie movies as a kid.
   And remember, these guys had passed the civil service interview, the background check and all the rest. That's why starting last year all recruits get a psychiatric exam. Culpepper said if we'd had to take one Considine would still be delivering mail.
   You probably saw on TV a couple of months ago this bunch of Negroes from Oakland calling themselves the Black Panthers march around the capital in Sacramento carrying loaded guns. They made speeches and wore black leather jackets and stupid looking black berets and the cops arrested thirty of them. Well, I just helped an Oakland robbery detective on a case and he knows all the players, and said this Huey Newton and Bobby Seale and Eldridge Cleaver can grab all the microphones they want, and can call themselves a political party, but he knows them as a bunch of murdering street hoodlums.

These Panthers stir up street riots like the one in Newark two weeks ago, now they're sitting in Oakland congratulating themselves because LBJ had to call 12,000 federal troops into Detroit this week.

And guess what, Jerome? I'm sorry to say hell is breaking loose in San Diego. We had twelve cops hurt in a mess at Southcrest Park and just driving around town and in talking to patrol, you can feel it building with the Negroes. We had another mini-riot yesterday at a park in Southeast San Diego, the black part of town, and the news media loves it.

I can't even get away from it when I go to my night school classes at San Diego State. Posters about Students for a Democratic Society are plastered all over campus. Don't they know it's already a Democratic society? If the dipshits don't whack out on dope before they turn twenty-one, they can go to the voting booth and change things they don't like instead of clogging traffic just because we're bombing Hanoi.

I don't mind straight subjects at school, like math and science, but sociology and poly sci classes are far out. I keep my mouth shut (believe it or not), because I'm just trying to get a passing grade and move on. This one teacher's a hippie herself and throws out terms like "system rejection" and students "wanting control over their college years" and stuff like that. She's stuffing it down the throats of these students.

Once I did speak up, I said, excuse me, but I never heard of the fifties being called the "Beat Generation," maybe I was too busy playing ball and being a sailor. A couple of long-hairs in the back of the room booed when I said sailor.

I have to go, Jerome. Sgt. Stanley just phoned and things are so bad on the streets in Southeast a bunch of detectives are going to report in uniform tomorrow to supplement patrol. The word is we'll work twelve hours on and twelve off, and the sarge picked me from robbery because I'm the newest, the youngest, and the only one who can still get into my uniform.

I don't need this, Jerome.

Don't mention this to Mom. To be continued.

• • •

August 7, 1967 – Monday

One of my managers in the Georgia-Alabama League warned us about the dog days of summer. Well, he never worked twelve-on and twelve-off in Southeast San Diego with a Santa Ana whipping the winds and the chin straps on these damn helmets rubbing your chin raw. It was a week from hell and I hope nobody has to do it again.

They had pulled forty of us from detectives and canceled all days off for patrol. The rest of the city made do with a skeleton crew of cars. Culpepper got yanked out of burglary and we ended up in the same three-man car. Chief Steele argued for four-man, but the city manager was afraid we'd look like "a police state" and wanted two-man, so they compromised.

As soon as we formed up last Tuesday morning I noticed they've changed from our old billy clubs to a new-fangled thing called an Ironwood baton. It's two feet long and skinny with no heft. Our old clubs looked like a sawed off Louisville Slugger. You needed to get close to nail somebody, but when you did, you hit a home run every time. The first two guys we battled were full of Colt .45 malt liquor and gin and they just blinked and called us the Gestapo. Culpepper said he wished he was the one with the Colt .45 and gin.

Here's how it all went down. Southeast San Diego is a big, big territory, but the trouble spots are confined to about a five square mile section. So it's nothing like Watts or Detroit but it's plenty for us. The hoodlums and activists stir up shit in these five square miles.

The trouble is centered in a couple of parks, and spreads from there. One of the parks is Mt. View Park at 40th and Oceanview and the other is Southcrest Park at 40th and Alpha. Combined they're not as big as Mill Creek Park in Youngstown and I'm grateful for that.

The trouble makers are street hoodlums but they're not dumb. They know a lot of families come to enjoy the park after work and on weekends. So Monday through Friday the hoodlums hang out at the park all day, but they cool it until the law abiding Negroes show up with their kids and picnic dinners. Then the hoods try to figure out ways to lure a couple of cops into the park, knowing if they can do that, they can take potshots at them or surround them which will make the cop cavalry come whipping down Oceanview Blvd and the party can really start.

For instance when the time is right, they'll drive a couple of cars up on the grass and peel around the picnic tables and play areas taking up patches of grass. They know we're not dumb either and they know we have surveillance on the park, so they just keep pulling our chain until they force us to come in. Let's say our surveillance team sees the two cars driving where they shouldn't be. They report it on the air but recommend it's not worth moving on.

So the hoods will add two more cars and drive them faster and dig up turf around the swing sets and the kids run away screaming and mothers and fathers start shaking their fists at the hoods. If we still decide not to come in, they'll stage a fight and fire a couple of rounds in the air knowing we'll get a "shots fired" call.

Now the department is facing a moral question. How much are we supposed to let them trample on the rights of the families using the park. I guarantee, the mayor and the city manager are not hanging out at the edge of the park taking part in the decision making.

Then we have to decide what our goal is. We can get on the bullhorn and declare it an unlawful assembly and order everyone to clear the park or be arrested. That's an easy way out for us, but it means we take the park away from the decent people.

Okay, we decide we have to make a move but we aren't going to declare an unlawful assembly, we're just going in and arrest the troublemakers. How many cops do we send in? Two?

Four? Six? Eight? The TV channels on the hillside hope we do a big show of force because a platoon of cops marching with their batons at port arms makes good footage on the news at eleven.

No matter how many cops we send, it's going to turn to shit. Rocks and bottles will fly and when we grab a prisoner, they'll try to take him from us. Then we start doing stick-drill and the TV station managers are clapping and the word is spreading real fast on the streets that the pigs are doing Police Brutality at Mt. View. Then the hoods down at Southcrest Park swing into action and extra units are being dispatched to go down there.

Darkness is our enemy because the bastards can take potshots at us. By now the law abiding people have scattered but more hoods are coming in with the darkness.

Saturday at 6:00 p.m. we hadn't been able to get off after our twelve hours shift because of everything going on. By then we'd ended up declaring both parks unlawful assemblies and made a bunch of arrests and a bunch of cops had been hurt. Then a patrol car got fired on over near Gompers school. And of course it's like chasing ghosts but a bunch of us got dispatched there and another bunch dispatched on fights breaking out at Otto Square, a shopping plaza in the 3500 block of National Ave. We have no way of knowing if they're fake fights to lure us in, or are the merchants getting assaulted by the hoodlums?

By now the cops are tired and hot and surly and hungry, and the fact is, they have us right where they want us because we can't win.

As soon as it gets dark, stuff starts happening at other trouble spots like 43rd & National, 30th & Imperial and 25th & Imperial. Mobs gather and unload their gunny sacks of stuff to throw at us, and then the same decisions have to be made. Go in and get them--or back off and evaluate?

Friday night a command post had been set up at 38th & Teak which is a couple of blocks from Mt. View Park, and we ferried prisoners to the C.P. All of a sudden, out of nowhere, a mob showed between the C.P. and the park and cut us off.

Every cop car starts with the same ignition key so it's not a
problem when you get into a riot and end up with cars parked
in all directions. Except I ended up in the back seat with two
prisoners because the flathead rookie driver had jumped out
when he thought four cops needed help in a fight right in
front of our car. My prisoners were cuffed behind their backs
so no problem there, but the rookie didn't think about the fact
that I was trapped, because he left me in a cage car with no
inside door handles. The mob picked up on that real fast because they've been in the back seat of police cars. So they
headed for my car and started crashing the windows and rocking the car. They figured they could accomplish two things.
Free the two prisoners and stomp your brother to death.

About the time they had my car almost tipped over,
Culpepper saw what was happening and came roaring up in
another car which made the mob around my car split. But
not before Culpepper had knocked a few of them silly with
the front end of his car. We weren't in a first-aid mode, so we
left them laying there while Culpepper yanked my door open
so I could jump behind the wheel and follow him out of
there. What that rookie was thinking I do not know.

By last night we had pretty much restored order, but Chief
Steele told us the cost was high in officer injuries and bad
press. The ACLU is teaming up with the NAACP and filing
complaints and the city is already saying it looks bad for cops
getting a raise next year because of the cost to repair police
equipment and defend lawsuits.

I'm sore all over, but Janet has filled the tub with hot water
for me, I've knocked back two beers and two shots of Old
Crow and with any luck I'll be able to get Janet into the tub
with me. Tomorrow morning I go back to robbery, and that
heavy caseload that I used to bitch about will sure look good.

So Long For Now,

Billy

P.S. Janet and I are creeping up on three years without smoking but I came close to lighting up a few times last week.

• • •

September 19, 1967 – Tues

Dear Jerome:
It's very quiet around the house tonight and on the next page you will know why.

Saturday I took the sergeants exam and felt real good about it. A lot of the questions I nailed. It's tricky to try and guess the outcome, I learned that from the first exam two years ago, but all that studying seemed to have paid off. I walked out of the test singing, came home and said to Janet, let's get Jimmie cleaned up and go to Lefty's for torpedo sandwiches.

Sunday I cut the grass, and then we went to Crown Point Shores, caught some sun, grilled franks and took swims in the bay. When I got into work yesterday morning I felt like a million bucks.

At quitting time the rest of the detail left and I stayed to push some paper. Then the sergeant who runs sex crimes tapped me on the shoulder and said the captain wants to see you. That would be the captain of detectives.

I go into the captain's office and there's the robbery lieutenant with him. They said sit down, and then the captain says, well, do you want to tell us about it? In nine years I've learned you never answer a question like that, so I said, tell you about what, Captain? The lieutenant says, about Miami. I said, Miami? Nobody says anything until the captain says, do you want to go the hard way on this, Considine?

Jerome, now I know what it feels like to be hit with a sledgehammer. I couldn't believe it was about the extradition six months ago, so I just said it again. Miami?

The lieutenant slid two pieces of paper across the desk at me. The voucher showing our plane landing at 5:04 p.m. and

the other was the city jail booking slip, time-stamped at 0027
which is twenty-seven minutes after midnight.

The other thing I've learned is don't bullshit them when
they've got you cold. I said what do you want to know? The
captain said, we want to know everything. I hoped they didn't
see my hands shaking but I looked at the captain and said, re-
spectfully Sir, I'll tell you my part in things.

Remember, I said in my letter we let the two suspects
shoot pool in Sergeant Stanley's game room in front of a brick
fireplace. Those bad boys had counted bricks. Every brick.
They figured that knowing the total was three hundred and
nine would work to their advantage someday. And the someday turned out to be yesterday afternoon.

The creeps are three weeks from trial and thought they
could get the charges reduced, thinking the department
would be too embarrassed about the publicity and want to
cover it up. They told their defense attorneys who told the
D.A. who called the chief's office.

So I sat in the captain's office and told them what I'd done,
but I never said Sergeant Stanley said to head for his house
from the airport or to come in when we arrived. I just told
them I went to a house in Ocean Beach and drank gin while
the prisoners shot pool and then sometime after midnight I
booked them.

The captain shook his head and said, give me your badge
and your gun, you're suspended. Be in the chief's office at
8:00 a.m. tomorrow. I felt naked walking out of the station.
When I got home and told Janet she got sick to her stomach.
But she never said anything nasty to me which almost made
it worse.

After he got drunk, Sgt. Stanley phoned me and said they
had called him in too, that they suspended him, and that the
chief planned to fire both of us in the morning.

You can imagine how I slept. It began sinking in and I
thought, I'm too good a cop to lose my job, even though what
we did was wrong and stupid. We didn't steal anything or beat

anybody up. Of course as Sgt. Stanley said, we did worse than that, we embarrassed Chief Steele and the department.

This morning at quarter to eight I reported to the chief's office and his secretary never looked up, just said report to the captain of detectives' office.

I figured the chief is so sore he doesn't even want to see me. I knock on the captain's door and there sits the captain and the lieutenant, in the same position they'd been in fifteen hours ago.

They looked up and didn't say anything at first, so I just stood there, and then the captain slid a piece of paper at me and said, sign this.

I picked it up and it said I'm suspended for forty-five days without pay and transferred from detectives to patrol for violation of this and that department rule and regulation, and for conduct unbecoming, and it detailed the whole trip to Miami and they had all the facts right, except one thing. It said we allowed the prisoners to drink booze.

I said Captain, this part about the prisoners drinking is wrong but he leaned forward and said, I guess you want to fight this, huh, Considine, and he reached for the paper I was holding like he'd be happy to take it back. But by then I was reaching for my pen and couldn't sign fast enough.

Nobody spoke again until the lieutenant gave me a copy and said, report to the patrol division on Friday, November 3rd, you're not to come to the station between now and then unless a supervisor orders you to do so.

I must have been in shock. I remember saying yes, Sir, yes, Sir, will that be all, Sir?

I'd taken the bus to the police station because Janet needed the car but I knew she'd be waiting by the phone. Jerome, I was too ashamed to place the call from the station, so I walked across the street to a phone booth in front of the surplus store and dialed.

Janet answered on the first ring and I said it's me, I've still got a job. I told her what happened, then I hung up and walked north on the railroad tracks to "E" Street where she picked me up. I'm still in a stupor and can't believe it happened only this morning.

By the way, when the two suspects made their pitch about having charges dropped or reduced, Chief Steele told them to stick it.

DeFreese telephoned and said keep your mouth shut, do your time on the beach and try and ride this out. He told me they gave Sergeant Stanley a bust to patrolman, a ninety day suspension and a transfer to patrol. But Stanley has his time in, so they let him take his retirement as a sergeant.

Then Jack Hackett and Culpepper came by the house and we sat on the patio. None of us had ever heard of anybody getting forty-five days. Thirty was about tops and anything worth more than that would get you canned. Culpepper said maybe Chief Steele decided to give me a break because I'd done good police work since 1958. Jack Hackett thought it was because I'd been with my sergeant.

Six weeks without a paycheck would kill us, so Janet and I sat around and tried to think of what kind of work I could get until November 3rd. There's not much call for a washed up second-baseman who knows how to delivers mail.

Just when I didn't think I could feel worse, Janet said she would call the credit union and arrange a withdrawal from Jimmie's college fund. She wasn't trying to make me feel bad, she was just being practical. I talked her into waiting until tomorrow, so now I'm sitting at the kitchen table writing this. Jimmie's asleep and Janet is laying on the sofa just staring at the ceiling.

I really fucked up, Jerome.

Billy

• • •

December 18, 1967 – Wednesday

Dear Jerome:
As you can see by the date on this letter, I've been back in patrol almost two months. Thanks to the three of you for the

letters of support. Amy said she loves me and that I'm a good cop, but added I'm a poster boy for allowing women to work patrol because no woman would have been stupid enough to do what I did.

I think I told you on the phone it was hard finding a job while on suspension because who wants to hire somebody for only forty-five days. After two days of looking, Sergeant Black (from my academy training days) phoned and said how are you putting beans on the table? He told me to go see a friend of his who runs an auto parts place on 30th Street. Sgt Black said, I told my friend that Billy Considine is a good cop and a good man who made a mistake.

So they put me to work and I busted my butt for him. Mostly I unpacked freight and stocked shelves and the rest of the time I made deliveries, scooting all over town in a white Chevy panel truck that backfires. A twenty-one year old kid named Tulley Brown worked there too and I'll tell you more about him later. Definitely a flake but I like him.

I'm assigned to a patrol beat in east San Diego next to Jack Hackett's beat, so it's like old times. With Jack there's no change except in his looks. He's thirty-five years old and looks ready for retirement because the whiskey has made him an old man.

Just before I got off suspension Jack got banged up in a Halloween riot at the corner of College and Montezuma which is next to the university. It started over patrol being called to a loud fraternity party and these days any time we show up things go downhill.

Then on my third night back, same place-same station, we did it all over again, only worse. The Wienerschnitzel is on the corner, and this time it started with a drunk kid standing on one of the outside tables taking a leak on the American flag his buddies had laid on the ground. A WW I vet with a bum leg went after the guy and we ended up being called. A five-keg party was taking place a few doors away and two cop cars got turned over before help arrived. I got hit in the shoulder with a brick they'd pulled up from some widow lady's planter box. The next day I couldn't raise my arm, but figured a guy just back from suspension doesn't go around submitting injured-on-duty forms. The less the administration sees my name the better.

Boy, Jerome, the hate in the eyes of these college students is too awful to describe. As the old veteran said when we were putting a bandage on his face, just think, they're gonna be the leaders of our country.

The night I reported back from suspension, the patrol captain reached in his drawer and pulled out an envelope with my badge and gun in it. All he said was, here's your stuff, good luck.

I stepped outside onto the patio and there's Frank Runyon, which surprised me because he's working day shift. Frank said, what's your goal, Billy? I said I hadn't really thought of a goal and Frank said, son of a bitch, you've only had forty-five days to come up with one.

Then he gave me a speech. He said there are two ways a guy like me can go. Get in that car and be the best patrol cop I can be, putting my detective experience to good use, and train the younger cops around me. Or walk around with a sour puss just doing enough work to get by, letting all the cops and the rest of the world know I got handed a shit deal. Frank said the department is more forgiving these days, not like when he got in the grease (for what I still do not know).

I've seen Chief Steele a couple of times in the hallway but he looks the other way. See, there'd been a five day period in which I could have appealed, but I'd let it expire, figuring you only appeal when you think you've been wronged. Of course we'd told Janet's folks about the suspension and the whole department knew, but as for neighbors and casual civilian friends, we just kept to ourselves and said nothing. I think the neighbors thought I was on vacation.

Then it happened. Jimmie's a first-grader now and a sports nut, so as soon as he gets out of bed he grabs the newspaper off the driveway and field strips it until he finds the sports page. Then he tosses the rest of the paper aside, spreads sports on the floor and kneels down and reads.

Anyway, on this day I stroll through the living room, say good morning to him and head for the coffee pot. Then something caught my eye and I'm still thankful it caught mine before it caught Jimmie's. Right on the front page is a big picture of your brother with a headline over it, Cop Suspended Over Prisoner Drinking Binge.

I scooped up the paper and ran into the bedroom. Janet hadn't cried for two weeks but went to pieces when I showed it to her. When I pulled out of the driveway to go to work the guy next door had the newspaper in his hand and he smiled and said good morning, Billy. You can imagine how I felt. So Chief Steele got me pretty good.

I told you on the phone I got notified I had passed the written test and would be going in for the oral board on the 26th. When I showed up at city hall for the interview the receptionist had me take a seat. The rules say nobody from our department can be on the oral board, and the board isn't supposed to see your service record, so I'm sitting there wondering and waiting until she escorts me into the interview room. She used the same fragrance Janet uses so I took that as a good luck sign.

It turned out to be a son of a bitch. There was an LAPD Captain, a Riverside Sheriffs' Office Captain, and a high school principal from San Diego. I hoped the San Diego guy didn't remember everything he'd seen in the paper.

The first twenty minutes went fast, they asked me things like why do I think I'd make a good supervisor, what are the biggest problems confronting police today, stuff like that. I felt nervous at the beginning but settled down and thought I was doing good.

The LAPD Captain finally said, do you have any questions for us, Officer Considine, and I said no Sir, figuring I was almost home free. The high school principal said well, I guess that's it, and I was half way out of my chair when the Riverside guy said, have you ever been suspended from duty, Officer?

I said, yes Sir. He said what's the longest you've ever been on the beach, so I knew Chief Steele had made sure word got leaked.

I leaned back, took a deep breath and said, forty-five days, Captain, and I'm doing it right now.

The lowest score the oral board can give is a seventy and that's what your brother got? The department gave me the lowest score possible on what's called Promote-ability, and since I don't write high test papers I had a very low aggregate score so I am candidate number forty-four on a forty-five man list. Which means Smokey the Bear and I have the same chance of being promoted to sergeant, because the list expires in November of 1969 and SDPD has never had forty-four sergeant openings in just two years. Jerome, I have to look at it as part of my punishment.

How can a guy complain when he has such a good family and terrific pals? One night while I was still on suspension Culpepper dropped over and plopped down a gift certificate for dinner for two at the Marine Room. He said he'd won it in a drawing but since it was only good for the coming weekend, could we use it because he had to go out of town.

The Marine Room is a fancy place in La Jolla and I figured my luck was turning. We got a baby sitter, washed the car and off we went. There's a huge window on one side of the dining room looking at the ocean, and from the tables next to it you're right above the sand. It rained like hell and the wind blew the rain so when the drops hit the wet sand they'd jump an inch high. The waves crashed and as it got dark the floodlights took over and what a sight.

Janet and I got a chance to talk. We had drinks before we ordered New York cuts, and I told her how appreciative I am about the way she handled the suspension. How she never crucified me. She leaned over and kissed me right in front of the waiter, and then when he spun around and left, she said she had a request.

She said when we met I hadn't been much of a drinker, but she'd seen a pattern developing. That now I was having booze just to have it, and would I cut down and talk to her when I'm stressed or have things bothering me. I promised I would and damn if I didn't get another kiss.

I asked her how her folks were doing about the suspension and she said they were, in their words, highly embarrassed. Janet said she's not embarrassed any more, she's still proud to be married to a San Diego police officer and we'll put this behind us and move on.

I'd been thinking about her folks. Having their daughter marry a cop was one thing, a Catholic cop quite another, and one that made the first page of the San Diego Union must have been the clincher.

We tipped the waiter real good and put our coats on, then I told the maitre d' we were glad our friend had won the certificate in the drawing. He said the Marine Room never participates in those things, that ours was a purchased gift certificate. That Culpepper!

And, how it happened I do not know, but I'll be off Christmas Eve and Christmas day. I called Janet right away from a booth by the ice house and when she answered, I started singing, I'll Be Home For Christmas. Janet screamed and called to Jimmie and he yelled then Janet called her folks right away. I'm a lucky man, Jerome.

Our presents should be arriving on your front porch any day now. Tell Uncle Denny I said to carve the turkey before he gets into the Jamison's so he doesn't cut his hand again.

So that's about it from here, I'm going to work hard and walk around the station with a smile on my face and try to make my way back into detectives someday.

That reminds me, one day after I graduated from the academy I was having a smoke in the patio and an old sergeant came up to me and said how long have you been on the department? I told him and he said…you're ruined for life, Rookie, because after you've been a cop there's nothing else worth being.

Jerome, being a cop who's been busted back to patrol is still better than any other job in the world.

Merry Christmas, Brother,

Billy

• • •

May 28, 1968 – Tuesday

Dear Jerome:

Are the Sixties ever going to end? Not many cops would have marched with Martin Luther King, but he was a peaceful man trying to make change. Then he gets gunned down like a dog. I've quit watching the news because all I see is dead and bloodied-up soldiers and cops knocking people around.

Culpepper made sergeant and Janet and I are happy for him. He's been assigned a patrol sector downtown and agrees with me that everything is different in uniform this time around. My vice and detective experience makes me a better patrol cop, because now I can size up a field incident and visualize how it's going to travel through the detective division and court system.

I remember from my rookie days the big mystery surrounding Frank Runyon when he got bounced back to patrol. Now some of the young cops keep staring at me, this big-shot robbery detective who's writing tickets now. The veterans horse me around pretty good. Like, Hey Considine, I hear you're going to be teaching extradition procedures in the next academy class. It gives me a laugh when I need one.

The mix of radio calls is all different. I might go from finding a lost kid to a call at the post office because some American Legion old-timer trying to mail a letter got into it with an anti-war picketer. All we do now, Jerome, is react. There's no time to cruise around, do police work and just be nice to people.

And everything that happens anywhere can set somebody off. Not forty-eight hours after the North Koreans snatched the Pueblo and its crew, the assholes here are blocking streets downtown. Waving signs saying "Capitalist CIA Dogs Spy On Korea." Patrol units get called in and when I got there five cops had already taken hits with bottles.

The kind of crime we fought when I came on the department plays second fiddle now to whatever's going on in the world outside of San Diego. You should have seen the donnybrook we had at the State Building down on Front Street because of the Tet Offensive. A bad scene.

Think about it. Marines are beating off attacks on the U.S. Embassy, our troops and the South Vietnamese are getting their asses kicked, which you figure would make these local creeps happy. Instead, they're breaking doors and windows screaming LBJ, LBJ, How Many Kids Did You Kill Today?

Their new trick is to activate movie cameras right after a cop gets hit with a brick, so when the cop comes after them with fire in his eye it's all on film, and they can run down to channels 8, 10 and 39 yelling police brutality for the late news.

Jerome, we have cops who fought in the Battle of the Bulge and cops who took islands in the South Pacific. Cops who have plates in their heads and pieces of mortar and machine gun bullets in them. Imagine what it's like for them, seeing their countrymen burning the flag and taking over a public building.

It's a different world and Frank Runyon says cops are supposed to know the answers before we even have the questions.

I'm thankful Jimmie is six because I'd hate to have a teenager right now. If a cop wasn't in favor of the Vietnam War before these hippie bastards threw bags of shit at him, he would be afterwards, because anything these people are against, the cop automatically wants to be in favor of.

Janet's stomach is bothering her and the Doc thinks she may be getting ulcers over all this stuff I run into on the streets. She told me last night if I wanted to quit the department she'd stand behind me and we'd make a fresh start. She said she could go back to work.

Maybe you're tired of hearing all this hippie stuff, but I've got to tell you about some payback last month in Ocean Beach. On a Sunday afternoon they'd blocked the sidewalks and snarled traffic so police units came flying in from all over, including me and Jack Hackett. A Command Post had been set up at Robb Field which is a big soccer and play area, so we got briefed on how to get in formation and march down the streets and clear them out.

The last time we marched down the same street, the 5100 block of Longbranch, the bastards had prowled the alleys which run parallel to the street, and lobbed bricks and bottles over the rooftops at us. This time, our sergeant put a dozen undercover cops from special units in the alley, and these cops look more like hippies than the hippies.

So while we're marching down the street, and the crowd is doing their LBJ chanting and giving us the finger, and glass is breaking in the street, the undercover guys in the alley are spotting the brick throwers. As soon as they see one toss something, they ease up to the guy and lay a punch on him like you and I saw Tommie Bell lay on Fritzie Zivic when we hitchhiked over to Pittsburgh for the big fight. They just leave the guy laying there and go find another one to punch out. One cop from fencing hit a bottle thrower so hard, tits came flying out of the tie-dyed tanktop and that's when he realized he'd smacked a girl.

All I hear the man on the street saying about the war is, get-the-thing-finished-or-get-the-hell-out-of-there.

Maybe I got a little soft over in detectives, because I got put on my ass the other day. When a rookie gets a fight call he heads for it as fast as he can, but a veteran takes it nice and slow, hoping it will all be over when he gets there. Jack Hackett and I got called to the parking lot of a bar and I was just around the corner. I wish I'd gotten a flat tire. A blacksmith from National Steel & Shipbuilding had taken on three guys, then I pulled up and told them the fight was over. Janet had to put a towel on my pillow because my face kept oozing blood all night. Jack Hackett said when they finish building a ship, this guy's job is to pick it up and put it in the water.

I told you I'd worked with a kid named Tulley Brown at the auto parts store. The first week he was nosy, asking all kinds of questions about where did I work before? How long had I been in town? That kind of stuff. My boss hadn't said anything to anybody about me being a cop, so I told this Tulley Brown that I'd worked in a job where people minded their own business.

He backed off, but when it came time to show me the delivery route, he was full of advice on the best streets to drive and how to avoid the cops and so on. Then the morning my picture made the front page, he said, you look familiar to me. I said yes, you pecker head, I'm sure it does, because when you swiped your neighbor's paper this morning you saw my mugshot and read about me.

He started laughing and said all he could think of was what a jerk he'd been, teaching me how to drive. We became pretty good friends and he said he'd tried to get on the department but with his driving record they wouldn't even let him take the written exam.

Tulley Brown was only twenty-one, so I told him to apply again when he'd gone two years without a ticket. I told him the department is a good job for guys like him and me who didn't have college educations.

My last day at the parts store he brought in a big cinnamon coffee cake his girlfriend had made and everybody chowed down in the lunch room.

Well, it's time to get some sleep. Have you figured out who's going to be the next president? You can't tell the players without a scorecard. Nixon is in, Wallace is in, LBJ is out and now Bobby Kennedy's in. Nixon being in makes Janet's folks happy and whatever makes them happy is fine with me.

Keep those cards and letters coming,

Billy

P.S. I told you last year that the deuce squad which pinches drunk drivers stakes out across the street from tavern parking lots which some of us think is chickenshit. Anyway, one cop told me he'd been watching customers come out of the Bar Of Music and one guy could hardly make it to his car. The cop stopped him in the next block and put him through the tests and the guy did them better than the cop. The cop says I'm taking you downtown for a breathalyzer, and the guy says,

I'll blow a zero-zero. The cops says, how do you know? The guy says because tonight I'm the designated decoy and all I've been drinking is 7-Up.

• • •

August 15, 1968 – Thursday

> *Dear Jerome:*
> Tonight I badly need to write this letter. On Monday we drove home from a vacation in Mexico, but can't believe it was only seventy-two hours ago. I'm trying hard to compose myself.
> Sunday-Monday are my days off, and since the city now pays for court overtime we decided to splurge, go to Mexico and stay at Quintas Papagayo near Ensenada--about seventy miles south of San Diego.
> Knowing the Democratic Convention starts in Chicago at the end of the month, and intelligence saying there's going to be trouble, our department is bracing for spinoff so days off will be canceled. Janet and I figured we'd better go while the ~~gettings~~ getting's good.
> Cops, and I guess everybody else, believe anything can happen since that son of a bitch killed Robert Kennedy. And even though nobody at the department is talking revolution, we know we've got to be prepared for the worst.
> At Quintas Papagayo they rent about twenty little cottages. Nothing fancy, linoleum floors throughout, but a kitchen and good beds and a fireplace + firewood and it's very clean and a maid comes in every day and all for only eight bucks a night.
> Here's the clincher. It's right on a rocky beach (the ocean, not the gulf side), and at night you get lulled to sleep from the wave action rattling the rocks.
> Since Sunday was our last night we barbecued steaks and corn on the cob. You mid-westerners won't understand this, but soak the corn in a bucket of sea water for a few hours,

then put them on the grill in their husks and you'll never reach for a salt shaker.

Jimmie had graduated to swimming without his float wings and we all stood in the patio drying off slugging down gin & tonics (the Mexicans make good gin and it's plenty cheap) and I know it was exactly six o'clock because I timed the corn on the coals. Exactly six o' clock, Jerome.

The thing is, while I was doing that, a lady on Lincoln Avenue in San Diego heard a shot. She didn't know it was a shot, but it was loud and scared her and she knows the exact time because she had turned on her TV program and jumped because she thought the TV had blown up.

Jerome, the lady lives next door to Frank Runyon and what she heard was Frank killing himself.

Jack Hackett had left a note on our door about it so we found it the next day when we got home. I felt sick about it and got on the phone and found out nobody really knew anything about why. He just went and did it. No note, no nothing. But that was Frank, he didn't figure he owed an explanation to anybody, even when it came to dying.

Janet said I dozed off about three a.m. but I don't think I did. I went to work and found out his ex-wife planned to bury him in a place called Adelanto where she and their kids live, and it would be the next day, Wednesday. Frank was seven years older than me, Jerome.

So I took the day off and got in the car. Janet offered to go but this I had to do alone. Adelanto is a four hour drive due north from San Diego over what is called the Tejon Pass which drops you down into the desert. George Air Force Base is there and Frank's ex had married a mechanic stationed there. Why else anyone would want to live in Adelanto I do not know.

When I studied for sergeant I learned most cops are drunk when they commit suicide, but Frank's blood alcohol read .00 when he ate his gun.

There were only eight people at the service and that included Frank's wife and kids. I was the only one from the department. His wife had hired some guy to do a eulogy but it wasn't much. When he finished, he asked if anybody wanted to say anything. Nobody did so people started to get up, then I called out that I had something.

So everybody sat back down and I went up front and it felt strange being at a podium talking to just seven people. Frank's kids stared up at me and his wife had her head down and I didn't know what in hell I was going to say.

I told them I loved Frank Runyon. I said that a guy once accused me of thinking Frank was Jesus Christ and even though that wasn't true, I thought he was damn close. I said I don't know what troubled Frank because he never let me in, and from what I've learned in the last two days he didn't let anybody else in either.

I said I've been lucky in my life to run into some very special people, but Frank Runyon is right there at the top. Then I started to lose it and couldn't talk. I finally told them, if Frank was here he'd say to me, Come on, Billy. You can do it. Jerome, all I could do was look at them and say, But Frank's not and I can't.

Then I sat down.

I'd started the engine for the drive home and Frank's ex walked up and asked if I'd come back to the house for coffee. So I did, and we talked for a couple of hours. She buried him in Adelanto because a couple of years before he had phoned her and said if anything happens to me take me out there. She figures it's because he didn't want any hoopla in San Diego, but I think Frank wanted to be near her.

She's a very fine girl. When they met, Frank was pumping gas and going to night school studying to be a pharmacist. There was family pressure for him to go to work with his father in the family drugstore. His wife said one day Frank came to her and asked how she'd feel about his applying for the police job. It shook her up, but she told him she loved him and if a cop was what he wanted to be, then that was what she wanted.

He'd been on five years when they broke up, which happened to be the year I came on. She said the job changed him and it was just a series of little stuff that made things go sideways until one day they looked at each other and knew it was over.

I got back to San Diego late and Janet came running outside as soon as she heard me pull in the driveway and hugged me to pieces.

I can't write anymore, Jerome.

Billy

• • •

April 30, 1969 – Wednesday

Dear Jerome:
Over the past few months, Janet has mentioned what Nixon said at his inauguration--that our destiny isn't in the stars, but as brothers on earth. Wouldn't it be something if we could pull that off?

I'm ready for the Republicans to get their shot at trying to patch up the country, and I like the way this Spiro Agnew talks. He won't be soft on crime and he's already yapping at judges to get tough on crime and calling on the demonstrators to work within the system. We can hope.

Those creeps at the democratic convention in Chicago who got their heads knocked had it coming because they should have dispersed when ordered to. I hope they convict all seven of them and set an example.

Just when you think maybe the country can put all the crap behind them, what happens? The radical bastards seize the administration building at Harvard and the admin building at Brandeis, wherever in hell Brandeis is, and then they use guns to grab the building at Cornell. Then it breaks loose at U.C.L.A. because the Negroes are fighting each other now, and these so-called Black Nationalists kill two Panthers in a shootout.

My sergeants' list expires in six months and crazy things are happening. Believe it or not, because of new budget positions and a shit pot full of retirements, they've made forty-three sergeants which is a record. That leaves me and one other guy left on the list, but Chief Steele has already sent word down that he won't promote me.

Sergeant's pay would be nice, but thanks to Janet we're doing okay. Since its winter our gas & electric bill reached $31 last month and haircuts just went up—2.00 for me and 1.75 for Jimmie. Last time we got haircuts, the barber worked on me as I snoozed in the chair. Janet walked in and Jimmie was reading Playboy. She gave us both hell, then started in on the barber.

Here's some good news. I told you on the phone Jack Hackett hadn't had a drink in two months. Well now it's up to six. He's running fifteen miles a week and he's met a girl. Janet says she's never seen him look so good. We've had them over a couple of times, she's a physical therapist who's never been married and eight years younger than Jack which makes her twenty-nine. He falls all over himself pulling out chairs and opening car doors. Janet says one of these days we'll see a ring on her finger.

One night Jack Hackett and I stood outside of Heavenly Doughnuts waiting for a hot batch. A cocky rookie working a one night stand on Unit 34 pulled up. Jack doesn't have as much hair as he did in the picture we sent you some time back, and the rookie makes a wisecrack about it. This kid's nose is bigger than Jimmy Durante's so Jack spends some time staring at it. The kid says what are you looking at? Jack says, I'm thinking there are two things in this world I'd love to have. The rookie falls for it and wants to know what. Jack says, I'd like to have a head full of hair and your nose full of nickels. I'd rather have your nose full of nickels than a suitcase full of dimes.

With that, Jerome, I'm going to get some shuteye. By the way, with the $$ you sent him, we took Jimmie to see San Diego open against Houston in the first big league game ever here. He came home with a Padres cap that he even wears to bed and his teacher had to impound it to keep it off his head in class.

Billy

• • •

June 27, 1969 – Friday

Dear Jerome:

I'm smarter than when I left for work this morning because now I answer to the name of sergeant. A lot has happened in the last two weeks and it all connects to Chief Steele. EX-Chief Steele.

The California Attorney General appointed a special prosecutor and a team of investigators to travel to San Diego and look at Steele and a couple of retired cops about allegations of taking payoffs to protect bookmakers. As the investigators were flying here from Sacramento, Steele announced his retirement and it will probably turn out he can't be charged criminally because the three-year statute of limitations is saving his bacon.

The whole town is shocked. I've told you retired Chief Hale had cleaned up the department in the 1940s. But it turns out Steele and these other three guys, who all came on in the 1930s, had fallen in with bad cops back then and could never shake loose of the old bookies that were still operating.

Steele must have gotten used to that extra $$ coming in and couldn't lay it down. I'm still stunned. The chief of police! All four of them, including Steele, took the Fifth when they got put under oath. It seems some suspect the feds wrapped up on an interstate gambling deal rolled over and started feeding them stuff, and as a result the feds started squeezing the bookies and then it all went downhill for Steele.

Nobody said anything out loud, but we sure started won-

dering about Soderholm. Remember him, the vice lieutenant. Apparently they cleared him, but I mean, Steele being
cozy with bookies, and Soderholm reporting directly to
Steele? And being Steele's puppet.

It happened so fast, Jerome. Steele was here one day and
gone the next. The city manager appointed DeFreese as interim
chief and we're all hoping it becomes permanent.

I wasn't even thinking how any of this would affect me,
but this afternoon the inspector of patrol calls me in. He's
standing behind his desk when I get there and he says, come
on Considine, we're going to the chief's office. My mind
started spinning and I thought, what have I done now?

We get to the corner pocket and the secretary waves us in
and there's DeFreese with a big smile on his face. He says,
congratulations, Billy. I said what for? The inspector smiles
and says, it's customary for the chief to congratulate new sergeants. Then they're shaking my hand and handing me a
sergeant's badge and telling me I better get my ass home and
sew on chevrons. Janet and Jimmie got excited and Janet even
sewed a pair of sergeant's stripes on my skivvies.

Tomorrow I report to the afternoon watch, but tonight
Janet and I are going to the Cotton Patch. On the way home
this afternoon I stopped and picked up flowers so she's walking around in a daze like me.

Until later, I remain,

Sergeant William Patrick Considine Himself

• • •

August 28, 1969 – Thursday
> *Dear Jerome*:
> I don't know about this sergeant business. As a plain old
patrol cop I just had to take care of myself. When he handed
me my badge DeFreese said I would make a good sergeant
and warned me it wouldn't be easy. I won't pepper you with

more stuff about the Negroes and the anti-war creeps, except to tell you things aren't getting any better.

The afternoon shift I got assigned to works 3 p.m. to 11. Being a rookie sergeant I float, meaning two shifts in Southeast, two in east San Diego and one in the beach. And during the beach shift I'm way too busy to even look at those golden girls strutting their stuff. (Wrote that in case Janet comes in and looks over my shoulder.)

Usually I'm responsible for eight patrol cars, but if the sergeant in the next sector is tied up I'll get called to handle a problem there. These are good young cops I'm dealing with, their heart is in the right place and they're trying to do police work while all the time the radio is keeping them hopping. I guess the mistakes they're making aren't any dumber than the ones I made eleven years ago.

One kid's activity is low and when I jacked him up about it, he said he has a five year old kid who's epileptic and that his wife is high strung and doesn't understand police work—she can't picture what he does for eight hours. I suggested he take a copy of his daily journal home plus copies of an interesting crime report or arrest and show it to his wife. I told Janet about my suggestion and she said too bad you didn't follow your own advice. So that's part of what I do although right this minute I'm not feeling much like a cop. Janet has the flu so I've done two loads of wash, shopped, heated her some soup, worked on Cub Scout mailings and kept an eye on Jimmie who starts school again (3rd grade) in a couple of weeks.

Yes, those Tate-LaBianca murders are terrible, but do you know what? A cop can understand how those whacked out suspects would think Manson is a messiah. We get calls, especially in the beach area from neighbors about noise or maybe some kid going tooty-fruity in the yard. You walk in the house which reeks of incense and here are these Manson type followers laid out all over the place. And the butthead who's running things greets you and is extra polite, but you know he's been telling those kids how evil cops are and how government is their enemy and how he's saved them from society's garbage heap. There may be a dozen of them in the pad, guys with hair down to their ass and girls with glazed eyes ready to spread their legs and you just know they're maybe one acid trip away from qualifying for a Tate-LaBianca murder.

You know how some of the girls end up in a house like that? We see more girls hitchhiking than guys and when a guy pulls over for one and she opens the door, he says ass or grass, which means I'll give you a ride if you're holding some marijuana or if you'll put out. Some world, huh? They should round them all up and hold another Woodstock, only this time put a barbed wire fence around the farm and padlock it.

Apparently there's nothing for any of us to worry about though. My sociology professor (she's the one that wears the tank top to class and could braid her underarm hair) said this New Left movement--and I'm quoting from my notes, Jerome--the New Left movement "rejects the system of democracy where citizens elect officials to govern them and that their cultural rebellion is contributing to a political awakening." Well from what I've seen they can all awake and kiss my ass.

Just about the time I'm working a shift and getting a belly full of hippies, I can't wait to get back to the Negro part of town and vice versa. The thing is, Chicago affected the way we handle riots and unruly crowds. Because the mayor's office knows the TV people are going to go for selected clips, we're being told to swing our nightsticks low and that's not easy in the heat of battle. It ranks right up there with shooting the gun out of a guy's hand. I'm hearing criticism about police I never expected to hear, so who can blame us for circling the wagons?

The other day one of my patrol cars found a dead guy in a car behind a building in the 3000 block of Imperial. I got there, and it looked for all the world like an overdose because we're seeing a lot of them. But you want to protect the scene and treat it like a homicide just in case, and do some follow up while you're waiting for the detectives.

Anyway, the car with the stiff is behind a building called The Crisis Center, and it turns out it's a federally funded thing for whatever ails you. We go up the steps to ask some questions about the car in their lot. When you walk in the room the first thing you see is a big sign on the wall, Eldridge Cleaver Welcome Here. Then under that is a blowup photo of a cop dragging a bloody Negro to a police car, and the caption under that, in big letters, is PIG.

The people working in the place are all Negro, most of them wearing funky African clothes, and the only white face is this girl in charge and she's a Code-3 bitch. Before we can open our mouth she orders us out, shouts instructions to the others that nobody's allowed to talk to us, and starts dialing some lawyer's number.

She wasn't there when the lawyer showed up, because we'd carted her off to jail for 148 PC which covers resisting, delaying or obstructing an officer in the performance of duty. If Earl Warren can interpret the constitution the way he wants then we can interpret the penal code the way we want.

Jerome, I'll continue this later because Janet just woke up.

It's 7 p.m. and an hour ago I almost pooped my pants. I'd gotten Janet settled down and started the dishes and from the living room I heard a voice on the TV and I thought, boy, that sure sounds like my sister.

I'm curious enough to go out there with a soapy pan in my hand and what do I see? Amy and three others getting interviewed by Dan Rather! My sister is working as a research assistant for that Commie attorney who's defending the Chicago 7. Which means she's rubbing elbows with Tom Hayden and Abbie Hoffman and Jerry Rubin and Bobby goddamn Seale. Worse yet, Dan Rather even named her and I'm sure half of the San Diego P.D. watched. She looked right into the camera and gave that Amy smile to Rather and said, Well, Mister Rather, at the Chicago convention, you had your rights trampled on when police unlawfully detained you for twenty minutes so you can appreciate the emotional trauma our innocent clients are suffering.

And while Amy's talking, her name is on a graphic on the bottom of the goddamn screen.

This rips it once and for all. I dialed Amy's number nine times but of course she's in Chicago. How she could do this to me and to her family and to her country I do not know.

• • •

August 29–Friday

Last night I got so upset about Amy I woke Janet up and told her about it. Then she couldn't get back to sleep and kept tossing and finally threw the covers back and stumbled to the bathroom and mumbled, I wish to hell people with the flu could go to the hospital where they'd be left alone to die.

I'll be glad to get back to work.

Billy

P.S. I'm on my fourth bourbon and got thinking, just last month, one man risked his life walking on the moon, while another man swam back to his hotel leaving some poor girl under water on Chappaquiddick. He can kiss his political career goodbye.

• • •

May 13, 1970 – Wednesday

Dear Jerome:

You said my letters make it sound like the world's going to hell in a hand basket, that I should look for ways to have events of the day take less of a toll on me. So I'll try, starting with news of my buddies.

Jack Hackett married that physical therapist on a hillside in Presidio Park. On a warm and sunny afternoon with pretty flowers and the smell of fresh cut grass and kids playing nearby. It couldn't have been nicer. We all like the new bride and Jack said his liver wakes up singing every morning because he still isn't drinking.

He and a couple of other cops tried to start an A.A. chapter at our department, they got the idea from New York and Boston cops. DeFreese went along but the city manager nixed it, says if we have our own chapter, the citizens will think cops take a drink.

The city manager hasn't lost all his marbles because he appointed DeFreese permanent police chief and the troops are happy. Speaking of troops, remember when I got suspended and worked at the auto parts place, I told you about a wild-ass kid named Tulley Brown. Well the other day I'm walking across the patio and who hollers at me, but Tulley Brown, all decked out in uniform. He's going through the academy and says I inspired him to become a cop. How that could be I do not know.

Tulley Brown is from a hick town in the Ozarks and said he came to San Diego to see the world. He claims his hometown population always stays at exactly 978 because every time a woman has a baby, a man leaves town. Tulley is a tall, good looking guy who brought just enough of that Missouri twang with him to make people smile all the time. I hope he can cut it because I like the kid a lot.

The other good news is that Culpepper got promoted and is working night patrol. Me and Jack Hackett told him now that he's a big-shot lieutenant he can quit studying and quit playing the field and get himself hitched. Janet says Culpepper doesn't need to find a girl who can cook because he makes the meanest pot roast and Boston cream pie she's ever tasted.

Now. About our sister. She's still sore and won't write or return calls. One time she picked up but when I tried singing a couple of lines from the Ray Bolger song, she gave me a two word message, then banged the phone down. Just another sign Amy can't handle the truth.

As far as the blast I got from Mom, I'm tired of the same old story about how rough Amy had it growing up with two older brothers and having to show off her independence. I was sore when they got the Chicago 7 off with a slap on the wrist, but I also got upset when Judge Hoffman put Amy in jail for contempt. Yes, she deserved it, but I hated to think of our sister being in that shithole, even for a little while.

One of the US members killed a Panther behind that Crisis Center building in Southeast that I told you about. It happened on my shift and when we finished clapping, we climbed the stairs to investigate and the same Code-3 bitch stood waiting for us. Only this time she didn't get in our way, so I guess she didn't like jail any more than Amy.

Boy, Jerome, that Mylai thing has been simmering for months and we've been grateful the San Diego protests didn't get as violent as we'd expected. Then last week we got Kent State and all hell broke loose the next day. Four of my cops got injured at San Diego State and the squad will lose at least eighty man hours. One guy's wife is all over him to quit because this is the third time he's been hurt dealing with so-called students. You can bet Kent State will be the swan song for the National Guard on campus.

On top of that, a twenty-three year old guy walked onto campus at the University of San Diego carrying a five gallon can of diesel oil. He doused himself, screamed something about Vietnam, and then put a match to his jacket. The homicide sergeant told me they log it as "self-immolation." (Homicide rolls on unusual deaths as well as murders.) This is a crazy world, and I hope Tulley Brown knows what he's getting into.

One day radio put out an 11-80 call (which means serious injury accident) at 49th and Imperial. That intersection is right outside Lincoln High which now is about ninety-five percent Negro and Sgt. Billy Considine just happened to be one block away minding his business. Of course school was getting out so everybody ran over to the corner. A car had run a stop sign, one driver not scratched, and the other hurt real bad. Both were Negroes and when I say thank goodness for that, I'm not being ugly. It's just that the crowd would have turned on a white driver.

It seemed like forever before any cover got there and a couple of rocks came zinging my way. The crowd is yelling out, you took your time getting here pig because it's Negro people that are hurt. The lady laying on the ground was in bad shape, I think she took the steering wheel in her chest, and some of the group started heading toward me and a pop bottle crashed next to me while I'm kneeling next to the lady who's coughing up bright red blood.

So I jumped up and yelled out, what do you want to do, mess over me and let this lady die, or get over here and help?

Then I held my breath and started giving orders as if we did this together every day. They looked at me and then at each other and all of a sudden they started directing traffic and keeping kids back and saying comforting things to the lady on the ground. It all worked out and my lieutenant told me I'd earned three weeks pay in three hours.

By the way, you said in your letter not to forget that Amy stood by me on the Miami extradition and I haven't forgotten. When you talk to her tell her I'd like a second chance.

Take care of yourself and tell Mom I love her.

Billy

• • •

December 16, 1970 – Wednesday

Dear Jerome:
Frank Runyon once mentioned an ancient Chinese curse—May You Live in Interesting Times. Janet thought that over for a while and said Billy, it all got started in Dallas.

Jack Hackett and his wife came over for hamburgers and Jack leaned back in his chair and said, when we first came on the department, all my relatives and friends in Oregon thought being a cop was special. I told him I remembered that mood, almost everybody rooted for us and even the movie cops were good guys.

Now one work day is like the one before. A sergeant starts his shift at a campus demonstration, then rolls to a violent "peace march," then gets called by an outnumbered cop in La Jolla because a crowd is smashing windows at a U.C.S.D. lab.

If we still have manpower, we form a wedge between the Brown Berets and the Black Panthers who are bad-mouthing each other in the park, knowing in a matter of minutes both will turn on us. But as Culpepper is quick to point out, it's job security.

I can't believe another Christmas is almost here and right this minute I'm supposed to be putting up outside lights. Which believe me I'd be doing if Janet was in the same zip code. But this is her day to serve on a review board that takes testimony on how things are working out for foster kid placements. Her part is all volunteer, and she spends two full days before the testimony reviewing case folders. She went through quite a screening process to get selected, then spent a week training in a meeting room at the Town & Country Hotel. I'm proud of her, but said I hoped her benevolence didn't cost me home-cooked dinners and clean socks. She threw a sponge at me, and Jimmie laughed so hard she threw one at him.

Jack Hackett quit studying and says he doesn't give a rat's ass about being a sergeant. He did organize an "unofficial" A.A. chapter for cops (Jack got a two-year cake last month) and spends much time supporting new members. He turned down a chance to go to Vice because he didn't want to be around so much drinking and also turned down Juvenile. Jack loves Patrol, and they've made him a Field Training Officer, so he works with young cops. What better man they could have picked I do not know.

I'm now working Unit 754 full time in Southeast, so no more jumping all over the city. I have seven cars, all two-man. Unit 16 plus Units 20 through 25.

Last week I did have to cover one call in another sector. A patrol cop who normally works the beach area had been sent to Kensington on a last minute relief. He's cruising around just after midnight and sees his wife's car parked on a side street. Figuring it's been stolen, he telephones home. No answer.

The cop stakes out the car and eventually another car pulls behind it with the cop's wife and some guy in it, and they're playing kissy-face. The cop punches him so hard the real estate salesman's face puffs up like a grapefruit. That's when Sergeant Considine arrives.

I pushed the cop back into his car and took his gun away. Then I talked the salesman into going home and forgetting it happened, reminding him his wife would be involved if it got any messier. After he left, I gave the cop his gun back and told him, all things considered, I would recommend he be counseled by his sergeant and a note put in file. But his captain overruled me and suspended him for six days.

When it gets close to midnight on New Year's Eve in my sector, cops find a closed gas station or any roof to park under, because the crazies celebrate by firing guns in the air. They either don't know or don't care that the bullets have to come down.

Jerome, by no means am I saying Negroes are the biggest problem. White people threw rocks at Nixon's motorcade in San Jose and the next day we had trouble here. A knee-jerk reaction by hippies all over town forming up and screaming about the war. More cops got hurt, including one of mine.

And a cop from intelligence filled me in on these Weathermen you may have been reading about. Most of them are white and they're an offshoot of Students for A Democratic Society. They preach and practice armed warfare and want the Commies to whip us in Vietnam because they say our government exploits people. A lot of girls from rich families are in the movement, and they've bombed government buildings and corporate headquarters in New York City. Supposedly their name came from a Bob Dylan song claiming you don't need a weatherman to know which way the wind blows.

I'm out of here.

Billy

P.S. If I'm not careful, one of these days I'll accumulate enough college units for a Bachelor of Science degree in Criminal Justice Administration.

P.P.S. The tobacco companies scream smoking isn't harmful. Do you think they wonder why after January 2nd they won't be allowed to advertise on radio or TV?

PART FOUR

Blood is a Homicide
Detective's Best Friend

• • •

June 27, 1971 – Sunday

Dear Jerome:
Well, Culpepper is a hero. The newspaper labeled him one
when they plastered his picture all over the front page. A cop
got shot answering a disturbance call and was laying on the
front lawn bleeding. Culpepper tried to drag the cop to cover,
but the guy opened fire again and Culpepper had to back off
after getting shot in the leg.

The SWAT team advised they were ten minutes away.
Culpepper said f... that. He limped around to the back door,
kicked it in, and confronted the guy in the hallway. Culpepper
got off five shots and put the guy in ICU at Mercy. The cop on
the lawn lived, so everybody's happy except the suspect's mother
who said Culpepper should have been equipped with tear gas
or done a John Wayne and shot the pistol out of his hand.

The troops love Culpepper, because even as a lieutenant,
he leads the charge in a riot or when they're backing the
paddy wagon up to the door of a party that gets out of hand.

It reminded me how the stress factor continually affects cops.
It influences their day to day dealings with people.

For instance, a patol unit in the beach area got an ambulance
needed call, and when they got there, the woman is washing dishes
and told them she'd miscarried in the living room and put it in
the toilet. My guys go look. A little fetus floating around. The
woman's still at the kitchen sink and my guys get emotional and
say to her, why didn't you just use the garbage disposal? She never
missed a beat, Jerome, just said, garbage disposal is broke.

These officers keep seeing human misery, and they have to stop
feeling or they won't survive. It can make them insensitive to the
suffering of others, which brings complaints, and since responding
to complaints is stressful they're back on the merry-go-round.

I'd been taking the bus to work since gas is up to .44 cents a
gallon, but it looks like I'll be driving again. There's a twenty

minute layover for a transfer on 5th Avenue, so I'd drop into the bar at the Hotel Sanford or The Bull & Bear for a quick one. Sometimes one led to two led to three and I'd have to face Janet when I got home. She checked her money book and is talking about picking up a used car as a second vehicle.

There's a lady named Pearline who lives in my sector, and she gets off the afternoon bus at the same time every day. I try to be there to give her a ride to her house in the 2900 block of "L" St. She's old and fat and works as a domestic like Aunt Kate used to, and watching her walk you know her feet are killing her. Her husband uses the car because he washes dishes at Navy Hospital in Balboa Park and the buses run too infrequently when he gets off.

Anyway, I dropped Pearline off the other day and she gets out and grins and says, keepin' this up, folks gonna be spreadin' news that I'm slippin' around with a white boyfriend. Then she told me to wait, and came out with a sweet potato pie for me to take home.

So long for now, Jerome. I'm going to see if I can sleep.

Billy

P.S. Four patrol cops and a detective got together and started a rock group, playing drums and electronic guitars and whatever. They call themselves The PD-5 and they're good. They play at junior and senior high schools and public functions and even at the Del Mar Fair. When they finish their final number, they rip off their wigs and the crowd goes ape shit when it's announced they've been screaming and clapping for a bunch of cops.

• • •

January 13, 1972 – Thursday

Dear Jerome:
Here's one about your favorite nephew who is now a seventh grader by the way. Turns out he got elected class president

and bubbling with excitement when he got home. He said to Janet, if you talk to Dad, don't tell him about it because I want to surprise him. Janet said Jimmie got to the door, turned around and said, well, if Dad calls, and if he's having a really bad day at work, go ahead and tell him. Boy, Jerome, could I possibly have been that compassionate in seventh grade?

At work, the good news is I haven't been called out of my sector as much for war games. Although late last summer, we had a brawl in Ocean Beach the day after John Mitchell announced the federal grand jury wouldn't be looking into Kent State. I got a uniform shirt ripped and three police cars got damaged.

I told you there are six or seven trouble spots in Southeast where they gather at night and end up tossing stuff at us when we drive by, most of it cooked up by the Panthers. My lieutenant and I figured out a solution and so far, so good. We did it by coaxing the midwatch commander into giving us six of their cars, all two-man. About an hour before the sun goes down we have a car occupy each of the trouble spots. It's easy as stepping in dog shit, and I don't know why we didn't think of it before. The cops drive in, cut the engine and pretend they're doing paperwork. The hoodlums pull onto the lot and as soon as they see the heat they keep driving. Of course the city manager won't let us occupy Ocean View Park and South Crest Parks. Never mind that we could keep the trouble makers out, he's afraid if the Union or Tribune got wind of it they'd label us Storm Troopers.

My own troops are doing good police work and we're getting to know each other. You understand they're the only white faces I see for eight hours. I have a contest going that works like this. Each of my cars submits a list of three places on their beat they think are most likely to be stickup victims. If a place on the car's list gets hit, I buy the two cops in that car barbecue from a place called Huffman's which is primo. It makes each car more aware of those spots, so they patrol them more, which increases the odds they'll run into a stickup in progress which is every good cop's dream.

Damn the fates. On day shift, an eleven-year-old boy was bouncing a ball on the sidewalk in front of his house when two cars collided. It would have been just a fender bender, but one car jumped the curb and killed this little guy. I covered the call but then avoided that street for a week and the first time I did go back a man stood out on the lawn looking at me and I recognized him as the boy's father, so I stopped. He was sweating up a storm and pointed to the garage end of his driveway. He said, I'm taking that down, don't want to look at it no more.

It was a basketball hoop, Jerome. I asked him if he needed help, then I ended up on a ladder while he leaned over from the top of the garage and we finally got it disconnected. We never said anything about the accident while we worked.

Afterward his wife brought us some iced coffee on the patio, and he looked at me and said, this is the worst thing can happen to a body. He walked me to my car and I put my gun belt back on and he said, why don't you take that hoop with you, I got no use for it.

I climbed into my car and said, why don't you put it in the garage and cover it up for a while, I have a feeling one of these days you might want to put it up again.

When I got home, Jimmie was shooting baskets in front of our garage and it tore me up.

So Happy New Year to you brother. I sure wish I was there or you were here so we could knock back a couple and talk about stuff.

Billy

• • •

August 28, 1972 – Monday

Dear Jerome:
One of the urinals at the police station has a cutout of Jane Fonda's face in it, and I've seen guys line up to use that

urinal even when others are available. See, a bunch of our cops got called up by their reserve unit and shipped to Vietnam. One is dead and another is a POW. When she got photographed sitting on a North Vietnamese anti-aircraft gun that tore it and now even Hollywood blacklists her.

As you probably know, a week ago Hanoi Jane and Bobby Seale stirred up a big anti-war crowd in Miami. The next day I'm coming out of the courthouse with two of my cops and fifteen of Fonda's disciples are on Broadway yelling "Baby Killer" to any serviceman who walks by. No law against that, but we stand on the top steps to watch, and just as a Marine approaches, one of the dirt bags reaches into a gunny sack and pulls out a big rubber baby with its throat cut. They've dipped it in red paint, and they heave it at the Marine.

The Penal Code defines that as Section 242 (Battery), so we start after them. The Marine doesn't see us yet, he's got paint all down the front of his uniform, and he lunges for one of them and goes down. Turns out he has what's called a prothesis instead of a right leg and is still getting used to it. A couple of sailors and three off-duty cops joined in and we got all of them in jail.

You probably know Amy and I talked on the phone (finally) and we have an armed truce. I'll try to be more tolerant and she'll try to be less of a chowder head.

As far as things in Southeast, I'd vowed not to tell you any more of the unhappy junk, but this is worth it. Remember when I first came on the department and told you the policy is not to arrest husbands for beating up their wives. Here's what happened.

We see so much of it in Southeast that I got frustrated and talked to Janet. She talked for a long time about why a woman stays with a man who beats her up. It boiled down to these women having no feeling of self-worth, they don't think they deserve any better, so they fall for the guy's bullshit about how it's because she messes up that he has to hit her, or that he smacks her because he loves her.

So I explained all of that to my troops and told them when
they run into a repeat offender or a first-time aggravated case,
throw the son of a bitch in jail and let me worry about the
heat. And I got a truckload of heat. The detectives squawked
about processing paperwork that would never result in charges,
and the city attorney complained to the chief's office.

But all the yelling stopped in a big hurry when a lady in
a white part of town got beaten to death by her husband. Because the neighbors told homicide and the newspapers that
patrol came out every time she got beat up, and when homicide pulled the paperwork, patrol had been called fourteen
times.

And of course nothing had ever been done to the husband.
The Tribune and the L.A. Times did a series on the murder,
and I swear the reports must have been listening to Janet explaining things to me. Now there's big-time scurrying going
on in the department and even talk of setting up a Domestic
Violence Unit as part of Juvenile Division.

The only other thing worth passing on is that one of my
guys in Unit 25 shot a fifteen year old who pointed a pellet
gun at him. I did the hospital end of the workup, and a rookie
nurse at Paradise Valley Hospital is briefing me on the kid's
condition. She says, Sergeant, thank goodness, the bullet went
through-and-through in the boy's right thigh and didn't do a
speck of damage. I said, we're trained that way and I'm so glad
it worked out. Jerome, she's a Raquel Welch look-a-like with
eyes like saucers and I thought she was going to cry. I said,
yes, Nurse, on leg shots, San Diego police officers are in-
structed to fire either above or below the patella, and to either
side of the femur and tibia.

The old charge nurse came in about that time and big eyes
couldn't wait to tell her. The charge nurse listened, put an
arm around her and said, Sweetie, there is one thing you're
going to learn about cops. They're all full of shit. Then she
winked at me.

I flunked the lieutenant's test, but it didn't bother me because

I haven't studied that hard. There's too much to learn about being a good sergeant.

The department is changing. More guys are coming on who aren't veterans, and they don't accept orders without question like the old-timers. And now, sideburns can be worn halfway down the ear. Still no mustaches which is fine with me, but there's talk of women working patrol. God help us all.

Janet sends her love to everybody and said to tell you the Sunset Cliffs story, Sunset Cliffs being a pleasant spot to park and look out over the ocean while you sniff salt air and hear wave's crash. Once, Janet and I parked next to a car with an old lady in the front seat and the hood up. A man with her told us they needed their battery jumped which we were able to do for them.

Turns out the lady was the man's mother, she was dying of heart failure and had never seen the ocean. So this fella up and loads her into the car and takes off from Eva, Oklahoma, which he says is in the panhandle. Janet said to him, that's a pretty good distance, and he said, 1,133 miles to be exact, Ma'am. Ever since that day, the view has looked even sweeter to us.

Janet is a pip. Payday we splurged on a five-pound eye of the round at LeClair's ($1.79 a pound) and had the Hacketts over. At the table I spilled a little wine on my shirt and Janet made me change it. Then she said to our company, when I met Billy, his idea of a clotheshorse was somebody who tucked their shirt in. I said, you can't make a silk purse out of a sow's ear. Janet rolled her eyes and Jack Hackett said, no, but you'd expect some improvement.

My best to Mom and the relatives and neighbors. Sometimes I just miss them like hell.

Billy

P.S. After two years in uniform, Culpepper is now a detective lieutenant.

P.P.S. Remember those Weathermen types I wrote you about. As I was writing the P.S. about Culpepper, the phone rang and it was Amy. There'd been a bank robbery in Cleveland pulled off by four Weathermen, two men and two women. Amy said they shot a police officer making their escape, and Amy's office is defending them. Amy told me if the cop dies, she's taking herself off the case.

• • •

December 27, 1972 – Wednesday

Dear Jerome:
There's something I couldn't tell you when we talked Christmas Eve because, well, because it was Christmas Eve. Then yesterday I started to dial you but got choked up. So here it is in writing, and I'll give it to you blow by blow instead of bottom line first. Maybe that way I can get through it.

Two days before Christmas, I switched one of my days off with a sergeant who works the east end so he could have more time for a visit from his wife's folks. That meant I took his sector, and I looked forward to a change from Southeast, even if just for one day.

Roll call went off at 6:40 a.m. that Saturday and everybody seemed pretty mellow. There wasn't much to read off to the troops because for once there wasn't much going on.

It took forever for the first six hours to go by. We had a lost two-year old who turned out not to be lost, just having a snooze in his mother's laundry basket, and a couple of other minor things and I remember thinking it seemed strange seeing all the white faces.

At 2:00 p.m. I'm buying Jack Hackett a soda at a 7-11 and we get a call about students causing a disturbance at San Diego State. Jack and I look at each other. What students? The place is shut down for Christmas, right?

So we follow each other up to the south end of the campus and don't see anything, then a girl on a bike pulls up and points toward College Avenue and says, it's a Don't Resume the Bombing Rally, and they're kind of crazy.

Just what we don't need, Jerome. Nixon's already said he's going to order a twenty-four hour moratorium over Christmas, but the papers are full of will-he-or-won't-he start blasting Hanoi again on the 26th.

We cruise over to College Avenue and there are maybe fifty of them, flowing out into the street, holding up banners and some of them still wearing their McGovern-Shriver shirts. I told radio to send me some cover and I told Jack Hackett I'd try to spot the rally leaders and talk to them--set up some ground rules. Sometimes that works and sometimes it doesn't. I mean only fifty people. This did not look like a big deal.

I spotted a guy who seemed to be running things, but he didn't look like a student. I said, how about having a talk? He said, how about fucking yourself? Cars started swerving to avoid them, and I said, at least keep your people out of the street, somebody will get hurt. A stringy-haired girl next to him gave me the finger and said, eat shit, Pig.

So I backed off and drove down the block to where Jack Hackett was and six other officers had shown up. I hadn't even gotten out of the car and I heard glass breaking. They were in the middle of the street now, blocking traffic, and smashing store windows. Not looting, just malicious damage.

I told radio what we had and told them we were going to move in on them. In my mind we'd make short work of it.

I got on my loudspeaker system and told them to disperse--told them they constituted an unlawful assembly and they'd be arrested if they remained. It was 2:37 p.m. because you have to note the time, but they stood there and kept breaking windows, all the time chanting, Stop the bombing! One-two-three-four, we don't want your fucking war-No more bombing, no more bombing!

I ordered my cops to get their batons, form a line and

move toward them. Usually at this point, facing eight of us, half of them will scatter as soon as we start moving.

But not this time. They let us get right up on them. Then, on cue as it turned out, the rest came roaring around a building. Probably three hundred strong, many definitely not student types. They peppered us with stuff as they ran, half of them ammo carriers toting sacks full of rocks and bottles for the others to throw.

Jack Hackett went down right in front of me and I grabbed him by the back of the gun belt and started dragging him away. They still had traffic blocked and started looking for more windows to smash.

TV cameramen got there quicker than my reinforcements, but as soon as the cameras started whirring, all of them split because they wanted no part of being ID'd on camera. They poured into trucks, all with license plates covered.

Jack Hackett's face was a bloody mess and he kept moaning about his eye. We got him to College Park Hospital in less than five minutes where they worked on him, bandaged him up and transported him to Mercy. But they couldn't save his eye.

Thirty or forty screwdrivers were found in the debris on College Avenue. The ophthalmologist said the damage is consistent with a screwdriver. Remember as a kid how you'd throw a jackknife to make it stick in a tree trunk? That's how they threw the screwdrivers at us.

Janet hustled over to the hospital to sit with Jack's wife, and I wondered how that made his wife feel. Sitting next to a woman who's the wife of the guy who caused her husband to lose his eye.

I had jumped too soon, Jerome. If I had sent a couple of units around back on a reconnaissance, or waited until they could deliver us face shields from downtown, or just let them have the damn neighborhood until we could load up our forces.

But I had plunged in, as if saying this is our city and you aren't going to tear it down. Jack Hackett is telling everybody it's not Billy's fault, it's not Billy's fault. But he's wrong, because I was in charge.

Do you know what I did yesterday on my day off? I put a patch over my right eye at 7:00 a.m. and kept it on all day. Everything got distorted. Distance vision, side vision, everything. Trying to brush my teeth I hit my nose with the toothbrush.

Jack Hackett's through as a cop. He lost his eye so he's lost his job. As for me, I'm sick of the war and I'm sick of hippies and yuppies and sick of Black Panthers and protests and marches and TV clips of soldiers in body bags, and it's been eight years now, and if it's still going when Jimmie turns draft age, and if he wants, I'll drive him to the Canadian border and see that he's got $$ in his jeans. He's the light of my life and I didn't raise him to die in some goddamned rice paddy in a war we can't win.

Poor Jack Hackett. And damn me. Remember when we were kids. We made our decisions saying eeny-meeny-mienie-mo, and all of our mistakes got fixed by do-overs.

Billy

• • •

April 30, 1973 – Monday

Dear Jerome:
I have little to report and am just wasting paper. The department is changing so fast who can keep up with it?

We now have a female in patrol. No, not one of the veteran policewomen from detectives, but a young clerk from the records division. She's a nice person and a fine looking girl, but some numbskull decided she can't wear a man's uniform, so they've issued her this awful looking tunic, and her Smith & Wesson looks pretty lonely hanging in its holster. This experiment is to satisfy these so-called feminists and it'll fall on its face as soon as this girl proves she's better filing arrest reports than doing police work.

Also, we now have what is called Community Oriented Policing, whatever the hell that is. It means getting out among the citizens and going to Rotary meetings and playgrounds. In other words, don't concentrate on busting criminals, just kiss as many asses as you can so nobody gets sore at you.

I guess we've been doing it wrong all these years. To me, Community Oriented Policing is when you get sweaty helping a guy take down a basketball hoop. Why give it a fancy name and set up a special office?

Everything is just ducky at home other than forgetting Janet's birthday in February and catching hell about drinking. It doesn't seem to matter to her that at least I'm doing it at home, not at Bernie's. I'll never figure Janet out. Sometimes I look at her and it's like she's not there and I don't know where she is and she won't tell me.

I may as well just stay at work and get yelled at since my lieutenant is all over me because my troops' ticket average has gone south. I told the L.T. if I'm not doing the job, just transfer me, or better yet, demote me. He says my leadership has slipped since the Jack Hackett "incident." I started to walk away, then I said an incident is a couple of people yelling at each other, do you mean the charge I led when Jack Hackett lost his fucking eye? But he just slipped back into his prepared speech which probably came from the captain.

Another thing, Jerome, I talked to a captain who does civil service interviews of applicants. Get this! They are now hiring people if they've been reasonably clear of drug usage for one year. That's how much dope there is out there. Well, these new wonder cops will fit right in with Community Oriented Policing.

I see Nixon's thanks for getting us a cease fire was to keep getting pounded on over this Watergate crap until Haldeman and Ehrlichman had to resign. The flatheads who are out to get him will end up getting the kind of government they deserve.

Jack Hackett has had a couple of operations and the city will pay him some $$ for a disability award. He's still officially on the roster but won't be for long. I don't see much of him anymore. All I want to do is get my time in and get the hell out of this business.

Billy

• • •

September 10, 1973 – Monday

Dear Jerome:
I'm hung over because Janet threw a surprise party for me last night. Since it wasn't my birthday I never saw it coming. I got home from picking up Jimmie and his friend at the stadium and twenty people jumped out of the hallway.

Jack Hackett and his wife ambushed me, along with a bunch from our academy class. Culpepper showed up with a knockout redhead, and we must have made thirty blenders of Margaritas because even Janet got tipsy. Jack Hackett had his root beer, but seemed to be having a better time than the drunks.

Jack is going to college full time working on a degree in social counseling or some such. What with the G.I. bill and his payoff from the city, they have the $$ to get him through school. He got his driver's license and says DeFreese wrote him a great letter for his resume. I'd seen Jack a few times since I last wrote, but Janet says I keep pushing away from him.

The summer dragged but football season's here, and it reminds me. Do you remember the game three years ago when USC pounded Alabama and that Negro fullback Sam Cunningham ran wild for the Trojans? Well, an Alabama cop told me he'd seen that game at Legion Field in Birmingham. The cop said Sam Cunningham did more for integration in Alabama in three hours than Martin Luther King did in ten years, because Bear Bryant finally convinced the state school system his team needed Negro players.

Who do you think is working for me in Southeast? Tulley

Brown, the kid I told you about who worked with me at the auto parts store. I can't believe he's been on the department over three years. Tulley is a good cop, my troops all like him, and the Negroes take to him.

So that's it from this end, Jerome. We look forward to your letters. One interesting thing. Janet and I reversed course. She thinks Nixon's an evil man and I say with all the serious stuff going on in the world, people should worry about something worthwhile. Him and Spiro are still okay with me, and cops I know feel the same.

Tell Mom I'll call one of these days.

Billy

• • •

March 22, 1974 – Saturday

Dear Jerome:
It is a month late but we're supposed to be leaving for the Cotton Patch to celebrate Janet's 38th, but she isn't ready, so I'll pour one and knock out a quick letter. On my lapel I'm sporting the fifteen-year service award the city gave me (nine months late), but it will end up on a charm bracelet Jimmie and I are having made for the birthday girl.

This Child Protection Services board is taking its toll on Janet, because there are so many sad stories with these foster kids, and all the stories come out during testimony. I tell her she's done her duty, why not back off and let someone else have a go at it, but it's like talking to the fence post.

Janet only gloated a little when Agnew resigned and pled nolo to his income tax evasion. Can you believe extortion, bribery and kickbacks? Not only while Maryland's governor, but even as the V.P. It was a shock like when Chief Steele tumbled. Guys like Agnew and Steele get used to that dirty $$ and can't let go. I sure was wrong about him.

Funny though. Agnew always bitched at judges for not
giving tough enough sentences, but you didn't see him turn
down probation and a fine. You and I would have ended up
on a chain gang.

It could be your brother was also wrong about the women
in patrol thing. They seem to be holding up their end, and a
couple of sergeants tell me they don't antagonize people like
some of the male cops. I wouldn't know because no women
are assigned to Southeast.

Remember that records clerk I told you about who was
the first girl in uniform? The cop who worked with her on
her first night out said she gave him a five minute lecture before they left the police garage. She wanted no special treatment and demanded to be treated exactly like male cops. The
cop told me he said nothing during the sermon, just
shrugged, pulled out onto Kettner, then said to her, I usually
stop for a cup of coffee to go at Lawton's, what do you take
in your f...... coffee, partner?

Provided it's a valid kidnapping, Patty Hearst's head will
be mush if these bastards ever cut her loose. Intelligence gave
us info on this Symbionese Liberation Army and they're just
another bunch of murdering street hoods. An offshoot of the
Panthers, and this Nancy Ling Perry is the brains. Cinque,
who's supposed to be the leader, is a street pimp out of Cleveland, and the Do-Good girls hooked up with him on their
visits to Soledad where they convinced him all Negro prisoners are oppressed.

I don't know if you followed it, but a couple of Cinque's
lieutenants gunned down a Negro man named Marcus Foster,
the superintendent of schools in Oakland. That wasn't enough
publicity for them so they kidnapped Hearst. The S.L.A. is
bad news, Jerome.

Speaking of kidnapping. You must have seen the news two
days ago where an attempt was made on Princess Anne in
London. Jerome, for a few days last week while you sat in
your undershirt knocking back a cold bottle of Iron City,

your kid brother hobnobbed with the future King of England. That's right, His Royal Highness Prince Charles. Here's the story and it's a good one.

Prince Charles came to San Diego aboard the HMS Jupiter where he's putting in his time as a Naval officer. The ship docked here and Scotland Yard had requested our department furnish a couple of cops to work with one of their sergeants who is assigned his protection. Our intelligence detail normally handles that stuff, but they were all jammed up and the corner pocket wanted a sergeant involved, so I changed into my suit and tie and got a break from patrol.

The protection was super low key, not like when the president comes to town. We buzzed around in two undercover cars, stopping for all the signal lights and acting like tourists.

He's a nice guy, twenty-five years old and not impressed with himself. One night we even had dinner with him at a plush eatery called Mr. A's. I mean, With Him.

See, the night before, he'd had a dinner date with a blonde Admiral's daughter, so my partner and I and Scotland Yard sat at the next table at Lubach's on the waterfront. But the next night when we walked into Mr. A's it was just the three cops, Charles and an aide. No reservations involved, we just walked in, and when they told the maître d' a table for five, my partner and I figured people had to be meeting them there. The maître d' didn't recognize him, told us there'd be a wait, so our group headed for the bar. But a few minutes later somebody took a close look at him and we got a table real fast.

Jerome, the table was for us, so Buckingham Palace bought my dinner. Much of the menu was in French so I just ordered what the guy next to me ordered. Charles described his Naval communications duty and told us how he'd pulled on the wardroom team in the tug-o'-war contest aboard ship. In short, he is a regular guy.

The reason I'm telling you this is because while eating we talked about all the violence in America and how different things are in Great Britain. They seemed real interested in

what it's like from a police point of view. That was on
Wednesday.

Then, the next day, when it was 8: p.m. in London, Charles
got called out of a luncheon because four people, including two
cops, had been shot during a kidnap attempt on his sister. As you
know by now, they got the suspect and Princess Anne is okay.

It turned out to be quite an experience and he'll make a
good king. I guess his life won't be too tough from here on.

Janet is ready and looks more beautiful than ever. We'll
toast you and Mom and Amy. Got to run.

Billy

• • •

August 10, 1974 – Saturday

Dear Jerome:

Nixon and I are both changing addresses. He's moving
from Pennsylvania Avenue to San Clemente and I'm going
from patrol to homicide. Monday I report and take over a
team, but feel rusty after five years in the field. DeFreese said
if he had any doubts about my ability to solve murders he
wouldn't have approved the transfer. He also said they had
something different in mind for me and I would find out
when I reported. That didn't relax me any.

DeFreese looked rough. He said, Considine, this chief's
job was fine once, but now I have a man patrol cop who
wants to wear an earring and a lady patrol cop who doesn't
want to wear a brassiere. He said no to both so they're ap-
pealing to civil service.

He also said no to a captain who wants to take us out of
uniform and put us in blazers so we won't be so "different"
from the citizens. DeFreese said, bullshit, we are different, but
as a concession he now allows mustaches and is getting ready
to make a decision on fingernail length of policewomen.

Women patrol cops now wear uniform pants instead of those goofy tunics and some of the wives are already bitching about their husbands spending their shift with young hard bodies.

You and I talked on the phone about the gun battle where L.A.P.D. killed those six S.L.A. members they trapped in the house. Since then I've learned how it went down and it's a beauty.

Bill Harris, one of the gang, shoplifted a pair of hiking socks and when an employee followed him out to the parking lot, Patty Hearst opens up with a semi-automatic rifle from their van. She doesn't hit anything, but they abandon the van and the L.A.P.D. and F.B.I. are all over it. Then the Feds pull a cute one. They find a local parking ticket in the van which of course gives an address, but decide not to cut L.A.P.D. in on it so they won't have to share the glory. But the house doesn't check out for them, so they have to show the ticket to the L.A. cops, and because cops know how to sniff around, they end up finding the gang on 84th Street.

Hearst and the Harris's weren't in the house, but coroner's tags got put on the toes of Nancy Ling Perry, Angela Atwood, Cinque and three others. In our lineup room the next day somebody put up a banner that read like a baseball score. It said, "LAPD-6: SLA-0."

Cops like to say the F.B.I. chased Hearst and her kidnappers for ninety days and came up empty, but when the gang headed south and stole a pair of socks, L.A.P.D. killed six of them.

My mind's still open as to whether Hearst is a willing victim. I know after she got kidnapped she took part in that San Francisco bank robbery, but studying for sergeant I learned about what's called the Stockholm Syndrome. Where victims come to feel a bond with their captors because the captors hold the victim's life in their hands. The Swedish case they named it after is very convincing, so who knows what the truth is. When Hearst is in custody someday maybe we'll find out.

Your nephew is fine and starts eighth-grade next month. Unlike his father, he does very well in school, and when Janet asked him if he wanted to go to college, Jimmie looked at her like, doesn't everybody? I told him if he kept working hard, his mother and I would send him to any college he could get accepted to. He said even Harvard, Yale or Princeton? I gulped and said, any one. Jerome, when I was in eighth-grade I'd never heard of those places.

When I get settled into this homicide business, I'll drop you a line. Wish me luck.

Billy

• • •

October 17, 1974 – Thursday

Dear Jerome:
Working homicide keeps me so busy my letters will be less frequent, and school is out the window, probably for a long time. When I will get my final three units needed to graduate I do not know.

Here's the setup. Our department has been working four-man teams in homicide for a long time, with a sergeant in charge of each team. When I heard about my transfer, I figured administration is adding a new team which would be #5. Well, I'll be team #5 all right, but DeFreese wants to experiment with two-man teams like L.A.P.D. uses, so they're hitching me up with an experienced homicide sergeant, and the two of us will catch cases and see how we match up with the four-man teams. The question will be, can we be as effective doing our crime scenes, morgue scenes, neighborhood checks, interviewing, interrogating, and liaising with the crime lab and the D.A., that kind of stuff.

They teamed me with Sergeant Otto Kos who's supposed to retire in six months or so. We're still getting used to each other. With Otto you know where you stand at all times. If he likes what you did he tells you, and if he doesn't like it he tells you LOUDER.

He's fifty-nine years old, been a cop since I started second-grade and a homicide sergeant for the last twenty-two years. In fact, Otto was the sergeant at that double suicide I rolled on when I was a rookie, where the old couple tied the plastic bags around their heads.

Otto remembers everything. Names, faces, places, incidents, what type of gun was used on a murder ten years ago. Our case folders end up thick as phone books but Otto reads stuff once and can rattle off who said what.

No one will confuse the two of us. Otto's shorter than me, pudgy, and looks like an unmade bed. His suits are decorated with cigar ashes. Drinker's veins like Uncle Aidan's are all over his face and he's got more chins than he needs. But Otto Kos has forgotten more about homicide investigation than I'll ever know.

Even people who don't like cops think Otto's okay. He makes peace with everyone quickly, and I've watched him sit in the interview room running his fingers through what's left of his hair, and some killer will all of a sudden decide this old detective is a man to be trusted.

We had a couple at Bernie's one night and through the cigar smoke, Otto said, remember Kid, respect brings respect and contempt brings contempt. Then he tossed back his vodka and said, if that's the only thing you ever learn from me, so be it.

I have to get some shuteye, Jerome, we've been putting in long hours. Thanks for your letter with the pictures in it. You look younger than me.

Billy

P.S. This homicide is the elite, but yesterday Otto stared me down and said, Kid, you're never as important as the cases you work.

P.P.S. Last week, a couple celebrating their 50th anniversary got into the bubbly, an argument started, she grabbed a steak knife and stabbed him in the chest. At the morgue, Otto said, we'll call this one the Anniversary Waltz where the woman cuts in.

• • •

July 30, 1975 – Wednesday

Dear Jerome:
Homicide is the best job on the department. Janet doesn't think so, because we get called out and sometimes it's thirty-six hours before I get home. Maybe then just to catch a few hours sleep, shower, shave and head back to the station. Janet said she never thought she'd need an appointment to see her husband.

Otto is smooth to work with and catches no heat at home because no one's there. He and his wife have been separated for ten years and for whatever reason neither have filed for divorce. He lives in a studio rental in what's called Little Italy and it's only a five minute drive to the station. Every morning Otto's the first cop in the squad room, puffing on his cigar and carrying a sack of bagels and cream cheese to pass around. I told you when I reported to homicide that Otto was going to retire in six months. The old-timers tell me Otto has been singing that song since Stengel managed the Yankees.

We're holding up our end with the experiment. Of course I never worked the four-man teams, but Otto likes it this way and the other day he winked and said, Kid, we'll make this work. If you're younger than Otto and if he likes you, he calls you Kid. Even the lieutenant, if there's not a crowd around.

We've worked thirty cases together and Otto says murders are different than when he came to homicide in 1952. He said then the suspect and victim usually knew each other, but with so much dope and gangs around now, everybody catches some tough ones. Otto says solving them still comes down to what he calls the Holy Trinity: Physical evidence--Witnesses--Confessions. Fingerprints are golden when you're lucky enough to get them, but blood at a crime scene can tell you a lot about what happened—how it happened. That is why Otto keeps saying that blood is a homicide detective's best friend.

If you can get to a suspect's family quick enough, they'll give you information because they're in shock. But unless the guy confesses to them, the family will eventually turn against you and claim you framed him. Otto told me you can say you don't mind that, but swears you never get used to decent people hating you.

When we get called out, Otto has usually been throwing a few down before the phone rings. I think that's another thing he likes about the two-man team, only half as many people to worry about breathing on. He says a stiff has never complained about booze on his breath.

We have a lot of outlaw motorcycle gangs in San Diego. Like The Hell's Angels, The Axemen, The Hessians, and The Gypsy Jokers. They get after each other once in a while so Otto and I caught one where a Hessian named Varmint had killed an Axeman and stuffed him in the trunk of a car.

We put five of them in jail for conspiracy but Varmint was in the wind, so we got a warrant and a couple of months ago he dropped in Oklahoma City. Otto and I went to get him and he didn't give us any trouble (your brother drank ZERO booze on the flight home).

Turns out Varmint had gotten to Oklahoma City, phoned his wife in San Diego, so she followed him with the clothes on her back and her nightshirt. They holed up in a trailer park for thirty days, sneaking out once a day to get junk food until a uniform cop got curious, stopped to talk to him, ran a warrant check and Hello San Diego.

Anyway, Varmint's a likeable little shit and on the flight home he looked down over the Grand Canyon and said, Sergeant Considine, I've been married for four years and I just fell in love. That ~~broads~~ broad's too good for me.

He told us they'd really gotten to know each other in those thirty days and tried to figure out what their lives

were all about. But it's too late for them now, because Varmint
did time in San Quentin before he pulled the trigger on the
Axeman, so they'll throw away the key.

That's it from here, Jerome. Seventeen years on the department already. Where did it go?

Billy

P.S. Be glad you're a steelworker making good $$. What
Otto and I keep hearing about on the streets is the high cost
of living and unemployment.

• • •

March 31, 1976 – Wednesday

Dear Jerome:
See, high-priced lawyers can't always get people off. The
jury told F. Lee Bailey to stuff it, that Patty Hearst is a bank
robber. So much for my Stockholm Syndrome.

The thing is, there are things defense attorneys don't have
to worry about. Like the truth. Prosecutors have to seek it
even when it hurts their case, but sometimes defense attorneys
have a legal right to conceal it. Their only mission is to get
the son of a bitch off.

For example, we convicted a guy just last week, and after
the verdict, a retired L.A.P.D. fingerprint man phoned me,
wanting to know the result. Turns out the defense attorney
had hired him to examine prints we lifted from a bedroom
window. After he examined them he told the lawyer, those
are your client's prints. The lawyer said, thank you for your
time, your check's in the mail, discuss this with no one during
litigation. All legal, but a prosecutor would go to prison for
that.

I forgot to tell you, when Janet and I celebrated our 15th
last December, I had the florist make up a bouquet that had

cotton candy mixed in with the flowers. The guy who delivered them couldn't figure it out, so Janet told him the story about our meeting at the Del Mar Fair. I am back on thick ice, Jerome.

I need points because I've started smoking again. Janet went ape shit and threatened to start again herself. There's a lot of stress in this murder business, and the hours are lousy and--oh hell--smokers can always find excuses. Luckies are too harsh for me now so I'm using a lightweight brand. The sixty cents a pack will kill me before the tobacco does. I'm going to try and quit again.

We're seeing more violence than ever. Drivers get into fights over who cut who off, or who had the right to a parking place. Then they break out the tire irons. The new term is Road Rage.

At Bernie's, one of the old-timers on team #3 told me it's bad for your head to spend time feeling sorry for victims or suspects, but I've got to tell you about an Iowa farm girl named Sally. Red hair, blue eyes, freckles, pug nose, nice shape. A naive little shit that comes to the big city for the first time and meets a guy she thought existed only in storybooks. He's a tall, handsome, quick-witted car salesman and for whatever reason they mesh and end up getting married. One night he comes home late, plops into bed and goes out like a light. Sally can't sleep, so she gets up and starts hanging up his clothes. Finds a love letter from her best friend.

She throws up on the floor before she kills him...before she even finishes reading the note. Jerome, she didn't kill him out of anger or revenge. Her heart just shattered. This corn pone girl didn't have it in her to wake him up and talk about it. Was incapable of thinking about counseling, or going to confront her girlfriend, or throwing his stuff out onto the front lawn, or packing her bag and heading back to Tootsville.

If you could have seen her sitting in our interrogation room. She looked like someone Pat Boone should be taking to the state fair. Part of me wanted to shake her and say, he came after you with a kitchen knife, didn't he? He's knocked you around before, hasn't he? But I just sat there and let her talk. After we locked her up, Otto and I closed Bernie's, because Janet and Jimmie would have been asleep anyway.

Maybe Janet and I can plan another trip to Youngstown in the fall. By the way, Amy and I talk at least once a month.

Billy

• • •

December 14, 1976 – Tuesday

Dear Jerome:

Only eleven more stabbing days left until Christmas, but I bring good tidings. Ernie Miranda, father of the Miranda Warnings and friendly neighborhood rapist, got stabbed to death in a bar fight in Arizona. The suspect wouldn't waive his Miranda Rights and without a confession, there wasn't enough evidence to charge him. Who says there's no justice?

Maybe the new president will pick the right judges for the Supreme Court if he gets an opportunity. Janet voted for Ford and was miffed that Carter got elected, so I told her Art Buchwald said with millions of Americans to choose from, the choice came down to two candidates. A peanut farmer and a guy who played football without a helmet.

Maybe Janet's training for the Boston Marathon. The more I smoke and booze, the more she runs. There's a nice course marked off on a sidewalk that runs along the bay behind the Hilton, and she's knocking off five miles a day. Talk about a hardbody.

Is everybody suing everybody in this new world? Otto and I drew a case where a guy came home and found his house ransacked, so he shot the burglar dead in the bedroom. Now the burglar's family is suing the homeowner who gets to put out big $$ for a lawyer. The homeowner must be shaking his head. If his tire had gone flat on the way home...or he'd stopped for a beer....

We now have our first woman sergeant and the patrol

troops tell me she's a good one. How those girls managed to survive in this chauvinist cop world I do not know, but I tip my hat to them.

Something else is new. Last year Negro officers got together and started what they call The Black Peace Officers Association of San Diego County. I talked to a friend of mine who's in it and he said the goal is to increase communication between black officers, the department, and the black community. Some cops say what's wrong with the communication now, but I respect this guy a lot and if he says there's a need, who am I to dispute it.

Jerome, a transvestite is someone who wears clothing of the opposite sex, and there are plenty of them in San Diego, mostly guys who want to be girls and take girl's names. It's quite a culture, and I talk pretty easily with them from my days on the downtown patrol beat and they're okay people. They wouldn't play too well at The Workers Tavern, although on our last visit to Youngstown, I talked to some of your boilermaker buddies in there. They consider themselves real connoisseurs of women. Yeah. Until the sun goes down.

The important things to these transvestites is their beauty, dough for silicone and hormones, then hopefully down the line, surgery for the sex change. To get the $$ they pick up guys (usually sailors) and do oral sex on them, taking them home if necessary. Sometimes it goes sour and that's when Otto and I get called.

One, named Diane, who I knew from my days working with Jack Hackett, got stabbed to death in her apartment. Like many of them, she lived in a dump because she was saving $$ for what's really important.

Otto taught me that a homicide cop has to treat all cases with equal importance, otherwise you get sloppy in your work. You can't go around saying this victim isn't as important as that victim, so let's just go half speed on this one.

Otto and I got on the streets and rounded up Diane's pals who are all willing to help because, for one thing, they want the guy captured so he doesn't carve them up next. We interviewed one named Paula the other night, and when we finished, Otto said, Paula, have you ever been straight?

She grabbed Otto's hand and said, Honey, I've been bent since I came out of my mother.

One of the group had seen Diane get in the cab with a sailor, but didn't get close enough to describe him and the numbnuts cabbie didn't remember shit.

We worked around the clock a couple of nights but have struck out so far. The suspect didn't get Diane's $$. The girls always get paid up front, then leave the guy in one room and go stash the dough in a hiding place before they get down to business.

Some of these guys know they're going home with a man dressed as a woman, and when that happens, the transvestites say the trick "knows the T," the letter "T" standing for truth. If a guy they bring home doesn't know the "T", and wants more than oral sex, they jack the price up so high he can't cover it.

Paula says she never takes a trick home she doesn't think she can whip, and if not, she takes a partner along with her. I wish Diane had.

She was pretty likeable, Jerome. Once she told me, listen, cutie pie, all I want is that surgery, and when I find a sugar daddy who'll buy me that gash, I'll do anything for him, even marry him.

So that's it from this end. Janet and I put presents in the mail yesterday. I remember what you did when we were kids, so just put them under the tree and NO PEEKING.

Billy

P.S. The Latino cops have an association of their own now too.

• • •

July 7, 1977 – Thursday

Dear Jerome:

7-7-77 is a lucky date for Otto and I but not so lucky for Harmon Hull, a sailor we found sleeping on the floor of an apartment on Fern Street and snapped handcuffs on. It is now twelve noon, I just got home and started to unwind, so please excuse me for a minute while I pour another couple fingers of Old Crow.

We'd been hurting on our case with Diane the transvestite because other murders had gotten in the way. Then it all came together within twenty-four lovely hours.

Yesterday morning a transvestite named Cindy came forward. She'd been in Los Angeles since the night of the murder and didn't hear about it until she came back to San Diego on Tuesday. She couldn't believe Diane was dead, because she'd been with Diane when she'd picked up her killer on "F" St. Cindy had been with the same guy a month before and told Diane he was safe, and that he didn't know the "T". Cindy watched them head for the taxi, then a few minutes later, she left for L.A.

Some of these girls remember everything and Cindy recalled this guy is on a sub tender, and was able to give us his rank and shoulder insignia plus a good physical description. Luckily for Otto and me, the ship had come back to port, so we hustled over to the Office of Naval Investigations and it went off like clockwork.

At the time Diane got murdered only a handful of the crew fit the physical, and good old Harmon Hull, the only one who wore glasses, never returned from liberty the night of the murder. Harmon must have figured he was a dead duck since Cindy knew him and had seen him leave with Diane.

Harmon's buddies gave us a few leads on the civilians he hung out with, so Otto and I came through his door at three o'clock this morning. He was more worried about what the Navy was going to do to him than what California had in mind.

We had one print from a beer can in Diane's kitchen

which matched with Harmon, and he said he killed her because he found out she was a man and felt tricked. He's a
cold-blooded son of a bitch and Otto and I figure he just
wanted to see what it felt like to snuff someone.

You know, of all the murders I've already worked, there are
maybe five that I consider death penalty cases. Opponents of
the DP think people who are for it want an eye for an eye
every time, but that's a lot of crap. The murder has to be really
aggravated. Like our stickup man who murdered the cashier
because he got tripped up by a witness once. Or our eight-
een- year-old laborer who lured a little neighbor girl into his
house, did awful things to her, then used a Louisville Slugger
to knock her around the living room until her blood was all
over the ceiling fan.

You probably saw where that Gary Gilmore guy stood up
before the Utah firing squad last January and became the first
to be executed in the U.S. in ten years. At least he had the
stones to say, I did it, kill me.

Stop reading while I pour myself one.

Well, Jack Hackett moved back to Oregon. Last month he
got his B.S. in human services and he and his wife packed.
He loaded up on courses about social problems, marriage and
family, and attended seminars and accomplished other things
that puts him on the road to being a counselor. Jack said the
county he's from in Oregon doesn't have enough trained personnel and he feels with his background he can reach a lot of
people who need help.

Jack said to send you his warmest regards. He's still got his
cop's sense of humor, because his last words to me were, I'll
keep an eye out for you, Billy.

Tulley Brown got transferred from patrol to vice and I can't
believe he's been a cop for seven years. I gave him a Do's and
Don't's talk the night before he reported and I look for good
things from that boy.

Things keep changing in this big city. There are maybe fifty
thousand Vietnamese refugees here, and they've settled mostly

in east San Diego and the Linda Vista area, a few miles south of where we live. They seem to be hard working people who stick to themselves, but they don't trust cops and its hell getting them to come across when they've been victimized.

I'll have to come back to this letter because Janet just came home and wants a sit-down. Guess I'm in the grease again.

· · ·

July 10, 1977 – Sunday

This is the third time today I've sat down to write this so you can see it's not coming easy. Janet sat me down all right, and she had a strange look. I said, am I in trouble, and she said no. I asked her what it was about and she said it's about infidelity.

Jerome, there's a secretary at work I flirt with now and then, so of course I figured Janet could read my mind. I said, I haven't been unfaithful to you. Janet said, I didn't think you had. Then she stared out the window and said, it's me, Billy.

I got that hit-with-a-sledgehammer feeling again and while I tried to recover Janet said, you're the only man I've been involved with since the day you bought that silly cotton candy.

By then I'm totally confused and I said, well what is it then? Janet said, I've met someone.

As soon as she got the words out it was like dying.

Turns out they'd had a luncheon honoring volunteers at her foster kid's organization about a year ago, and some guy dropped in to see his sister who serves with Janet. He's in and out of town from Gallup, New Mexico, where he's a salesman for some supplier of heavy equipment. Janet said after a bit there was just the two of them at the table and they gabbed about this and that.

A month later he came by the meeting and Janet told him his sister wasn't attending that day. He said, I know, I came to see you. The meeting broke up, so Janet went for coffee with him.

Since then it's been kind of an unplanned, but planned thing, because they both make it a point to show up at the coffee house on the first Thursday of the month.

Janet said one day recently they paid their check and walked outside and he said, I've kept my motel room an extra day. She told me she was tempted, and if he hadn't of been married she might have gone with him.

I couldn't believe what I was hearing. I said Janet, I never saw this coming, never saw it coming at all. She said, Billy, you've been too involved in your work to see anything, or even care about anything, especially me and your son. She said, this man actually asks me questions about myself, how I'm feeling, what I'm thinking, what are the things I care about.

I said maybe he has his best foot forward so he can get you under the covers. Janet threw a magazine across the room and stormed out.

A couple of hours later we talked some more, and she said last week she'd researched marriage counselors and found one with a good reputation, would I go with her for a consult. I told her there wasn't anything really wrong with our marriage, and even if there was, no third party had any business getting their nose into it.

That night I hardly slept.

I called in sick the next day. The next day, Saturday—hell that's yesterday, isn't it—Otto and I got called out. I told Otto about Janet and he said she's firing a warning shot across my bow.

All I know is everything's spinning.

Billy

· · ·

August 10, 1977 – Wednesday

    Dear Jerome:

Do you ever feel like you keep getting socked in the jaw?

Monday night Chief DeFreese went on TV to settle once
and for all this controversy over whether he'll hire homosexuals to be cops. I say controversy, though there really isn't one
except what the media creates.

It made big news that San Francisco P.D. is hiring them,
but believe me, Jerome, if you'd ever been to San Fran, news
like that wouldn't surprise you. But this isn't San Francisco,
and in answer to media queries, DeFreese has consistently
said homosexuals would not be hired. But he's always said it
without explanation.

Until Monday. The TV channels and newspapers have
been hounding him so the city manager told him to hold a
press conference and get it over with. When the cameras
rolled, DeFreese said homosexuals lack the emotional stability
required of police work, and during the Q&A he gave ex-
amples of incidents and stresses cops encounter, then explained why they wouldn't cut it. Some of the questioners
used the word gay instead of homosexual which from what
I've been hearing lately means the same thing.

Janet and I watched and thought it went well. That was
Monday. Then the next night—last night—Culpepper phoned
and said, are you sitting down, Billy? I said my feet are propped
up but I have a death grip on a bourbon.

Culpepper said, I'm calling to give you a heads up, because
tomorrow I'm holding a press conference. Nobody but command officers hold press conferences, so Culpepper had to be
kidding, right?

Then he said, Billy, I'm a homosexual, and I have been for
as long as I can remember, you're a valuable friend, and I want
you to hear this from me, not while you're channel switching
tomorrow night.

I didn't believe what I heard and still thought it must be a gag, but there was something about how Culpepper sounded. He said, Billy, I like and respect DeFreese, but I can't stand by and let him hand out this emotional stability crap, and besides, I'm weary of the stress involved hiding my sexuality.

I said, Culpepper, let's get together and talk right now, I need to talk to you, let's meet at Bernie's. He said, Billy, you don't want to be seen in public with me the night before I go on TV. I told him I don't mind being seen with him anytime, anywhere, and anybody who doesn't like it can kiss my ass at 30th and University.

So we took a table at Bernie's, just the two of us. We talked about a lot of things, including something that happened one day during our rookie year. Jack Hackett and I and another cop had been out drinking and happened to be driving through Culpepper's neighborhood. We got the brilliant idea to round him up and hit more nightspots.

We'd never been inside his place, and when Culpepper opened the door, a guy was messing with the venetian blinds in the living room. Culpepper told the guy to leave him an invoice, then Culpepper left with us.

Well, last night at Bernie's, he told me that was his lover of the moment. That they'd looked out the window, saw us piling out of the car, and cooked up the venetian blind story.

And all those trips to L.A. to see the airline stew was just cover so he could get out of town. That's why Jack Hackett and I never got any of those little airline whiskey bottles Culpepper kept promising us. The stew was cover, just like the bimbos he took to the police parties were cover. He said he could get lost in a gay crowd in L.A. or Laguna Beach or Palm Springs, though he always sweated being recognized.

We threw down a bunch of drinks and I told him not to resign, to stay with it and who gives a shit that he's homosexual, that he's a great cop and a great human being and that I'd talk to DeFreese for him. I talked fast. I was stunned.

By closing time Culpepper convinced me he couldn't stay. He could live with some of the cops trying to make his life miserable, but the media attention would be constant and intense. They'd never let it die. Every promotion he got, every transfer, they'd drum up a new angle about the homosexual cop with the Medal of Valor.

So tonight Janet and I watched channel 10 and there he was, sitting tall and looking right into the camera, and all the beautiful memories came back. We had told Jimmie what was happening so he watched with us. Hell, he's almost sixteen. Jimmie's a fan of Culpepper and said it was no big deal.

Culpepper had alerted Jack Hackett, so I phoned Jack. Jack said I've loved that son of a bitch Culpepper since we were in the academy and I'll always love him.

Life is something. Just when you think you have things sorted out.

Billy

P.S. I had planned on writing to say Janet and I are trying to smooth things out about you-know-what, then this came up.

• • •

September 23, 1977 – Friday

Dear Jerome:

I was shocked when you wrote about the Campbell Works closing. How in hell do they get off putting 5,000 people out of work, and what in hell are Campbell's two locals doing about it? That's crap about closing and saying it's because the open hearths are obsolete. Sure it takes longer to crank out a batch of steel with the hearths, but I'm not a steel guy and I know they could have gone to electric furnaces. Or installed the BOP shop they'd promised.

If Youngstown Sheet & Tube still owned Campbell by themselves, instead of hooking up with that conglomerate, this wouldn't have happened.

I was relieved by the clipping you sent from the Warren Tribune where U.S. Steel says the Ohio Works and McDonald Works will continue to operate. You've been loyal to U.S. Steel and to the Ohio Works since you've been nineteen years old, and it's good they're going to keep taking care of you. You've come a long way since you worked that first year at Republic as a riveter's helper.

What I didn't tell you in the last letter is that Janet and I are off to a fresh start. On Sunday mornings the two of us get on a city bus and just go. There are usually only a handful of people aboard, and we transfer whenever we feel like it and just ride around town talking about things. When we see a place we'd like to grab a bite or take a walk, we jump off. Janet said she's seeing parts of town she didn't know existed.

I talked her out of that marriage counseling stuff but promised I'd try to quit smoking and cut down on my drinking. Not that I ever drank that much, but sometimes she goes overboard trying to take care of me.

Janet's commitment with Child Protection is up so she decided to quit. She said that salesman guy from New Mexico called her at home once and she told him they were through communicating, that she'd told her husband about it. It burned my ass, Jerome, that he even called.

Culpepper moved to L.A. and is trying to decide whether to take what's called a deferred retirement, or draw out his pension contributions. We had him over for dinner before he left and he said he misses police work already. The night before he held his press conference, he told his mother and father and they're taking it pretty well. His mother told him she'd suspected for years.

Otto and I needed to interview a bunch of employees at an industrial complex the other day, and when we got back in the car, he pointed out that we're seeing more women in the work force than ever before. Otto got all worried about who was staying at home with the kids, and launched into a sermon. I got all worried about how to get out of the sermon.

I have to run, Jerome. Thanks for not mentioning any of the personal stuff to Mom or Amy.

Billy

P.S. When Elvis died last month we saw mature women crying. Otto said they'll do the same when he retires in six months.

• • •

April 24, 1978 – Monday

Dear Jerome:
Otto recently took up fishing and says when he retires he'll outsmart bass and catfish full-time at Lake Henshaw. The workload has been a pisser and it might have been the reason I got into it with Jimmie recently.

Otto and I had stopped at Bernie's and promised we'd have two quick ones then head for home. As luck would have it, we ran into a retired homicide cop I'd never met, but Otto had worked with. His name is Foley, and he shouts when he talks because he's deaf as a doorknob. Of course we had to buy him one and you know what that led to, and anyway, this old guy is getting pretty sloppy. He looks at me and says, I think of some of my young victims who got cheated out of their time and wonder how they'd look if they were alive and what they'd be doing today. Then he signals for a round, and he says, Considine, escape while there's still time.

After the old guy left, Otto said, Foley's a sentimental prick, don't listen to him.

Anyway, I got home a little late and Jimmie's waiting up at the kitchen table because he has to fill out something at school for a college counselor. That surprised me because I thought the kid was only in his sophomore year, but he's a junior. So Jimmie says, I need to talk to you, Dad, about this Criminal Justice Administration major. I said why would you be interested in that? He said, because I'm thinking about being a police officer.

Jerome, I was floored. Being a cop is the last thing I'd want for my son. Maybe I could have handled it a little better, because then he said something and I said something and he said something and you know how that goes. Janet hears us and comes out of the bedroom about the time I'm telling him he's not going to be a cop, and he's telling me I'm not going to run his life like I try to run everybody else's. What he meant by that I do not know.

I said, do you want to be a cop and end up like your Uncle Jack Hackett with one eye, or dead in your garage like Frank Runyon? But that didn't even slow him down. He snapped right back and said or walking around half-drunk all the time like Sergeant Billy Considine.

Janet ran over and got between us and steered me toward the bedroom, but I looked over my shoulder and said, that's a cheap shot, I've cut down on my drinking. Of course Jimmie had to get the last word in, so he yelled not that anybody would notice.

The next day I got thinking about how hard I've tried with Jimmie. Never pushed the kid toward baseball because it's no kind of life, a guy can spin his wheels for a few years losing valuable time. But Jimmie took a liking to football, and his high school coach at Kearny told me the only reason he didn't cut Jimmie is because he's such a hard worker and full of spirit. He's never missed a practice, and the coach uses him as an inspiration to the talented players who aren't putting out. That being the kid's makeup, I didn't get too upset with him for treating me disrespectfully that night in the kitchen.

Of course Janet landed on me. She said, Billy, you're going to make Jimmie afraid to talk to you about things a kid needs to talk to his father about. You can see how Janet's overreacting.

How can I, on one hand, let everybody know how damn much I love my job, yet tell Jimmie and Janet I don't want him to be a cop? How can I explain that?

Is it because I don't want him rolling around in the gutter wrestling drunks and whores? Or getting in the way of a bullet? I need some help here, Jerome.

Enough of my problems. I caught ABC's documentary on the Youngstown Religious Coalition's Save-Our-Valley campaign. They even showed the Sheet & Tube chorus singing Battle Hymn of the Republic over at the Boardman Methodist Church. Hooray for anything ABC and the Coalition can do to keep the Brier Hill Works from being shut down. They also showed the second clipping from the paper where the U.S. Steel official says the Ohio Works and McDonald Works will be doing business in Youngstown for a long time. Damn it, Jerome, if it's true, why do they have to keep saying it. Youngstown steel is one of the things in my life I'm supposed to be able to rely on without having newspapers confirm it.

Incidentally, Culpepper is training for an air traffic controller's job in L.A. so those passengers are in for safe rides. He says in different ways, it's as stressful as police work.

Two weeks ago, DeFreese got Otto and I in private. He said I'm going to lay something very heavy on you, but I want a lid kept on it until the two of you get up to Parker Center and get me the facts. He said, Lieutenant Soderholm is dead in his car in Hollywood—with his throat cut.

Jerome, you remember Soderholm. He's the scar-faced lieutenant I worked for on the vice squad. Parker Center is the headquarters building for L.A.P.D. and the Robbery-Homicide unit who works out of there had the case. By the way, Hollywood isn't a separate city, it's part of Los Angeles.

We drove it in two hours scratching our heads all the way. Otto said, you need to wear your drinking shoes when you work with Robbery-Homicide. I said, what do you mean, and he said, Little Tokyo is right next to headquarters, Chinatown is just a few blocks north, and they're both watering holes for L.A. cops.

Turns out Soderholm had picked up a black hooker that

the other girls call Rene the Razor, and while she serviced him, Soderholm found out how she got her name.

There'd always been rumors that Soderholm could get pretty rough with the girls. Hollywood Division Vice put the case together for Robbery-Homicide, and obviously Rene the Razor knew how to handle tough guys. Rene is on the run, but Otto and I drove out of Parker Center with the two Robbery-Homicide cops to look for her. Of course, it's always rush hour traffic there so the L.A. guys suggested we wait in Little Tokyo until it thinned out.

The oriental music was soft, the egg roll tasted good, and the longer we sat there telling them what an asshole Soderholm was, and discussing why four dignified guys like us would go out to chase down a hooker, we said piss on it, Rene will drop somewhere, let's have another.

Janet and I will be thinking of you, and U.S. Steel had better do the right thing. As the documentary pointed out, Youngstown made cannonballs for the Civil War, metal for tanks and bombs, and steel for the gates of the Panama Canal. You and all of our ancestors made that metal come alive, and that's why steel must always be there for the Mahoning Valley.

I'm out of here.

Billy

P.S. In this job, you get an up-close look at people's priorities. Otto and I handled an officer-involved-shooting where a young patrol cop killed a daytime burglar inside an apartment after the burglar shot and missed the cop. The cop's excited and the burglar's chest looks like Swiss cheese with blood spurting out, and the cop is doing all he can to stop the bleeding. The apartment house manager came in when it was safe, and the cop yells to him, get some towels, get some towels!

The cop is applying pressure to the chest wounds and after a couple of minutes he yells out, where are my towels, where are my towels?

Honest to God, Jerome. The manager says I've got them, I've got them! The cop looks up and the manager is using them to blot blood off the carpet.

• • •

August 5, 1978 – Saturday

Dear Jerome:

How would you feel about Jimmie coming to Youngstown for a week? He needs a change of scenery and the influence of his uncle. It's no secret he thinks you're a top-drawer guy.

Stuff is going on and I can't figure out why. The first clue should have been when he announced he's not going to play football this season. I was just puzzling that out when I came home one day and hear Janet and Jimmie screaming at each other in Jimmie's bedroom. I listen up for a minute, and it turns out that the week before Janet had found a marijuana cigarette in his room and hadn't told me about it. Jimmie is yelling that she always backs me during a beef, and Janet is yelling over him saying that's untrue and unfair, that she tries to understand and support both of us.

Jerome, I couldn't believe what I was hearing. I barged in the bedroom and now we're all yelling. Janet screamed, STOP-STOP-STOP, I can't take this anymore. She runs out to the garage, guns the car engine and takes off. As I was chasing after Janet, Jimmie must have gone out the patio door because all of a sudden it's me, myself and I in the house.

Three hours later Janet comes home, looking a mess which is hard for her to do. I was so worried about her that she had no trouble calming me down about the dope. After I made her a cup of hot chocolate, she said, Billy, Jimmie gets peer pressure, he's a kid doing kid stuff and you're outfitting him for prison stripes.

God damn it, Jerome, Janet's a cop's wife so wouldn't you figure she'd get the picture. If you don't get control of stuff like this, next thing you know your doorbell rings in the middle of the night and some cop is standing there getting ready to tell you something awful.

How many times have I seen it in patrol and in homicide? Jimmie's peer pressure buddies—Hey, Jimmie, my man. Meet my friend, Charlie Dipshit. We're goin' over to Bennie Pissant's pad and kick back, you'll like, Bennie, man, he's cool.

Next thing, Jerome, they've knocked back a dozen beers and Charlie and Bennie are mugging some lady at an ATM or kicking in the door of a warehouse, then when patrol nails them Jimmie's life changes forever.

Anyway, Janet gets me to drink some hot chocolate and by the time Jimmie gets dropped off, she's been saying things that make sense, so the three of us were able to talk it out. Jimmie said he's tried smoking a few joints and it's no big deal. I told him a few joints lead to heavier stuff and bad addictions and he listened but I don't think he was buying.

After Jimmie went to bed, Janet said, don't you remember what it was like being a teenager? Then she talked about hormone changes and what all. She said Billy, this is a kid who was taught early on in school to hide under the desk in case of nuclear attack, try to imagine for a minute the insecurities that promoted.

I guess it was my turn to look like I wasn't buying, because Janet pointed her finger at me and raised her voice. She said, he was old enough to watch the horror of Vietnam on the news and have some of the dirty politics rub off. She said that Jimmie and his friends ended up saying screw you to the older generation, that they were saying I'm not going to stand for this kind of world. Janet is sure that in Jimmie's mind, the older generation turned on him and his buddies.

Jerome, does any of this make sense? Let me know. We'll put him on the plane and you could pick him up in Cleveland. Jesus, we've got to do something.

Billy

• • •

November 24, 1978 – Friday

Dear Jerome:
Janet's folks came down yesterday for Thanksgiving. See, my mother-in-law thinks it's terrible if the family doesn't spend the entire day together. The plan was to get the turkey in the oven, pile in the car, then take a spin to La Jolla Cove and the Shores. Otto and I were third in line for a callout, so it looked unlikely we'd be bothered.

The five of us were walking out the door when the phone rang. Murders had been flying all over the place for thirty-six hours, and Otto and I ended up in Del Cerro where a guy named Eddie had killed his wife, his mother-in-law, father-in-law, and sister-in-law. I guess he didn't want any bullets left over, because finally he turned the gun on himself.

A neighbor in the next apartment heard the shots at 10:30 a.m. so we came in right behind it. This house of death had a turkey in the oven. When he started shooting, one victim had been opening a can of cranberry sauce and another was putting the filling in a pecan pie. He shot his sister-in-law last, in her sleeping bag on the living room floor. Hell, she was seventeen and might have slept through the first volley of shots.

In this business, you continually see fate deciding who's going to live and who's going to die. This kid in the sleeping bag had gotten into an argument with her boyfriend, otherwise she'd have stayed in Oceanside and had dinner with him and his family.

When patrol broke the door down an audio tape was playing, so we listened for anything significant. The family had cut the tape the night before, singing songs and all, and then they'd passed the mike around, each of them telling what they were thankful for. The mother-in-law said she was grateful her family was back together again, the seventeen- year-old said when she had her own family someday she was going to maintain the tradition of passing the microphone around on Thanksgiving Eve. Eddie the shooter said tomorrow would be a special day for all of them, and he was looking forward to it.

By the time I got home, Janet's folks had gone to bed and I didn't feel like eating the dinner they'd warmed up for me. I drank a few bourbons, spent too much time thinking about the girl in the sleeping bag, and then fell asleep at the kitchen table.

The next day Otto and I stopped at Bernie's for a quick one and who drifted in but Tulley Brown. I said, what' the Vice Squad doing hassling Bernie's, and Tulley said, I'm not in Vice anymore, I report to Robbery tomorrow. A good step up for Tulley.

By the way, your kid brother wears glasses now. What put me over the edge was trying to read something in the car one night when the dome light wasn't strong enough. When I lifted the piece of paper close enough to the dome light to illuminate the writing, I couldn't get my head in a position to read. So I ended up standing outside like a fool, reading in the headlights.

Janet and I are doing fine though she got sore at me last week for questioning why she'd gotten home late from a movie with her girlfriends. She said, Billy, do you doubt I was at the movies? That's Janet, fire the torpedoes, hold nothing back. All of a sudden I felt like a shit for saying anything. We've slacked off on our Sunday morning bus rides but intend to start again.

As for your nephew, he's gotten into two fights at school which is two more than ever before. I don't know what's going on. He can do school work in his sleep because he's knocking down straight A's. I think his new friends convinced him being a football player wasn't cool, and I told him so. He came right back at me with something smart-alecky. Boy, Jerome, when they're seventeen they know it all. Why Jimmie would not agree to visit you in Youngstown I do not know.

Janet told me I've cut way back on things Jimmie and I used to do together, pointing out that if I'd knock off going to Bernie's, I could put that time to good use. Of course, she had to stick the knife in, reminding me that a few weeks ago I stood him up when we'd planned to take in a movie.

San Diego has been christened the meth capital of the world. If Amy practiced here she'd make a million. It sounds like she's doing well in the private firm she hooked up with, and maybe you heard, she represents a Cleveland cop who the D.A. has charged in the shooting of a stickup man. Amy told me the killing is totally justified and said she's going to kick the D.A.'s ass into the middle of Lake Erie.

You asked on the phone about the PSA crash in September, and you're right, 150 dead make it the worst air disaster ever in the U.S. Because a Santa Ana had blown in that morning, it took the firemen a few hours to put out the flames. A bunch of houses got leveled when the plane used Dwight Street for a runway, and Otto and I got assigned to help with the identifications at the scene. I didn't tell you that before. All I'm going to say is it's the worst thing I've ever seen. Ever.

I'm sick about the Brier Hill Works. You sounded certain it will close, even though the announcement isn't formal. Fifteen hundred jobs! Don't those bastard bean counters know what that does, not only to those workers' families but to the rest of Youngstown?

I told Janet I can't find the words to describe how I feel. She said try fear and guilt. Fear U.S. Steel will close down the McDonald Works on you, and guilt because I'm not there to suffer through this with you.

As usual, she nailed it.

Billy

• • •

30, 1979 – Saturday

Dear Jerome:
I told you briefly on the phone about what I now call the Day from Hell. There is still no word from Jimmie and it's been over two weeks. You had suggested he and I go out of town for a father-son weekend to sort things out, and Janet and I planned on doing it. In fact, I intended to propose it to him on the evening of that day. Here's what happened.

The day before his graduation, I was at a murder scene in Ocean Beach. I got paged to call a number I didn't recognize, and it turned out to be the Narcotics bureau of the National City P.D. (National City borders San Diego on the south.)

National City cops had been with narcs from our department sitting on a dope buy, and when the buyer left the apartment house by himself and drove away, they stopped his car around the corner. Who do you think was one of three guys in the car? Sitting in the back seat with an I-don't-have-to-tell-you-shit attitude. Yep, our boy Jimmie.

One of the narcs from our department had looked at his ID and recognized the Considine name and asked him about it which is how they ended up paging me.

It had to be the low point of my life. Walking into the National City P.D. and checking in at the front counter like every other asshole parent whose kid is jammed up. How I could have known it would get worse I do not know.

I talked to the narcs first and they said they recovered four ounces of meth from the guy who'd gone in the apartment, that none of the three would talk, and if I wanted, they would cut Jimmie some slack and not book him, though they had plenty of probable cause. Translated, that meant the third guy who also wasn't holding would ride Jimmie's coattails and walk also. I told them thanks and accepted the courtesy.

They had Jimmie alone in an interview room, so in I go by myself, and he's sitting there like some big shot with his

hair hanging over the collar of his leather jacket and a pack
of smokes sticking out of the pocket. I didn't even know he
smoked. I said, what are you trying to do, break your mother's
heart? He gave me a wise guy look and shrugged and said,
I'm only going to say this one time, and you can tell your cop
buddies in the other room—I don't do crank, and I didn't
know anything about a buy going down.

I said, for a guy who doesn't do dope, you sure speak the
goddamn language. I think you're a liar. Then he really tore
it. He looked right at me and said, well you must be right,
because your judgment is so good about everything.

That did it, Jerome. I made a grab for him, but he moved
fast and grabbed me, pushed me against the wall and doubled
his fist. He's a little bigger than me and I didn't realize he was
so strong. I said, go ahead, give me your best shot. Then I realized maybe I couldn't take his best shot, so while he thought
about it, I went for him and we bounced off the walls until
cops ran in and got between us. My glasses fell on the floor
and somebody stepped on them, and Jimmie had yanked off
my breakaway necktie trying to pull me down. The cop who
had me in a bitch of an arm lock was a woman cop, so how
did that make me feel?

I pointed to Jimmie with my free hand and said, don't ever
set foot in my house again until you're ready to tell the goddamn truth. Then I went back to Ocean Beach and tried to
concentrate on running my murder case.

He didn't come home that night and he didn't show up to
get his diploma the next night. Janet and I sat in the front row
and she worried herself sick, but I told her he'd be home
when he got hungry.

But when he didn't come home Janet started looking at
me funny, and I figured she knew I had watered down my
part of what went on in the interview room in National City.
I had told her my glasses fell on the floor but left out some
of the other stuff. She hounded me until I told her what I'd
said to Jimmie about not setting foot in the house. Boy,

Jerome, she really lit into me. Maybe I was a little hasty, but then again, Janet wasn't the one in that interview room. Looking back, I wish she had been.

If you hear from Jimmie, please call right away. I asked the same of Amy and she said she would, unless Jimmie made her promise not to. Always the goddamn lawyer, isn't she?

Billy

• • •

November 30, 1979 – Friday

Dear Jerome:
We still don't know where Jimmie is—more later.

So the dirty bastards at US Steel shut down the Ohio Works. After the company hosts a party at Sokol's for the crew in the burning yard and lied telling them their hard work saved their jobs. After you and officers of 1330 go to Cleveland and the PR guy for US Steel said they had no plans to close the Ohio Works. Then last Tuesday the board of US Steel says—surprise—you're all on the soup line.

Tonight the news showed your bus load that went over to the national headquarters in Pittsburgh and picketed. Janet and I couldn't help comparing your demonstration to the anti-war kids who'd never done anything worth a damn in their lives. But your people fought three wars, got up and went to work every day, have mortgages and kids in school. They get screwed royally but demonstrate peacefully.

Janet looked at me and said it's ironic. Ten thousand steel workers are out of jobs, but it doesn't get wet-eyed attention like Vietnam and the Civil Rights Movement.

Oh, Jerome, my stomach hurt watching you walk the line in Pittsburgh snow while I'm in San Diego sunshine. Janet and I are in excellent standing at our credit union and whenever that chicken shit severance they give you runs out, we're going to help from this end. No argument!

The shutdown goes along with the news from here which is all bum. As Janet told you in her letters, Jimmie has been gone five months and the only clue we have is a couple of postcards addressed to Janet. One got postmarked Washington (state), the other Oregon. He just said he loves his mother and he's healthy—no mention of what he's doing, who he's with, and of course I don't exist.

BUT...twice he's phoned her. First thing he does is tell her if she mentions my name, he'll hang up. Poor Janet is torn. There's two things she wants in this world. Get me and Jimmie reconciled so she can hold her boy in her arms again, and...keep him on the phone so she can hear his voice and tell if he's okay.

One of Jimmie's long-haired buddies came by the house recently and wanted to talk to me, so we sat out back for an hour. He swore he doesn't know where Jimmie is, but he wanted to tell me Jimmie was no doper like the rest of them. He said I don't know why your boy hung out with us, Mr. Considine, he was angry most of the time and none of us could figure it out because he wouldn't talk about it.

This kid is very decent, but he wouldn't promise to tell me if he heard from Jimmie. Since one postcard came from Oregon I called Jack Hackett in case Jimmie had looked him up, but no dice. It was embarrassing telling Jack the chain of events.

The only good news in this whole letter is to tell you Jack is doing fine. Besides working for the state, he started a program tied to the community college in Coos Bay having to do with alcoholism and gambling addiction. What a guy Jack Hackett is!

Jerome, the 1970s started with everybody talking about Vietnam and they're ending with everybody talking about our hostages in Iran. I can really identify with those families, yet my boy isn't even in danger. At least I hope not.

Billy

P.S. Mom urged us to see China Syndrome so we went and Janet was pleased but surprised I would watch Jane Fonda. I told her everybody deserves a second chance. If the department hadn't given me one Lord only knows what I would be doing today.

• • •

May 10, 1980 – Saturday

Dear Jerome:
Wait till you hear the doozy Janet pulled yesterday. She's been getting on me lately as if I'm a lush.

Just last week she said, when is the last time you went twenty-four hours without a drink? I said, what in hell is that supposed to mean? She said, come on, Billy, I'm your wife and I have a right to talk to you in an adult fashion and I expect you to sit down and answer my questions. I told her I'd just come from a day of interrogating hostile witnesses in a double murder and didn't feel like coming home and having my wife treat me like a suspect. She must have realized she was out of line because that ended it.

At least I thought it had. But the next day, Saturday, she wanted me to drive her to the market. We're backing out of the garage and she said, Billy, why do you have to have a can of beer between your legs when we're just driving ten blocks away? I told her it was habit but she came right back and said, when you drive with that beer you're breaking the law. I said I am the law. So that was that.

Anyway, getting back to what she pulled yesterday. At 7:00 a.m. I got to the morgue to watch the autopsy of a two-year-old who'd died in the ER. The ER staff had screamed child abuse and they were right, because not only had someone smashed him in the gut with a blunt object (probably a fist) but the little tyke had a couple of cigarette burns under the armpit. When a liver is only two years old it doesn't take much to make it bleed out.

The suspect is the sailor-sweetheart of the victim's mother, and after I left the morgue I spent four hours being nice to that prick, making him think I'm an understanding guy and wanted to be his friend. He stunk the place up with B.O. and tapped his finger on the table till it drove me nuts. But he finally copped out to playing Ali-Frazier on the boy's tummy.

We take the sailor through the homicide processing at the lab, then my lieutenant decides it's time to chew my ass and write me a reprimand because I didn't make a deadline on a budget update.

It looked like I'd get home on time, but a detective replacing Otto for a few days asked for Monday afternoon off because his daughter is giving a piano recital. Well, I couldn't give it to him, because we have three things going Monday, including doing a search warrant with La Mesa P.D. that may solve an old case for us. The detective takes the news poorly and sasses me, and it's only because he's a helluva cop that I took his crap.

That made me a little late, and going up 5th Ave I spotted a parking place in front of the Sanford Hotel, which is the one with the old-fashioned bar I may have written you about. So I dropped in for one to relax me on the drive home.

It turned out to be more than one, but anyway, I head for home and as soon as I pull onto Dellwood Street, here comes Janet flying out of the kitchen into the garage. I figure she's sore, but she gives me a hug and I go in the kitchen and pour myself a drink.

Janet's acting kind of funny and five minutes later I know why. The doorbell rings and who's standing there but Culpepper and Jack Hackett. The same Jack Hackett who's supposed to be in Oregon.

Have you ever heard of an intervention, Jerome? Well, I hadn't until the three of them sat me down and proceeded to tell me what a stew bum I am. I got sore, then Janet started crying and then I'm hearing stuff like tough love and how worried they all are about me.

They started to psychoanalyze me, giving me a hundred reasons why I drink. Stress at work. My relationship with Jimmie. His being gone. Guilt over leaving Youngstown. The mills closing. They said my choosing not to take the last couple of lieutenants tests showed I didn't want to move forward in my life.

I started yawning but they kept it up and kept it up and when they got to the part about taking vacation time and going into a treatment center, that did it.

I jumped up and said I'd been being leaned on all day and didn't need to come home and have my wife and a one-eyed ex-drunk and a gay air traffic controller lecturing me just because I take a couple of drinks.

Jack Hackett started to say something and I said there's the goddamn door, take it on the way to Oregon. So he and Culpepper left and then as you can imagine, I gave Janet a piece of my mind. I said do you know how embarrassing this is for me, having you cook this thing up with my two best pals? Janet said, don't you think I weighed all of that, Billy? She said, don't you think I'm at my wit's end and have been for a long, long time?

I grabbed the car keys and drove up to the Sands Hotel which is only a mile or so away and had a couple, figuring Janet needed some time to think this thing out. Then I still wasn't ready to go home, so I drove down to the Caliph and ran into a couple of guys from narcotics and one from fencing and we had a few laughs.

Janet was asleep when I got home, but I'm not sure she wasn't pretending.

This morning I got up and before Janet came into the kitchen I put a dash of bourbon in my coffee since that circus the night before had been pretty unnerving. She didn't look at me until noon, then she told me a couple of things I'd said to Jack Hackett and Culpepper that I don't remember saying.

Nothing new from Jimmie except a couple more cards and another phone call. How about asking Amy if she's heard anything.

Billy

• • •

May 21, 1980 – Wednesday

Jerome:
How comforting to know my own brother chimes in with all the others and calls me an asshole. Luckily I have Otto, plus my pals in the squad room who never kick a guy when he's down. At least I can head for work knowing if I hold up my end and be a regular guy, nobody's going to take pot shots at me. Right now I have a few more important things to do than write a goddamn letter.

• • •

May 25, 1980 – Sunday

Dear Jerome
As you may have guessed, I'd had a few drinks when I wrote the last letter and am sorry if I said anything nasty. Truth be known, I can't remember what I wrote.

I made calls to Jack Hackett and Culpepper. Culpepper said I ought to try managing my life for a change, and Jack said I'm the type of guy who has to hit bottom before I admit having a problem. They were short conversations.

I appreciated your suggestion about Janet and I using the beach to talk. We went to the long stretch south of Del Mar and walked for a long time without saying anything. As the sun went down, we plopped in the sand and I told her I knew she had done that intervention thing for my own good. I also told her I'd be cutting down on my drinking. Whether she believed that or not I do not know.

I got a little uptight when she listed affects drinking has on a person's health, then she talked me into letting her schedule physicals for us, because it's been a number of years for me and I've put on a little weight. Janet gets checked regularly, scales out at five pounds less than when we got married, and with all the running looks ten years younger than forty-four. She said I was full of crap when I told her that, but smiled a little, then skimmed a stone over the water.

By the way, Janet wears specs now too, so when I lean over to give her a kiss, clinking glasses takes on a whole new meaning.

You're right, the steel companies threw fifty-thousand lives on the garbage heap when you count families, plus stores that have closed. It must be awful to drive downtown and see guys you worked with standing in line to sell their blood. Janet said it's so sad—men who made a useful product now getting together only to talk about their troubles. We're glad some men found jobs at the G.M. plant in Lordstown seventeen miles away. At least G.M. will always be there.

You said some are leaving their families behind, going to California and Texas looking for computer jobs. But as you pointed out, all they've ever done is operate machinery that became obsolete in 1910.

Still nothing solid from Jimmie. We keep hoping and praying.

Billy

P.S. Do you remember Theo Sinkwich? The guy I went to school with who got hired at the Campbell Works right after we graduated? He called and said he's coming here to look for a job, so we're going to put him up for a week starting tomorrow. Theo used to say the only difference between an Irish wake and an Irish wedding is one less drunk.

• • •

June 3, 1980 – Tuesday

Dear Jerome:

I know it's only thirteen days since I wrote, but I'm upset and want you to know you can't get away with pulling a fast one on your kid brother. Theo Sinkwich snitched you off, though he thought I already knew.

Why didn't you tell me that in February you drove one-hundred miles over to Clyde and stood in line all day in fifteen-degree weather with thousands of other applicants competing for two hundred jobs? Because you're trying to spare me worrying, right?

Amy said you're questioning your self-worth, but anybody who knows Jerome Considine will tell you that's a crock. It's natural for a guy to do that when he's been a hard worker and provider all his life, then finds himself on the street. But family is supposed to be there for each other, and you know Janet and I are. So please knock off the secretive stuff. 10-4.

There's good news about Theo Sinkwich. Remember the auto parts store I worked in when I got suspended thirteen years ago? Well, the guy who hired me is still there, so Theo has a job. He's a workhorse like you, because forty hours a week isn't enough for him. He's also pumping gas on the night shift at a Shell station at 16th and G.

The two incomes give Theo enough to rent a place, and he's sending for his wife and kids. The night he arrived at our house Janet cooked a pot roast, and when we finished eating, Theo's eyes got all watery talking about his family. He got up from the table, looked out on our patio, and said Billy, the guys in suits are raping Youngstown. Then he got choked up and couldn't talk.

The next day he told me about the dead storefronts in Federal Plaza, that he counted twenty homes boarded up on Ford Ave over by the University. He said a lot of them are getting torched, and when he got a job boarding up vacant ones, his crew averaged twenty-five houses a week. Theo said it got too depressing and that's why he lit out for California.

I have to go. Don't shut us out, Jerome.

Your loving brother,

Billy

P.S. I have a feeling in my bones Jimmie will be home in a couple of weeks.

PART FIVE

Heartbreak

• • •

July 1, 1980 – Tuesday

Dear Jerome:
Turned out it was wishful thinking about Jimmie coming home. Janet and I handle this in our own way and hardly speak about it, which keeps her from getting sore at me all over again.

Well, we went for our physicals and the doc chewed me out for having too high a count in what is called an SGOT test. It has something to do with the liver, and he says if I don't quit drinking I'll be in trouble. He says my blood pressure is way too good for someone who lives the way I do.

When he examined Janet he found what he called a mass in her breast that hadn't been there the year before. He made a mammogram appointment for her, but said that 80% of these things are benign. So she kept the appointment, then had to wait for what is called a wet reading. A few days later the doc said it does show a little mass, but couldn't tell if it was solid, maybe it could be a cyst. So he set her up for an ultrasound which she'll have next week, because the 4th of July weekend slowed things down.

I worried at first, but Janet does regular home exams and felt nothing, so this cyst is new, and I remembered you preaching to me that 95% of the things a person stews about don't come to pass. With that and the doc's 80% I like the odds. Typical Janet. Instead of worrying about herself, she's all over me about my liver test.

At work, these computer things are changing the way we do business. Now every report form has a million squares to check off. Where we used to write down "girlfriend" or "boyfriend" (the old timers wrote "shack jobs"), we now check off "significant other." How would you like to be referred to as Significant Other Considine?

The civilians feed all this stuff into the computers and supposedly we'll have them in the detective division someday, then all we'll have to do is punch a button and the suspect will jump out and handcuff himself.

Another thing changing is the type of down-and-outers we're seeing on the streets. Instead of the old winos, we're getting lots of young people, and thanks to the media, they're calling themselves "the homeless". Most of the time when we ask one what they're doing to find work, they kind of stumble and mumble, which tells Otto and I all we need to know. When we run into one who seems legit, we try and steer them onto something.

I have to go, Jerome. Hold the good thought for Janet. I know it'll be okay.

Love to all,

Billy

P.S. I know I'm getting to be an old goat because the young office secretaries are starting to confide in me about their love life.

• • •

July 24, 1980 – Thursday

Dear Jerome:
Things are not that good. Janet had the ultrasound and it won't a cyst like we'd hoped. The doc said we'd better get it out of there, that it was no big deal, they'd do a biopsy and learn more. He gave us the name of a surgeon he works with and said the guy does a lot of breast surgery. Then he told us we could check around for other surgeons but Janet said no, if the doc liked this guy, he'd be fine with her.

We made an appointment for a few weeks down the line, but they had a cancellation and got us in three days after her ultrasound. The first thing the surgeon's office did was set up an appointment for two days after surgery to tell us the test results. The surgeon told us some doctors give good news over the phone and bad news over the desk, but he likes to see people in his office no matter what, because then patients aren't on pins and needles at home waiting for the phone to ring and not being able to sleep when it doesn't.

The day of the surgery I took off work and drove Janet up to Scripps Memorial hospital on Genesee. They admitted Janet to what's called the surgical prep area, then got an IV started and asked a bunch of questions, then wheeled her off to the operating room.

The surgeon came out to the waiting area an hour later and told me it went fine, now we'd have to wait for pathology reports. He's a tall guy with sloping shoulders who'd played basketball at Penn State, and when he found out I worked homicide he had all kinds of questions so we got to know each other. Then he said I may as well go home because Janet would be out awhile, but I didn't feel right leaving, so I stayed and snoozed in the lobby that night and took her home first thing in the morning.

We kept the follow-up appointment and he asked how Janet felt and checked the incision. Then he looked at her and said unfortunately it is malignant, but he thinks they got it early. I said does this mean Janet has cancer, and he said yes, then I said well how serious is it, and the doc said we won't know until more testing gets done.

I couldn't believe what I was hearing, so I said, Janet's not going to die, is she? The doc said whoa, you're getting way too far ahead here, he said we have a lot of wonderful treatment today, chemotherapy and radiation is better than ever, and the next thing we'd do is a surgery to sample the lymph nodes. He explained it would be a biopsy type of surgery, that they would take ten nodes and Janet would have a drain afterwards and they'd show me how I could manage it at home. Janet told me later she thinks he got talking about the drain to get me off the doom and gloom stuff.

But before we left his office I said, do you ever do this type of surgery and the lymph nodes are okay, and the Doc said yep, and that's good news, we love to have that happen.

But it didn't happen this time.

Janet had the surgery a week later and spent two nights in the hospital. In her room the day after, the surgeon came in and told us that four of the nodes had evidence of metastasis, and he said while that's not a good thing--it meant it had spread a little outside the area--more testing would be done and then he'd want to send us to what is called a medical on-cologist for consultation.

And he told us again there's some terrific treatment avail-able now, and the medical oncologist would talk to us about that, and maybe they'd also have us see a radiation oncologist. Janet did a lot better than me and asked him a bunch of ques-tions, but when we finally got home I couldn't remember a one of them. I swear, Jerome, I don't know how she does it.

We're going to keep the positive attitude and will let you know more after we see the medical oncologist next week.

So long for now. Make a novena for Janet.

Billy

P.S. A forgery detective told me he always stops for at least one beer after work. He said if he goes home without police breath his wife will think he's fooling around on her.

• • •

August 10, 1980 – Sunday

Dear Jerome:

Hey, finally some good news. This medical oncologist is a lady doc and we both like her. She's way too pretty to be a doctor, but I kept that opinion to myself. Anyway, she ordered a bone scan for Janet that they did in the nuclear medicine department of the hospital, and we really held our breath, thinking what if this stuff had metastasized more. But the test came out real good and Janet will be starting chemotherapy tomorrow.

The doc said we know you have positive nodes, and especially at your age, we think chemotherapy would be appropriate, so they did a bunch of what they call staging tests, blood work and all, and now Janet goes back in the hospital for five days for this chemo. Then she comes home and three weeks later I guess they may have to do more. The doc said the same thing the surgeon said, that treatment has never been better and they have lots of supportive drugs to help Janet get through this. From what I understand, medical science picked up some good dope from Armstrong walking on the moon and other space flights. We're both feeling better about things.

Nothing about work has seemed important lately, but I got quite a jolt the other day when Otto announced he's retiring. None of us could believe it. He's been a cop forty years, and when he told me, I started to say Otto, I really need you now, what with everything Janet's going through. As usual the squad room was full of people and typewriters clicking away and phones ringing.

Otto knows what I'm thinking before I do. He said, Kid, I wouldn't leave you in a lurch, I went to DeFreese on the sly and he's agreed to give you Tulley Brown from robbery.

Otto said, Billy, you don't need me anymore, you need to occupy your mind teaching someone the homicide ropes, and Tulley Brown will soak it up like a sponge the way you did. Jerome, all of a sudden it seemed okay, because if Otto had to go there's no one I'd rather have replace him than Tulley Brown.

I don't think I told you, but a few months back, Otto got some chest pains and I made him go to the docs, and though Otto wouldn't say much, I know he went on medication.

Otto packed up the stuff from his desk, shook my hand, took one last look around and said, Kid, if my heart is going to explode, I want it to be in the middle of a trout stream, not in the squad room with a bunch of ugly cops drawing straws to see who has to give me mouth-to-mouth. Then he was out the door.

Tulley and I caught a mystery right off and a detective from Team 3 tried to convince Tulley to spend the night in the morgue sitting next to the body. He told Tulley the image of the killer always returns and appears in the dead man's eyes. Tulley said bullshit, but he didn't say it real convincingly.

So now you're up to date from this end. Janet and I are going to slip down to the A&W and treat ourselves to something nutritious, like a Papa Burger, greasy fries and a root beer float.

Love to all my family and friends,

Billy

P.S. Where the hell is that Jimmie?

• • •

September, 29, 1980 – Monday

Dear Jerome:
This will be a short one to let you know things are going well and we're on our way to licking this damn cancer. The price Janet pays is enormous though.

She's had two chemo sessions now, each one lasting a week, and like the doc warned us, she's starting to lose her hair. The other night I saw her scrounging around in Jimmie's room and she came up with a Padres cap. Why women look so cute in hats I do not know.

The thing is, Janet comes home after five days of chemo sessions and gets sick as a dog. Spends all day clutching her stomach and moaning and making trips to the john to throw up. Then, after a week or so, she starts feeling better, and eventually almost human again. She'll grab her ball cap and we'll go do groceries together, or go to the park and take a little walk.

Three weeks after treatment she's actually feeling good, then she says to them, okay, do it to me again, zap me with that poison and make me hurt some more so I can throw up all over the place. She has more courage than anyone I've ever known.

By the way, I hope you're sitting down because your kid brother has quit drinking and smoking. Last week I lay in bed trying to sleep, thinking of things I could do to make Janet happy. Guess what topped the list? The more I thought about it, if Janet has the guts to handle what she's going through, then how big a deal is it for me to quit booze and cigs?

I decided not to go to A.A. because when I'm not working, I want to spend every possible minute with Janet while she's going through this treatment. I just flat quit, and yes, it's been a bitch at times (especially when I can't sleep) but I feel better and Janet is so grateful.

Besides, in this health happy, run-don't-walk town, you light up a smoke and people look at you like your pecker's hanging out.

So long for now. Janet said when her hair grows back and she's through with treatment, we're coming to Youngstown and she's going to run Mill Creek Park.

Love from us both,

Billy

• • •

November 16, 1980 – Sunday

Dear Jerome:

Yesterday I caught the Buckeyes on TV and they don't look like a Rose Bowl team which brings us to rooting for A.B.M.— anybody but Michigan.

We're in the second week after chemo #4 and the aftermath doesn't get any better for poor Janet, but the next time I hear her complain will be the first. Apparently the doc tries different formulas for the dosages, but Janet says they're all the same to her. She lives for the postcards from Jimmie and lights up like a Christmas tree when one arrives.

The postcards are more frequent than the calls, and Janet decided to say nothing to Jimmie about the cancer. We got in an argument over it, but she said why worry him when it's going to be cleared up anyway, and also she's skittish about Jimmie thinking she's trying to lure him home. She did get out of him that he's making good dough. Tulley Brown said he hopes it's not from growing pot or sticking up banks.

Speaking of Jimmie, several months ago, Jack Hackett saw a hitchhiker who looked like Jimmie get into a car, and knowing his cards are postmarked Washington and Oregon, Jack followed them. He stayed behind for forty miles until they stopped for gas in a burg called Myrtle Point and checked the guy out. Is Jack Hackett a pal or what?

Amy calls once a week and I can't even remember the last time she and I got into it. She and Janet have long talks and Janet says they've become soul mates.

Otto calls regularly to check on Janet. He says there is life after the police department and suggests I try it as soon as I have my time in.

A detective from auto theft came by the office, he'd heard about Janet, and said his wife had the same thing, went through all the chemo four years ago and has been fine ever since. So we just have to tough it out like they did.

Everybody at work is very supportive. The other teams have volunteered to take my call-outs when Janet's in a chemo week, and they take Tulley Brown with them so that his homicide education doesn't suffer. They tell him the only thing Considine can teach him is how to drink.

DeFreese is doing something the other chiefs never did. Busy as he is, once a day he walks around the station and plops himself on the corner of somebody's desk and shoots the shit for a few minutes. He's always asking about Janet.

As for Tulley Brown, the Missouri farm boy is learning fast, except he's still not used to keeping his hands in his pockets at crime scenes. I told him the first time his prints show up on a lab report, his ass is grass. He's spending more time at Bernie's than he did when he worked Robbery, so I see a lot of me in him. I told him a person's brain starts working the instant he's born and stops when he takes the first drink of the day. He didn't come right out and call me a reformed whore, but he had the look.

Tulley pulled one last week. A guy on Team 2 came in with a box of baby Cocker Spaniels because his wife wouldn't let him keep the whole litter. He'd been trying to give them away with no luck and complained to Tulley. Tulley said, give me the box, they'll be gone before lunch.

Tulley gets into the evidence drawer and pulls out numbered tags, then puts one around each of their furry little necks. He goes all over the building telling secretaries, want to get in on the pool? A buck a chance. Of course, they say what pool, and why are those little puppies wearing numbers?

Tulley told them these are the ones we couldn't give away, so after work we're going across the street and throw the whole batch into the harbor, and the numbers are to ID the last one to stay afloat—winner take all.

Jerome, in less than an hour, they all had new homes.

I have to go check on Janet, she's down for a snooze. She's been having a little shortness of breath which I think is from the chemo and the stress, but the doc has ordered another lung scan.

Thanks for all the calls and letters, much Love,

Billy

P.S. Jack Hackett is tickled I've quit drinking but wants me to call him day or night when I get the urge.

P.P.S. I'm on a good habits roll so Janet made me promise to go back to San Diego State and get the three units I need for a bachelor's degree.

P.P.P.S. Seems like yesterday we kidded about an actor being governor in crazy California--now he's president.

P.P.P.P.S. You can tell things are better because I'm writing P.S.'s again.

• • •

December 8, 1980 – Monday

Dear Jerome:
The scan showed some spots on the lungs. When the doc gave us the news, she put her hand on Janet's arm and said, it looks like this chemo just didn't hold it, then real quickly she said there are alternative chemotherapies we can swing into.
Janet nodded with that sweet look on her face and told the doc okay, but she wants a week off right now. Of course we'll go for the new chemo, but it was a shock and we both need time off.
Strange, I heard on the news today about John Lennon being shot, and even though I never had time to be a Beatles' fan, I cried like a baby.

Billy

• • •

December 15, 1980 – Monday

Dear Jerome:
We went back to see the doc today. Janet and I had stayed up all night talking about what Janet would say.
The doc began explaining about an alternative chemo and

Janet let her get a little way into it, then Janet said, Doctor, I've spent two days in the library reading, and I've got this thing figured out—this isn't going to have a good outcome, is it? Before the doc could answer, Janet said, I'm not going to beat this, am I?

Janet and I had agreed we would look real hard at the doc's face when Janet said that, wondering if the doc would say whoa, we're nowhere near that point. But the doc didn't say anything and I think I saw a look of relief, like she wouldn't have to be the one to hit Janet with a sledgehammer.

Janet said, I am terminal, aren't I? The doc said the involvement on the lungs is quite significant and based on my medical experience, the answer is yes, but we still have treatment to offer. Then she started telling us about more stuff until Janet interrupted her.

Janet said, I don't want to try anything else. I want quality time. I want my hair to grow back. I want to be alert when my son returns home. I want energy. I want to feel good and pull the threads of my life together. Christmas is ten days away and I want to enjoy it.

Jerome, the doc's eyes got watery and she told Janet she respected her decision, but wanted her to remember there are other things we can try.

Then Janet just out and said it, how long do I have? The doc said nobody can answer that and I don't want to try, but if you stop all treatment, I would say you are talking months and not years.

When we got ready to leave, the doc handed Janet a pamphlet and said there's an organization called Hospice which hasn't been around our country too long, but they're having good results with it. She said Hospice has wonderful ways of keeping patients comfortable, and she suggested we take the pamphlet with us and look it over when we feel like it. The doc wanted us to know this Hospice is there for us, and that her office could set up a meeting any time.

We didn't say anything on the way home but I kept thinking about something Janet had told me about her library research. Because the cancer had spread to her lungs, the medical term is she had failed chemotherapy. I think chemotherapy failed Janet.

Everything is kind of unreal right now.

Billy

• • •

December 18, 1980 – Thursday

Dear Jerome:

Please, please tell Amy if she hears from Jimmie, have him call home right away.

We figured he'd call for Christmas, and he did this morning. But the connection was bad, and just as Janet was starting to tell him about her cancer, the static got so loud neither could hear. Then she got cut off completely.

Ten minutes later, he called again, but same thing.

I ran out and bought an answering machine, then we set it up for Janet's voice to say, "Jimmie, there is an emergency— please come home. Please come home NOW!"

Jesus, a week from today is Christmas.

Billy

• • •

January 16, 1981 – Friday

Dear Jerome:

It's been one helluva thirty days. I don't know whether we've laughed more or cried more. And your surprise visit! I had asked Janet just the day before what she wanted for Christmas. Another Christmas, she said, as she put her arms around me.

When you and Mom and Amy knocked on our door carrying packages and wearing Santa Claus hats, we started forgetting our troubles.

On New Years Eve, I told Janet I would arrange a transfer out of homicide. She squeezed my hand and said, oh, Billy, let's not suddenly do change just for the sake of change. She said, I want you to stay in homicide because our lives will be normal. She's so brave, Jerome. She said, what I need from you is love and comfort and you're so good at that when you want to be.

One day we talked about that guy who'd driven his mother the eleven-hundred miles from Oklahoma so she could see the ocean. Janet said, I've seen my oceans, Billy, I don't need to go to Athens or Fiji or the Riviera, because I've seen the world through my wonderful books.

My mind races all the time. All Janet ever wanted from a husband was a guy who would love her and treat her with respect and come home after work. I broke her heart too many times to count. Will I ever forgive myself?

Janet is feeling pretty darn good which makes it harder to believe what lies ahead. At least we've gotten to the point where we can go an hour and not think about it.

Today a stranger came to our house, and we sat and sipped coffee and talked about Janet's dying. As casually as if we were picking out colors for the living room. Later I fell apart.

When I say casually, I don't mean it wasn't dignified. Our visitor was a nurse from this Hospice place, and she couldn't have been more professional. Janet had called the doc's receptionist who we've gotten to know pretty well, and said we'd like to know more about Hospice.

I should tell you the doc herself called Janet a few days after our visit of Dec 15th and wanted to know how we were, is Janet sure she didn't want to start additional chemo?

Anyway, this Hospice nurse turned out to be what is called the team leader. One of these women with a hyphenated last name we're starting to see. Her name is Ruth, and she caught me by surprise when she said, Hospice uses a team concept like you do in homicide, Sergeant. I asked her how she knew

I ran a team and she said she'd seen me on TV and in the newspapers. She explained how their core team consists of a nurse, social worker, home health aide, and sometimes others, like a volunteer or chaplain can be tacked on. The care is intermittent, not hourly, though the nurse and social worker are available on a twenty-four hour call basis.

Janet said to Ruth, the doctor says I'm looking at months instead of years and Billy and I are working up to accepting that, will you be my nurse all the way? Ruth said yes, and the same core team would be in place the whole time, then she explained that Hospice doesn't hurry up or slow down death, but their strength is what Ruth called symptom management and providing palliative care which she said makes the pain more bearable.

We both felt a little better after Ruth left. Didn't feel quite so alone, maybe.

Janet and I don't dwell on Jimmie or we'd be on the mat. She did get a postcard apologizing for the poor phone connection on the call just before Christmas. Postmarked Oregon like some of the others. Jack Hackett said the telephone troubles could mean Jimmie's on a fishing boat or in a logging camp or on a firefighting crew, all of which are only educated guesses.

You said the family in Youngstown wanted to be kept posted so now you have it. We can feel your prayers across the miles.

Billy

• • •

February 21, 1981--Saturday

Dear Jerome:

We're getting a good rain today and I was afraid it may sink Janet's spirits, but on the contrary, she dug out our raincoats and hustled me out for a walk. I swear, it's so strange, going out doing chores, shopping, picking up cleaning--seeing people going on with life not even knowing Janet's sick.

On our walk, we saw a guy on a motorcycle waiting out the heavy rain under a gas station roof. Janet reminded me that years ago I'd been drooling over a BMW, but we'd decided to stick more $$ into the college fund instead. A car splashed us good crossing the street and we laughed about that, then Janet started crying, saying she'd been selfish not letting me buy that motorcycle in 1970. She kept crying and nothing I said did any good.

Ruth telephones frequently and comes by a couple of times a week. I told her she's a real comfort, and she said Billy, when I knock on a door, I know the people inside need more from me than what's in my nurse's bag.

The social worker is a young Dartmouth graduate who wears granny glasses and she's been here twice. Now we'll see her on an as-needed basis.

The home health aide's name is Cora and she couldn't be nicer. They got her started a little earlier than normal, she's in and out about twice a week, does some personal stuff and chats with Janet. With Hospice we don't feel hopeless any more. We know Janet's not going to get better, but it made me quit denying and is giving us the strength to bear up under what's ahead. So far at least.

Ruth gives Janet lots of options, then supports whatever she decides. It's very apparent these Hospice team members have camaraderie like cops.

Janet figured if she called off treatment she'd begin feeling better and she was right. She talks to her folks every day and we're going up to Whittier for an overnighter next weekend. Sometimes though, when Janet doesn't think I can hear, she goes into our bedroom and cries. I start to rush in there, then put on the brakes because Ruth convinced me Janet needs time alone. The two of them talked about a volunteer joining the team and Janet said she'd like to give it a try.

That's it from here.

Love,

Billy

P.S. Nothing else seems important. At work Tulley Brown and I sit down with people who kill other people for stupid reasons, and I see it as a waste of life more than I ever did before.

• • •

March 27, 1981 – Friday

Dear Jerome:
Working homicide over the years, I haven't taken much vacation, so I took this whole month. It has been some wonderful time, I'll tell you. We've taken bus rides like we used to when Jimmie was a squirt, and we've been to Balboa Park three times, and heard a day concert in the Organ Pavilion. Twice we sat on the sand at Crown Point Shores, and Janet reminded me we were at the shores when I said Just the Way You Look Tonight should be our song. She wanted to know if I remembered that, and I told her I did remember, that one day I got in line for cotton candy at the Del Mar Fair and all heaven broke loose.

We went from the shores to that Carnation ice cream store at Ohio and El Cajon where you made those banana splits disappear, Jerome. We looked out the window and talked and talked and talked.

I will never forget March of 1981.

Another postcard from Jimmie arrived. It said he'd be home "soon," whatever that means. A homicide cop in Seattle is running Jimmie's name for me through records and driver's license bureaus in the Northwest. It's not a legal use of police resources, but time is against us now.

Another wonderful person came into our life. Her name is Celia Waters, a black lady about fifty-years-old who is the Hospice volunteer. Celia is the kind of person who makes you feel better as soon as she walks into the room. She and

Janet talk for hours and Celia is a great listener. She has a voice like an angel, and sometimes Janet will request a song and Celia makes the whole house soft and mellow. They play a lot of cribbage and talk about books they love.

I was holding Janet one night and she said, Billy, there is one good thing about dying. It forces you to rewind the film and recount the wonderful things that have happened in your lifetime. Then she told me all the reasons she was so lucky.

Everything isn't rosy though. Once she laid there looking really tired, and I asked how she felt. She said, like a condemned man listening to them build the gallows. Then she started talking about grandchildren she'll never see.

For twenty years, eight months and twenty-five days Janet has made me a better man. Now part of me is dying because I'm losing her and another part because of all the times I let her down.

I don't know what in hell's going on with me physically. I average about a headache a year, but lately I've been getting them regularly plus muscle pain I've never experienced. I feel guilty when I complain. And truth be known, Janet is slowing down. Her breathing is a little labored, and she's feeling some discomfort in her chest. Ruth has stepped up her visits, but Janet has been resisting medication.

God help Jimmie to hurry home.

Billy

• • •

April 11, 1981 – Saturday

Dear Jerome:
Thanks again for the flowers. They're still blooming.

Well, Janet's no longer mobile, but Ruth arranged for a wheelchair so she scoots around in it, though we don't go outside much. She sleeps more now, her breathing is somewhat limited and her energy level has fallen off dramatically.

Ruth told me the pain-management goal is to allow alertness, but also allow sleep. Cora is here more frequently and bathes Janet. How we'd get along without her I do not know.

Janet and I still have good talks and she hasn't lost her sense of humor. Her pals drop in for short visits, mostly cop wives, but also a couple of women from the library. Everybody loves her.

I think I'll sign this one off now,

Billy

• • •

April 26, 1981 – Sunday

Dear Jerome:
This is the letter I've been dreading. I don't know why I'm writing it, because I talked to you last night at midnight your time. But the hell of it is I can't remember anything I said.

Janet died at 7:30 last night. She'd been in a coma for two days, but was obviously restless and uncomfortable so I called Hospice and Ruth came right away. She showed me how to put small doses of liquid morphine into Janet's mouth with a small syringe, and after that she rested very comfortably right up to the end. I played her favorite music and sat with her and sang songs to her, some silly ones plus the one Mom used to sing. With someone like you, a pal so good and true…I'd like to leave it all behind and start anew…

Janet spent the last week in bed, and I'd moved the bed into the living room where she could see the flowers in the yard. All last week she seemed to be withdrawing and getting a little confused. She also took less food and fluids. Ruth said maybe Janet needed me to tell her it was okay to die.

Boy, Jerome. That's the hardest thing I've ever done. I lay next to her and it was hard for her to talk. I got my face right up next to hers and could smell her hair. She whispered things to me, but it took a while because she could only get out a few words at a time.

She said, here are your marching orders, Sergeant Considine. Make up with our son. Find someone else to love. When we get grandchildren, tell them their grandmother loves them.

Then she slipped into the coma.

Ruth and Celia Waters were there at the end, and Jack Hackett had come down from Oregon in his RV and parked in our driveway. When Ruth called the mortuary, Jack put me in his Winnebago so I wouldn't be able to see them take Janet away. Jack and I sat drinking Dr. Pepper and I confessed something to him. After we learned Janet was terminal, I had told myself if our positions were reversed, I'd shoot myself. In the Winnebago, I told Jack how wrong that would have been, how I would have cheated Janet and myself out of tender moments and memories.

Janet had written notes to certain people and I'm going to hand them out next week. She told me she needed to do it so people would know how much they meant to her. Jerome, she even had one for the lady at the dry cleaners, who in the old days used to let us wait until payday to settle up when we were short.

What a privilege it was to even know Janet Williams Considine.

Billy

PART SIX

New Beginnings

• • •

May 11, 1981 – Monday

Dear Jerome:
Have only sixteen days passed? Everywhere I look I see
Janet. People suggest having her clothes removed from the
house, but damn it, Jerome, those are Janet's things!

I made the mistake of taking a walk last night. So what happened? Soaked up big-time memories of walks I took with Janet
and with Jimmie. Hospice keeps checking on me and giving info
on survivor support groups, but I'm not ready for that. Celia Waters
told me she continues being a volunteer because—in Celia's
words—the work keeps showing her the wonders of the human
heart and the human spirit. I can't say enough about Celia Waters.

Janet's parents told me they were grateful for the way I
cared for their daughter during the darkest times. Her father
said, I guess it's no secret that you wouldn't have been our
first choice, but Janet loved you and now we know why.

And by the way, Jerome, no more of your guilty talk because
you didn't come for the services. All three of you came in December when we needed you most. After you left Janet picked
out mementos for all of you and I'll stick them in the mail.

I'm trying to get back into homicide-cop mode but it's not
easy. DeFreese told me my life will never be the same, but it
will be good again. I told him I'm glad Janet went first, because I wouldn't want her going through this kind of pain.

Billy

• • •

May 15, 1981 – Friday

Dear Jerome:
I know, I just mailed you a letter two days ago. We worked
all last night and all of today on a body under the Adams Ave

bridge. A kid had overdosed and been dumped by his so-called friends. The kid's father is a somebody in town, so we needed to get all the questions answered early. My heart wasn't in it and Tulley Brown said I stood around like I'd never been to a crime scene.

I was going to hold off telling you this next thing for a while, but I can't keep it in. We wrap up the bridge caper and just before dark, I'm driving up our street and who's on the sidewalk in front of our house talking to a neighbor? Yep, Jimmie! I won't even try to describe the feeling in my gut.

Just as I pulled into the driveway the neighbor told him Janet was dead. He went berserk. Once or twice I got him calmed down, but only because he needed me to give him details. I can't believe he'd been gone for twenty-three months, then shows up twenty days after his mother dies.

I stayed calm for an hour, Jerome, then it blew up. He screamed that if I hadn't thrown him out of the house he'd have been here for his mother, and I tried to convince him the best thing we could do for Janet is make up.

I got him quieted down so at least the neighbors couldn't hear. He asked more questions about the cancer, but it was like talking to a stranger. As he opened the door to leave, I told him thanks to his mother's planning, we had college money for him, but he said he didn't want any money I was a part of.

Then I lost it, and yelled that his mother kept hanging on and hanging on, hoping she'd see him one last time, and why in hell couldn't he have made a better effort to get through on the phone. He stormed out, got to the sidewalk and yelled at me some more. Then he walked away.

I hardly knew him. His hair is short and he's filled out and has to stand at least 6-4.

An hour later he knocked on the door and I didn't know what to expect. He didn't want to come in, just stood next to the Philodendron and spoke softly. He told me he didn't hate me, just didn't want anything to do with me. That when he got a place to stay he'd mail me his address and that's how we could keep each other advised of address changes.

He told me some other stuff, but he wasn't inviting a two-way conversation. He'd been working on the Alaska pipeline between Prudhoe Bay and Pt. Valdez, on a crew repairing damage to the forty-eight-inch lines caused by backhoes and hairline cracks and what have you. To keep me off his trail, guys going on vacation mailed Jimmie's postcards from Washington and Oregon.

As I said, he spoke softly, kind of looking through me. I asked if we couldn't talk things over, but he cut me off and said, no, we look at life far too differently for that. I could see his eyes getting all watery before he walked away.

Don't ask me what I'm going to do now.

Billy

• • •

October 28, 1981 – Wednesday

Dear Jerome:

Sorry for this crybaby letter, but things just don't get better. Janet's been gone six months and you'd think some of the pain would be diminishing. Instead, I find myself getting angry at the world and God help me, a couple of times I got angry at Janet for dying. My Hospice friends still call, but I clam up which I don't understand because I used to babble on and on to Ruth and Celia Waters. Enough already about me.

I feel terrible about what you are going through. An analyst on the news said the bottom line is, steel companies want their spending to go to businesses like oil and chemicals and hotels, that provide a higher rate of return. Those bastards don't care that Jerome Considine is working at a hardware store at a third of what he used to knock down.

At least those ninety-nine senators swallowed smart pills and confirmed a woman for the Supreme Court. DeFreese appointed the first woman lieutenant here, and she's a good one, unless you ask a few of the deadbeat sergeants who competed with her and are crying foul.

Jerome, I mentioned a friend of Jimmie's that talked to me once after Jimmie ran away. Well, I've made it a point to see this kid a couple of times, he's really very decent and I guess the dope didn't pickle his brain. Here's the scoop as this kid laid it out.

Jimmie started college at Cal-Berkeley this fall. It's a high-end place, but California residents get a break. How is he affording it? It seems when he worked the pipeline he was in the middle of nowhere with no place to spend the good salary. A boy he worked with has a father who handles investments, and he steered Jimmie and his son into a Minnesota company who makes pacemakers. Jimmie and his pal made $$ and still are.

Jimmie thought about UCLA, but wanted to get farther away from me. Nice, huh? Using this kid as an intermediary, I tried one more time to make up with Jimmie, but no soap. Janet charged me with making things right and I can't even do that for her.

Jerome, I remember all the sweet father-son times Jimmie and I had together. I guess all he remembers is me being gone a lot and the drinking and my yelling at him. What more can be done at this point I do not know.

I'm going to get through this because I promised Janet I would.

Billy

P.S. Amazing, isn't it? This hard-core bunch of fanatics who won't let the 1960s die. Did you see where the Weather Underground pulled an armored truck heist and killed three in Nanuet, New York.

• • •

July 23, 1982 – Friday

Dear Jerome:

Well, DeFreese announced his retirement yesterday, so we've lost a great cop and a great chief. He's taking a big job in Nevada having to do with state regulation of casinos.

So they're all gone now. Jack Hackett and Culpepper and Frank Runyon and Otto...and now DeFreese. Last night I got so melancholy I wanted a drink, but phoned Jack Hackett instead--told him how DeFreese had taken me aside a few months ago and jacked me up. DeFreese said, you've taken a couple of pretty good hits, Considine, but now you need either a kick in the ass, or a transfer out of homicide, because you're not getting the job done. He told me to look in the mirror at my shave, haircut, and frayed shirt collar. Then he put his arm around me and said, get yourself straight, then go be a good influence on Tulley Brown.

We'll never see the likes of DeFreese again.

Since I turned fifty this year, I qualify for retirement agewise, but I'm still a year shy of service time. Dead bodies get to me more often, and when I saw a PBS documentary about some retired plumber teaching kids to play baseball, I wanted to trade places. Let the plumber attend autopsies and I'll explain the infield fly rule.

Work is pretty routine but Tulley Brown keeps things lively. He's coming along and is a top-drawer interrogator. Some carpenter murdered his girlfriend's mother, then torched the house to destroy evidence. We were hurting going into the sit-down but three hours later the guy had written out a confession after Tulley told him what it was like growing up in Missouri.

Here's some more stuff about Jimmie. He wants to be a doctor. According to my source, Jimmie had an epiphany of sorts in Alaska. Jimmie told this kid that one night after work, he stood outside in the cold, looking at his hands all grimy and bruised, and said to himself, God gave me a wonderful brain and God gave me these hands and it's up to me to do something worthy.

Jimmie latched on to some books someone shipped to another kid and read the discourses of Socrates and Plato where they spoke of the benefits of a life of service. This friend I see told me Jimmie's more motivated than anyone he's ever seen.

Jerome, he wants to be a doctor. The kid's going to be better than his old man.

Maybe things aren't so bad after all.

Love,

Billy

P.S. I wasn't going to tell you this, but hell, you know everything else. When I called Jack Hackett, I was crying. About failing with Janet and failing with Jimmie, and told Jack I'd decided the best thing I could do now is respect Jimmie's wish and leave him alone. Jack told me the worst thing I can do is fall into self-pity. Jack said Billy, you've fucked up twice, so don't do anything to make things worse with Jimmie.

• • •

May 29, 1983 – Sunday

Dear Jerome:

Another Memorial Day weekend and Tulley Brown and I are first up. He's a work horse and never complains about call-outs. Tulley is spending less time at Bernie's and more time at home the past year. His wife is from Germany, and I regularly get invited over for schnitzel. She'll only buy her veal from The Sausage King in Mission Hills and if guests go hungry at Tulley Brown's house, it's their own fault.

My letters are slowing down because there isn't that much to talk about. But, one piece of news. Your kid brother has a Bachelor of Science degree in Criminal Justice Administration. That's right, and I put on a cap and gown, but only because Janet slipped it in there with the other promises. Truth be told, I almost backed out. The graduation ceremony is held on campus at the Aztec Bowl, and I felt pretty silly until I saw some grandmother with a walker in line next to me. Tulley Brown said Janet was there too.

Along with my final three units, I had to write a paper, so selected domestic violence for my topic. A few years ago, the department set up a DV unit in Juvenile where they already had a child abuse team in place. The abuse team handles abuse plus neglect and sexual exploitation of kids, and works with social services, educators, doctors etc. The DV team follows their pattern. We're not going to have horror stories like the rest of the country where cops get complaint after complaint, but don't react until some dirty son of a bitch puts his wife in the morgue.

In my rookie year I responded to a radio call where a woman had written the police phone number on the wall in crayon right over the telephone. Her lifeline. So the kids could phone when she was getting beat up. Our DV unit is a far cry from when we handed a woman a band-aid and walked out on her.

I reached the twenty-five-year mark this month, but think I'll hang around awhile. Funny, a cop loves the department and thinks what he's doing is so important. But when he leaves, it's Billy who? A long time ago, Janet had me read From Here to Eternity where a soldier named Prewitt loves the Army and tells someone that it's okay for a man to love something and not have it love him back.

I've been thinking a lot lately about what Prewitt said—as it applies to me and the department. To me and Jimmie. I just have to come to terms with it.

Love to Mom and to Amy if you can catch her,

Billy

• • •

August 4, 1984 – Saturday

Dear Jerome:

Where did the year go? We're busy as hell, and when I'm home, I'm either reading or watching M.A.S.H. reruns. And finally, finally--I'm sleeping well.

My weight is down and I've even been swimming in the surf like old times. Very scary the first time out and I got knocked around pretty good when I tried riding a few waves. Jimmie and I did a lot of body surfing in the old days. Then we'd bundle up in sweatshirts, roast wieners on a stick, then sit on a blanket and talk and watch the sunset.

DeFreese offered me a job with the Nevada Gaming Control Board. A helluva good job for a single person because they go all over the world doing backgrounds on gambling license applicants. All on the applicant's dime. It was tempting but I'm not ready to leave the department and I want to be closer to Jimmie just in case.

I'm looking forward to my trip to Youngstown. We'll have a catch in the middle of Hampton Court for old time's sake.

Billy

P.S. There is one more thing. I went out on a date. A woman who works in the library at San Diego State. No wisecracks about my having a librarian fetish. She's widowed and very nice, but nothing seemed right, and we looked at each other over dinner and started laughing about it. We said goodnight in the restaurant and that was that.

Billy

• • •

October 16, 1985 – Wednesday

Dear Jerome:

Jimmie doesn't know it, but I drove up to Berkeley to see him graduate. It was clear and crisp the day I crossed the bridge, so I got a good look at Alcatraz and Treasure Island where I'd spent a little Navy time. (At the latter, not the former. Ha-Ha!) The graduation class was so big they didn't hand out diplomas, and I never did spot Jimmie. Janet was in my thoughts all day.

From my source, I've learned Jimmie has been accepted to medical school at the University of California at San Francisco. No undergrads there--all medical--and he wants to be a surgeon. Only about one applicant out of twelve even gets an interview, and they put Jimmie through three in one day. They're looking for academic ability. Can they stand up under the grind? And the personal side. How motivated is he? Jimmie's Alaska time must have served him well, because one of the interviewers said to him, you're a young man with a tale to tell.

Jimmie is twenty-four and I suspect San Diego will never see him again. In case you're wondering, this friend of his that talks to me doesn't consider himself a snitch. He's reconstructed a good relationship with his father and feels bad about our mess.

Here's one for you. The wide-world of coincidence that any cop who wants to be a homicide detective had better get used to. A lady and her husband visiting from New Jersey. She's manic-depressive and for a month has refused to take her meds. He goes down to the hotel bar for a few belts while she's taking a snooze. So far so good.

She decides to jump from their 6th floor room. He's walking out of the bar onto the sidewalk at the same time. She lands on him! He's in the morgue--she's going to survive. Interviewing witnesses and doing the reenactment, there's no way she knew he was walking out of that lobby door. So sad all around.

Don't think I've already told you this, there is a very sweet lady who calls me about every six months. Her son was a murder victim five years ago and we haven't solved it. He was gay and took the wrong guy home with him. Otto and I worked it hard, and when we get a new lead, Tulley and I re-interview people and keep digging.

Anyway, when I pick up the phone this woman always says the same thing. I'm so sorry to bother you Sergeant Considine, but I wonder if anything has come up on Dwight's case? Jerome, you don't know how bad it makes me feel, and how much I'd like to say, Mrs. Blake, we just locked up the man who murdered your son.

With that, I'm out of here. Tell Mom she's way too glamorous to be turning eighty.

Billy

• • •

January 9, 1987 – Friday

Dear Jerome:

It's been a long time since I've written since we're talking more on the phone these days, but sometimes I need to write my brother.

Last month we made the move I've been dreading--from Market Street to the new headquarters building at 14th and Broadway. A seven-story concrete, steel and glass monstrosity that looks like a hotel. Now there's no interaction between cops in different units because people come and go by way of elevators and each floor has its own closed society. It's the pits.

Jimmie is living in the Haight-Ashbury District which is just down the hill from the medical school. Thank the Lord Haight-Ashbury is a shell of its former self. I hope he's being smart because I see this AIDS thing has caused over 11,000 deaths. How it sprung up all of a sudden I do not know. Now that it's spread to the straight community, there are plenty of people in San Diego blaming the gays for delivering it in the first place. I notice Reagan is blind to the epidemic.

Six months ago Tulley Brown and I drew a case in east San

Diego where a suspect pulled a young woman off the sidewalk, raped her and cut her throat. As she was dying he marked up her privates with his knife. All too ugly to describe.

We faced a homicide detective's dilemma. On one hand we hoped we'd never hear from the guy again, but the more he works, the better chance we have of nailing him. Five days ago he hit again. In Ocean Beach, nine miles to the west of job #1. A high school student a block from home. Both cases occurred after dark but before 11 p.m. Both victims on foot in a residential area. He pulls them into bushes, probably shows them the knife and tells them if they don't scream, he won't hurt them, then does his dirty work. We have nothing, Jerome, absolutely nothing. If I'd have done my job and caught the guy last July, that sweet girl in Ocean Beach would be doing homework tonight.

I put in a hurry-up call to Jack Hackett and he told me all the right things. When I hung up I didn't need a drink.

I guess I told you I don't take the lieutenant's examination anymore. Why I would need more $$ I do not know. I had been helping Tulley Brown get ready for the sergeant's test but this series killer has put studying on hold.

Guess that's about it from this end.

Billy

P.S. I said we had nothing on our two murders. We have semen, but it won't do us any good because analysis shows the suspect is not a secretor. Therefore we can't determine his blood group from the semen. Knowing a blood type helps us eliminate a lot of suspects.

• • •

March 17, 1988 – Thursday

Dear Jerome:
I get weary of death. Last month Tulley and I worked one

where a cop from Forgery sat at the bar in Bernie's, polished off his last vodka, looked at the detective sitting next to him and said, well, I think I'll go home and blow my brains out. That's exactly what he did.

About our series. He hit again, three months after the high school girl, which makes it eleven months ago. In a different part of town than the first two cases.

This time it was a hair stylist walking home from work. All three of our victims were between seventeen and twenty-eight, all had very good figures. But that's the only common denominator. As far as we can tell, none of them knew each other and no similarities in where they'd been before he grabbed them.

We've knocked on hundreds of doors in all three neighborhoods trying to find someone who saw something. Checked out all of our sex offender parolees. Looked over every traffic ticket and field interrogation made in the crime scene areas.

One of the assistant chiefs who has trouble finding his way to work suggested we put out a composite photo of an artist's sketch. I told him we'll do that, as soon as one of the dead girls comes back to life so we can interview her and find out what the son of a bitch looks like.

Stakeouts are out of the question because of the time between cases and the distances involved. Tulley and I are trying to pluck a suspect out of a county of three million people with the square mileage of Connecticut.

Jerome. Dealing with the survivors. Parents, husbands, brothers, sisters. They're heart broken and look to Tulley and I to make things better. Closure's the word we keep hearing. We need closure on this, Sgt Considine, we need to know who this beast is and why and...on and on and on.

Janet used to put these things into some kind of order for me, make me believe we're decent, competent detectives doing all we can to solve cases. It's tough being on my own.

Billy

. . .

October 24, 1989 – Tuesday

Dear Jerome:
Doctor Considine has returned to San Diego.

He graduated from med school, and here's my info which is sketchy. Apparently the head of the Dept of Neurosurgery at UC San Francisco saw something in Jimmie he liked and steered him to the Univ of Calif-San Diego Medical Center. He told Jimmie he hated to lose him, but the neurosciences group in San Diego is so strong it will give Jimmie a better chance to get published, thus a better chance to make the faculty, which I understand is Jimmie's goal.

If I got it right, he's looking at nine years of training. The first seven of surgical internship and residency. Then kind of a triangle thing kicks in that involves teaching, research and patient care. Then the final two years would be a fellowship consisting mostly of research. IF he has the smarts and the motivation and the character to get through all of it. Now you know all I know. I'm betting on Jimmie.

I don't care to talk about the cases, but our suspect has hit two more times. Cases number four and five. Still no pattern. The last one occurred eleven months ago. We still have zero. What this guy does between crimes I do not know. I'm thinking of asking out of homicide. It doesn't look like I'm up to the job anymore. That's all from here.

Billy

. . .

February 4, 1990 – Sunday

Dear Jerome:
It's eleven a.m. and I just got home. Missed two nights sleep

but I'm too tired to go to bed, if that makes sense. Today is what? Sunday? On Friday night, two hours before midnight, after a fifteen month layoff, our murder-rapist hit again. Case number six. This time a twenty-year-old community college student walking from the bus stop to her apartment in east San Diego. Yep, he came back to the east end of town as in case #1.

But this woman got lucky--if you can attach the word luck to such a horrible thing as rape. Exact same M.O. He grabbed her off the sidewalk, pulled her next to some bushes, held a knife to her neck and raped her. But when he went to cut her throat, she screamed, and we caught a break. Finally.

The guy whose house they were in front of came out with his dog for the evening walk and almost stepped on them. The suspect took another swipe at her throat with the knife, but because he was in a hurry to get out of there, the wound wasn't fatal. He ran, but the witness is gutsy, so he and the mutt gave chase. He'd already yelled for his wife to call 9-1-1. I don't think he really wanted to catch the guy, but he got a partial description of a car the suspect got into. Finally we have something to work with.

Anyway, the girl is taken to the hospital and I go there to interview her. A kind, innocent kid with a bandage around her throat and a welt on her cheek where the guy slugged her to get her under control. The poor thing kept apologizing to me for crying.

When I finished talking to her, I needed coffee and went to the cafeteria. I got my cup filled and had just sat down when I saw Jimmie sitting with a bunch of other doctors across the room. I slipped out of there before he saw me, because I didn't want to upset him. He looks good, Jerome. It looked like they were talking serious stuff, but he broke into that great smile of his a couple of times.

When I got to the parking lot, I sat in my car for a few minutes thinking about that kid on the third floor with the bandaged throat. Then I started crying.

When I came to homicide sixteen years ago I wouldn't have done that. Now almost anything makes me cry. Like thinking how old one of my murder victims would be now, or seeing a boy in the shopping mall. If he's holding his father's hand, I think of Jimmie at age three. If the kid's bopping down the sidewalk with his shirt hanging out and hair over his ears, I think of Jimmie at thirteen. Any old Christmas carol will set me off. I'd cry at the grand opening of a super market. I'm getting too goddamn old for this job.

Billy

• • •

April 28, 1990 – Saturday

Dear Jerome:
This is a good news--bad news letter. The bad being our star witness (the guy who chased the suspect) is colorblind. Tulley Brown and I did a nighttime reenactment with him, using cars we borrowed from dealers, and the guy is hopeless.

He had told us the suspect got into a blue car, but after the reenactment, admitted he said that because the shade looked like his aunt's car and he's been told it's blue. I don't think I told you, there was no moon the night in question, the suspect had a watch cap on, and even though the witness got close to him on the lawn, he only saw the suspect's back.

Our victim had her eyes closed the whole time and who can blame her for that?

The good news is, we found a tire gauge in one of the streets the suspect ran in while being chased, the kind that clips onto your shirt pocket. Since east San Diego is the only area he'd hit twice, we found seventeen tire stores in that part of town, including used and recapping, retreading and repair. We eliminated gas stations. I don't know about Youngstown, but here they're all self-serve, and the next time an attendant checks my tires will be the first.

So our witness struck out on car color, but he runs four

miles a day, and said our suspect ran like a deer. He described the guy as lean, with a great stride. That description helped when we checked out tire store employees, because so many look like couch potatoes. Anyway, Tulley Brown and I hit all seventeen stores and used the old cop ruse of working a hit-and-run case.

You know, Jerome, these sociopath bastards stack all the odds their way when they're doing their dirty work, but the sweet part is, some things they can't control. The owner of one shop happens to be a police reservist, so we could level with him and not get burned. The owner remembers every dime he spends, and said he had to issue an employee a new tire gauge on a Monday in February. That Monday fit perfectly with our last case.

The employee turned out to be a guy named Orson Eldridge, aka Orson Hope, aka Orson Welliver, an ex-con out of Fresno for residential burglary who'd gotten out of the joint about three months before our first case. We did a quick workup on him and he lives with a very attractive young woman in her place on McClintock Street, which is nicely situated for our two east San Diego jobs. She's a dental hygienist.

The Fresno cases are what cops call hot-prowl burglaries, taking place when people are in the house asleep. It made us suspicious, because hot prowls are often sexually motivated. In case you're wondering, our experience tells us that Orson getting regular sex at home doesn't diminish him as a suspect. The shrinks can spend hours explaining that to you, but it all comes down to power and control over women.

We haven't approached Orson or anybody connected to him, because we have nothing, and if it is him, and we spook him, he'll back off, change his M.O. and find another way to terrorize women.

We've tailed him the last three Fridays since our last two jobs fell on that day, and we've been on him other nights as well. It may not be Orson, but it's nice having somebody to work.

So long for now,

Billy

P.S. The lab guys are talking about something called DNA, and tell us if this Orson is our suspect, we'll be able to make him. They say DNA is a genetic fingerprint, whatever that means. We'll take anything we can get, because the damn clock is ticking.

• • •

June 23, 1990 – Saturday

Dear Jerome:
This time I bring only good news. For one thing, Tulley Brown passed the sergeants test, so I'll be losing him. Glad for Tulley but hate to think of breaking in a new partner.

I thought you'd like to know we caught our suspect and yep, it turned out to be our boy, Orson. It only took a few weeks of surveillance to know we were looking at the right guy. Most of the time when he left the apartment his girlfriend would be with him, and he'd drive directly to the restaurant or theater or store or wherever. But alone, he'd be all over the place. Usually to the store to pick up smokes (our victim told us the suspect reeked of tobacco). He'd cruise up and down residential streets, slow enough to see everything but not slow enough to attract attention.

We worked the surveillances using a minimum of five undercover cars. There is one cardinal rule of surveillance. Your suspect may not have moved for hours, but as soon as you put an open can of soda on the dashboard, or spread a pizza on your lap, the son of a bitch will fire up his engine.

Tulley Brown and I made the rounds of patrol lineups and detective offices, looking for lady cops who fit the profile of our victims. We had experimented with men cops dressed like women, but that was like trying to disguise an elephant by putting sunglasses on it.

Jerome, can you imagine the guts it takes to walk down a dark street, knowing a guy with a knife who's murdered five women is going to jump out at you from behind and put you on the ground. We can't mike the women up to hear us. Of course I had arranged tight cover, and Tulley told our decoys, if he jumps out at you, we'll be on him like dew on a June bug. But still.

Last night at exactly 9:00 at night he and his sweetie got home from a Sizzler Steak House. An hour later the lights went out, but we always stay till at least midnight. Near eleven he came out by himself and Bingo!

He cruised Mountain View Drive, so we put a lady cop from Juvenile out and he liked her right away. He parked on a side street two blocks north and hid in the bushes. We hid too, using earplugs so our handie-talkies couldn't be heard. Our decoy was twenty feet from him when a car full of teenagers drove by whooping and hollering, so Orson backed off. End of decoy #1.

On Orange Avenue we used a woman from Forgery, and I swear, he was five seconds from jumping her when the last city bus of the night made a stop across the street. That ended the work night for decoy #2.

Then it appeared he intended to go home, but he made the block twice on Landis Street, so we put out a rookie from Patrol named Ginny Backus. My heart was pounding so loud I figured he'd hear it.

He hid behind a Eugenia hedge running perpendicular to the sidewalk, but Ginny didn't know what we knew. When she got three steps past him he jumped out, got her in kind of a choke hold with his arm, knife in his free hand, dragging her onto the lawn.

But Ginny was still on her feet, and Orson must have heard our feet pounding because eight of us moved in on him. You could tell he was making up his mind whether to run, but by then we were almost on him.

He kept his arm around Ginny's neck and put the blade right under her chin, screaming for us to back away. We put the brakes on and started talking to him.

I told him he wasn't going anywhere, just put down the knife and let's keep things simple. After ten minutes of talking, Orson got the idea he was running the show, and that's when Tulley Brown gave him a good look at Tulley's .44 magnum.

Tulley said to Orson, quit squirming, I can't get a clean shot at your head. Orson said, you don't dare take a chance, I'll cut her throat. Tulley moved real slowly, got to about five feet from them, and aimed over his rear sight just like at the pistol range.

Ginny Backus put her head down, slumped so she became dead weight, and yelled, shoot the fucker!

When Ginny said that Orson screamed you don't dare, you don't dare, his knife still on her throat. He'd been watching too much TV, because those turned out to be his last six words. Tulley cranked one off and put it right through the hem of the watch cap, between his eyes. Orson died before he crashed face up on the lawn, then Ginny Backus spun around and kicked him in the balls three times. I think I forgot to put that on the report.

After the medical examiner finished, we went down to the station and did our reports. Then, after the shooting team and Internal Affairs interviewed everybody, Ginny and the surveillance crew went to Bernie's. I even joined them. For iced tea. First time I'd been in there since I went on the wagon.

Jerome. It used to be, after making a case like this, I'd be on a tremendous high as soon as the jail door slammed. But not this time. Maybe nothing will ever be the same.

Billy

P.S. Orson must be comparing pitchforks with his new friends and telling them how important it is to hang onto their tire gauges.

P.P.S. Boy, did I get my ass chewed by Jack Hackett. He said

next time I go into Bernie's, I may as well bring an axe with
me and hand it to the bartender, then lean over and put my
face on the counter so the bartender can do it in one swing.
Jack said a guy like me is cutting my head off when I sit
around a gin mill.

• • •

August 15, 1990 – Wednesday

Dear Jerome:
Tulley Brown will make sergeant in November, so I'll be
breaking in some other poor bastard who wants to spend sixteen years of his life looking at dead bodies. Yes, Jerome, I've
been in Homicide since August of 1974. If I can't get pumped
up after we put Orson Eldridge six feet under, what will get
me excited? Nothing feels right. Last week we worked a wife-
doesn't-like-her-husband-any-more murder, and as we arrested
her, Sergeant Billy Considine forgot to impound her diary. In
it she had spelled out how she planned to drill hubby with the
family shotgun on the pretense of mistaking him for a burglar.
By the time I realized it and tore back to the house, her lawyer's
team had been through the place. Surprise! No diary.

What other news? Oh, yeah, my old partner Otto Kos didn't
get his wish about dying in the middle of a trout stream. But he
got second best. Otto had a massive heart attack tying bass flies
at his kitchen table. So RIP Otto, and thanks for everything.

Let's see, last week Desert Shield troops took off for Saudi
Arabia because Iraq invaded Kuwait? Jerome, if this thing isn't
all about oil, then as Uncle Denny would say, I'll kiss your ass
at the entrance to Mill Street Park.

Billy

• • •

September 1, 1990 – Saturday

Jerome, You Sneaky Rascal:
Exactly five minutes ago, Jimmie shook hands with me, said goodnight, and closed my front door behind him.

I was stunned when he phoned a couple of hours ago. I'd been sitting around wondering what in hell I was going to do with my evening. He asked if he could come to the house for a few minutes. Of course I told him yes, come ahead. Then I started shaking.

When I answered the doorbell we stood looking awkwardly at each other, then I let him in and we took seats on opposite sides of the living room. Me in the leather chair by the patio door.

Except for that time seven months ago when I saw him from a distance in the hospital cafeteria, I hadn't seen him in nine years--when he came to the house right after Janet died. It turns out he'd seen me interviewed on TV several times.

Jimmie got right to it. He said as far as he and I were concerned, if he had it to do again, he'd do some things differently. I said, me too. Then he let the conversation drop for a bit.

Jerome, twenty-nine years ago tonight I was painting his bedroom, the night before he was born. But I decided not to mention that. You have to understand I walked on egg shells the whole visit, afraid I'd mess something up.

He's in the second year of that long surgical internship and residency, and he said things are going well. I mentioned that I hadn't had a drink or a smoke in ten years but for some reason that didn't seem to surprise him.

He turned down my offer of coffee or a soda pop, and I thought he was getting ready to leave. Then Jimmie said he had never heard the story about cotton candy at the Del Mar Fair—how I had written his mother a speeding ticket.

He got up and looked out the sliding glass door. He's so tall, Jerome. Then he said, a package came to me at the hospital last week from Uncle Jerome, and when I opened it, a bunch of letters tumbled out, all from you to Uncle Jerome, starting in 1958.

Jimmie told me about the note you wrote inviting him to read all or any of the letters. Well, somehow he'd found time to read every one, and he started telling me stuff in bits and pieces.

I don't know how long we talked, but his love for Janet came shining through. He said one of the things that influenced him to leave home was seeing what affect the infighting between he and I had on his mother. Jimmie said when Janet would run out of the room crying, he'd go into his room and bury his head in the pillow. He said neither of us was being fair to her.

I started to answer back about Janet but he raised his hand to hush me, so I let it drop. He got up again and went back to the same spot at the patio door and he said reading those letters from a cop made him understand me somewhat. Neither of us said anything for a while, then Jimmie said, I got to know you before you were a cop—was able to understand what police work does to a cop's soul.

Neither of us said anything for a long time, then Jimmie said, I read letters about how you'd talk to me while I was asleep after you'd come home working the night shift.

When he got up to go, he said, if I hadn't run off to Alaska, I'd never have had the solitude that came with working the pipeline, would never have searched my soul, would never have become a physician.

At the door, I went for it and said, I know you're busy, but maybe we could grab a cup some time. Jimmie said, that would be good. That's when we shook hands.

Jerome, thanks to you, the world looks like a different place. I love you.

Billy

• • •

October 2, 1990 – Tuesday

Dear Jerome:

What a difference a month makes. Ten days ago Jimmie and I got together at the hospital for that cup of coffee. It only lasted two minutes because his pager went off. He apologized and ran toward the elevator, but we agreed to try again the next day—same time—same place.

And that one worked out fine. We met for almost an hour. Talked a little about where my head was back in his teen years, and where his was. He said the letters brought back a lot of good memories; that he learned what made me tick. He said he shipped the letters back to you as promised.

I told him I was burned out at work, and Jimmie said, why don't you pull the pin? It really startled me, Jerome, and I said something like pass the sugar, then Jimmie said, you know the old story, you think you'll be missed, but stick your finger in a bucket of water, then remove it, still the same amount of water. It was like he wanted me to retire.

When it was time to end our visit, a couple of doctors sat down as we were getting up. And Jimmie introduced me, said to them, this is my Dad, Sergeant Billy Considine--he works homicide.

Jerome, I had my car door open before I realized he'd called me Dad. I wasn't worth a damn the rest of the day.

When I got home from work that night, I thought about the department. Lord, I've got thirty-two years in. Knocking down something like forty-five grand a year plus overtime. I don't even look at my pay stubs. And the house is long paid off. I couldn't get to sleep and calculated my retirement would come to something like thirty-five hundred bucks a month.

As I was getting drowsy I thought about Jimmie's finger-in-the-bucket crack. But I'll tell you this, there are a lot of guys in Folsom and San Quentin and Soledad who know my finger's been in their bucket

When I woke up, I drove out to Sunset Cliffs. The water was like glass, and I stayed there a long time. Then I went down to the retirement office and filled out the paperwork. While I was filling in the blanks I remembered how Jack Hackett and I, a couple of strangers, stood next to each other at the counter filling out applications at the old Civic Center on Harbor Drive.

So that was that. I made the retirement effective within five days. As soon as the word got around I got offers for pretty good jobs, but why that would appeal to me I do not know. Besides, I'd be taking a job away from someone who needs the $$.

Jimmie was pleased when I called him, and encouraged me not to make any other big decisions for a while. He said don't be selling the house or buying a herd of giraffes.

Yesterday I went down to the station for the last time. Didn't go in, just stood back and kind of hung out on the sidewalk. A couple of young patrol cops who didn't know me from Adam were having a smoke and I heard them complaining how the rookies today aren't very savvy. It made me think of Frank Runyon putting up with me. Frank said police work is drama without a script.

Then I drifted over toward the main entrance where the memorial is. Dedicated to those cops "Who Walked The Point."

I read over the names. Ten of them got murdered on my homicide watch. Hell, I never liked this new building anyway, so I felt okay turning around and walking away.

But I did pause next to my car for one last look. A lot of memories started washing over me. I saw the faces of my academy classmates and realized what special people they were. In our rookie year they'd load five of us into a transportation car to take us out to our walking beats, the whole carload acting confident, but not knowing what in hell we were doing. It's a good thing the citizens didn't know.

Now those classmates who are still alive have grey hair and lines in their faces, some of them with a head start on getting pretty sick.

I worked with wonderful people, Jerome. My special pals

were people of large talent and small ego. I loved them all. I hope they loved me back.

Billy

• • •

February 27, 1991 – Wednesday

Dear Jerome:
How did I ever have time to be a cop?
Tomorrow I'm driving to Yuma, Arizona, which is four hours away and just over the state line where I'll grab a motel and spend a few days sitting in the sun watching the Padres work out and play intra-squad games. Pitchers and catchers have already reported. When I leave Yuma I'll return to my "work," but more about that later.

Jimmie sends his regards. After a few more coffee meetings, we had dinner at an Italian place near the hospital. When he talks about work his eyes light up, but even when he tries putting it in laymen's terms, it's hard to follow. He was tickled to hear his Aunt Amy had been appointed to the U.S. Court of Appeals for the Sixth Circuit. She's a helluva judge and I'm proud of her.

One heartwarming thing came out of the dinner. He agrees I should take the money Janet and I had set aside for his college and put it into a college trust for the kid he expects to have some day. What would make Janet happier than that I do not know. How Jimmie has time to date the ladies given his schedule is beyond me, but he's managing it.

Jerome, there are scads of little leagues in San Diego, including a few in the lower-income neighborhoods. But little league is very structured, and there are kids in Southeast San Diego and Logan Heights whose families aren't into that culture.

I got talking about this to a friend who's with Boys' Clubs of San Diego, and as a result I have an unpaid position and bounce back and forth between two playgrounds coordinating ball games. Most all of the kids are black plus a few Latinos. No uniforms. No scorebook. No age limit. I bring two duffel bags full of equipment, choose up sides and away we go. Just like when you and I were kids--play until dark or until too many players have to go home.

More and more kids are coming around because word's getting out. And the thing is, two minutes after the last out is made, nobody cares who won or lost. Some of these kids are blue chip athletes. I've got a shortstop who fields like Ozzie Smith and hits like Jim Rice, but he can't stay out of the grease at school. Tell Mom since I've been figuring on a trip home soon, I'll tie it in with the wedding of Johnny Angelini's boy. That way I'll get to see a lot of old faces at the church and the hall. Jerome, did you know it broke Johnny's heart that he never got offered a pro contract, because he always thought he was a better ballplayer than me. Hell, maybe he was.

There is one more thing. I've dated someone a few times. A widow ten years younger than me who's a counselor with Social Services. In fact, we met when I showed up with my shortstop at a session that the Juvenile Court had directed him to attend. I may or may not see her again. I have to go now.

Billy

• • •

March 20, 1991 – Wed

Dear Jerome:
How things could be going better I do not know. Jimmie has been out to the playground twice to watch games and meet my kids and had to put on his doctor's hat when there was a collision at second on a double play. Boy, is he good with kids.

We meet for lunch pretty regularly now, most always at the

hospital, and I'm getting a little tuned in to just what he does there. Our visits aren't all smooth because a couple of times something from back-when popped up and it got awkward, but we work through it.

I'm not going to fly when I come to Youngstown next month (no need to tell the following to Mom--she'd give me an earful), but will ride my new motorcycle. Well, not new-new. It's a 1970 BMW 750cc R75/6. The way you remember engine stuff you've figured out it's the bike I drooled over with Janet so many years ago.

Jerome, I've never really gotten a good look at our country. When we traveled in the minor leagues I was sleeping on the bus and on extraditions who sees anything at 35,000 feet? The sergeant in charge of training motorcycle cops agreed to put me through the paces and I'm doing good though the sarge said when you get too comfortable is when you'll go down.

I'll tell you about this woman I've been dating, though not too much or you'll get the idea I'm overly interested.

She's an Arky and sixteen years ago, her husband, who was a Navy commander, got killed flying a F-4 Phantom over a California desert on a training mission. He'd been stationed at NAS Miramar here which a movie buff like you remembers as Tom Cruise's Top Gun school. The hell of it is, the guy had flown combat missions in A-4 Skyhawks in Vietnam and never got a scratch.

She said after her husband died she refused to look beyond their seven-year-old daughter's graduation from college, so she went back to San Diego State and got her degree--her title is something like LCW or LCSW, I'll have to check on that. They had just the one kid who recently graduated from Stanford and since that happened she said she's taking life day by day.

I think she's very attractive, 5-5 with light brown hair and brown eyes. She said she needs to lose ten pounds but I think she's just right. I watch her at court hearings, and figured out that when she smiles inappropriately it means she's mad and the more she smiles the madder she's getting. She's fun to be with, never tells jokes as such but likes to laugh at her own wisecracks. Even though in her work she sees mostly negative stuff she manages to look at the bright side of life.

We go to lots of movies and antique stores because antique furniture is one of her self-described four passions. The other three are her daughter, her work and certain jazz pianists. She doesn't smoke or drink so how about that?

So there, now you know a little about her.

Billy

P.S. Her name is Naomi. Nice, don't you think?

• • •

May 5, 1991 – Sunday

Dear Jerome:

It's Sunday evening and I'm pooped! Rode back into San Diego yesterday ending my big trip and because today is Cinco De Mayo, Naomi and I went to a celebration downtown and another in Old Town. In between dances we stuffed down as much Mexican food as we could and still shoehorn ourselves into the car.

We had arranged with Jimmie for he and a date to meet us at the Bazaar Del Mundo and I'd been feeling strange. He had not met Naomi and I wondered what his reaction would be to my holding hands with someone other than his mother.

It went fine. We spent an hour talking and knocking down taquitos topped with guacamole. Afterwards Naomi said Jimmie is gorgeous.

Yesterday, when I hit the San Diego city limits I rode straight to Naomi's and she seemed distant. I thought maybe she'd brought work home with her, but after a while it was evident something else was bothering her. It took a pry bar to get it out, but she said when I'd phoned and told her I was extending my trip by a couple of weeks, Naomi figured I was saying our relationship is over. How she got that idea I do not know.

The more I talked and tried to explain the more confused it all got, and finally Naomi said, stop talking, let's take a walk.

Everything turned out fine.

The two weeks in Youngstown were too wonderful to describe and I'm sorry you had to be in Cleveland on business the last three days and miss the wedding and not see me ride off. Of course you get to go to receptions and wakes frequently, but for me it was like stepping back in time.

When everybody moved from the church to the hall I sat and talked with all the guys. There was Giczy and Accardo and Hogan and Simmons. Then, who comes storming in but the three bad Czechs, Janik, Klapka and Soucek. They're as loopy as they were when we were kids. That made eight of us at the table and we had a great time but could hardly hear each other what with the younger set dancing and partying.

San Diego is a transient place and sitting around that table made me realize how many Youngstown people never leave home. They don't think they're missing a damn thing and you know what? Maybe they're right.

And Johnny Angelini. I talked to him when he wasn't making a toast to his son and the bride or banging on the table yelling for a foxtrot to be played or pouring somebody a boilermaker. Johnny looked like an old man and all he wanted to talk about was the mills closing. His lungs are full of cinder dust and I swear he wheezes louder than he talks.

When I was worn out and talked out and ready to go I hugged and hand-shaked my way across the room, then took the outside stairs down to the parking lot. Just as I reach the bottom I hear the commotion and look up. Harold Murphy's kid is making like he's going to jump off the roof. He had a bottle of beer in each hand and he's singing A Nation Once Again. I screamed no, no, don't do it, don't do it. I'm waving my arms to get his attention and I'm still waving when he decides he can fly. Jerome, it's a thirty-foot drop if it's an inch. Augie Donatti's boy drops his own bottle and staggers over to try and catch him.

I did what I could, then stood by until the ambulance took them away. Donatti had one eye open and Murphy wanted to know if anybody'd gotten a picture, so I figured they weren't busted up too bad.

Every day I was there the differences between San Diego and Youngstown kept jumping out at me. I don't think I ever took my sun glasses out of my pocket, and I was conscious there were no beaches or much choice of movies or big time sports. And not that much of a restaurant selection. San Diego must have a couple of hundred Chinese places and even more Mexican joints. In Aunt Hazel's yard I looked at the sky and used the word dingy so Mom snapped at me. Youngstown could shut down their Chamber of Commerce as long as Mom's alive.

The day you left for Cleveland, Amy and I stood on the rim of the valley, in the same spot we'd stood as kids. We talked about the days you watched flames jump against the sky and could smell the roasting iron ore and look down on the white clapboard row houses on the hills above the mills. Amy said do you want to go see the remains of the dead? I hesitated a minute, threw a stone down the hill, then said, yeah, what the hell, let's do it.

We got in the car and made our way down and noticed the row houses were mostly boarded up. Then Amy took me over to where they'd dynamited the Ohio Works. Just a damn war zone. A couple of scarred up old desks and file cabinets laying on their side among the rubble.

I was shocked at the Brier Hill Works, it's just a shell. It was so odd, staring up at the top of the ten-story blast furnace but not hearing a sound. Amy waited outside because she'd seen it once, but I went in and walked through the Blow Room which was eerie, then found a locker room. It's like the world had just stopped. A few hard hats and gloves and shoes laying around, but everything mangled. Pants and shirts on the floor all rumpled like a guy had gone out the window because the husband just came home. Stepping through cement dust and broken glass there were even two or three lonely playing cards scattered around on the floor.

That did it for me and I said to Amy, take me downtown to Federal Plaza so I can see the monument to the steel workers. Even that turned out to be depressing. We got out of the car and the first thing I saw was The Paramount theater all boarded up with a for-sale sign stuck to it. The monument was nice, but the bad Czechs told me everybody hates it because it reminds them of when times were good.

But Jerome, I gotta tell you, walking around those wonderful tree-shaded streets made me realize you find very few like that in San Diego. And the solid old homes looking like they'll last forever. I got nostalgic more than once, just seeing somebody reading The Vindicator, or walking by a particular house or store that made me remember something very sweet.

One of the highlights of the trip wasn't planned at all. I was strolling down Hartford Avenue over by the cemetery and saw this old lady fighting to keep her balance, all stooped over with a death grip on her cane. I nodded to her and was a couple of steps past when I heard this voice say "Billy Considine."

Jerome, it was Mrs. McGill. She gave me that same stare she'd given me a hundred times and said, I didn't think you were ever coming home. She said if I wasn't the worst English student she'd ever had, I was a close second. Then she gave me a hug as best she could and said, I'm proud of what you did with your life, Billy. I guess I must have looked surprised because she said, I keep up with all my kids, though when they move as far away as California I have to use binoculars.

What a grand ten minutes we spent together. They ought to put up monuments to the Mrs. McGills of the world.

Anyway, the day I left Youngstown I was sitting at a long signal light and decided, what the hell, why don't I detour over to Iowa and see Culpepper, how many more chances will I have? I don't know if I told you but Culpepper had gone on strike with the other air traffic controllers and lost his job when Reagan fired them. So Culpepper got it in his head to take flying lessons and now he's a crop duster. I stayed with him for two days, met his partner who I liked a lot, and even flew the fields with him. Quite an experience. Banking and turning and all the time a Chopin polonaise piping away and making all the farmland below look structured and green.

Culpepper said life is good. Like me, he keeps in touch with Jack Hackett and told me Jack just published a second book on coping with alcoholism.

The trip will stay with me forever, Jerome, and I thank you for the large part you played in welcoming me home. Now it's time to grab some sleep.

Love to everybody,

Billy

P.S. Reading over my letter maybe I was too hard on Youngstown. Riding across Arizona, it struck me that as nice as San Diego is, nothing beats sitting under the arbor in Mill Creek Park munching a baked ham sandwich and sour pickle from Isary's.

• • •

June 27, 1991 –Thursday

Dear Jerome:
A reporter I've known for many years got wind of my playground work and did a piece in the Sunday paper. Next day the Padres volunteered a duffel bag full of batting practice balls and some catchers gear. This is still the pure joy of sandlot ball and some of my kids can flat out play.

A few days ago I'm hitting ground balls to my infielders and notice a Mexican man and a kid standing behind first base--I figure it's a new ballplayer. When I finish, they walk over, the man smiles and the kid who's maybe twelve or thirteen says, can I play?

I told him sure, anybody can play at this ball park and he says I have a glove and he holds it up for me to see. The man is still smiling and I look the kid over closely and I said, let me see that glove again. He hands it to me and I look at the glove and then I look at the man who says it's good to see you again, Billy.

Jerome. It was Hector Morales and he says that's the glove your wife bought for me. I almost lost it right there behind home plate.

I fell all over myself apologizing for not looking him up but Hector said he could have done his part as well. He'd seen the story in the paper about me.

So I told him about Janet, then learned Hector is an architect and did the major work on a building in the financial district. We promised to get together--no fooling this time. The kid looks just like Hector when he followed me around Unit 51's beat and as they were leaving the kid says, it was nice meeting you, Billy.

Well, now I know how Jimmie feels about Naomi and me. Last month he said 'Dad, I'm buying you dinner at Mr. A's.' I asked why such a fancy place and said the hospital was fine with me, but he insisted so I met him there. Jerome, I walk off the elevator and get escorted to a table and what do I see? Jimmie and his date, Naomi, and Naomi's daughter who's down from San Jose for a few days.

All this for my 59th birthday which I'd forgotten about. Jimmie planned it and I didn't even know he knew how to get in touch with Naomi. It was a beautiful evening and a week later she had Jimmie and I to her place for dinner. So how do you like them apples?

Speaking of Naomi, I'd been real happy with the way things were going for us, then one night I'd done a roast on the grill at my house and while we were clearing the dishes, she said I'm making a trip to Arkansas, how about coming with me to meet my parents. I almost dropped a plate so I said isn't that rushing things a bit and Naomi spun around and said don't fall apart, Considine, I'm not proposing to you.

Well, what could I say to that so next thing we were at the airport piling onto a plane for Little Rock. We rented a car and just took our time going north, making it about a four-hour drive through the Ozark National Forest and on into her town, Harrison, which is very picturesque with a lot of pasture land and trees and hills.

Naomi's mother and father are pushing eighty and treated me nicely, except they couldn't let the religious thing drop. See, they had sent Naomi to this small Christian college just over the border into Oklahoma and told her go and hear from someone other than her parents that the Bible is the word of God—told her the goal of this college is to educate the head, the heart and the hand.

The hell of it was, her folks had never even taken a look at this college, just put her on the bus and said come back with your diploma. Anyway, Naomi attended for two years, intending to get a bachelor's degree in family and human services. But she'd met her husband-to-be who was two grades ahead of her, and they got married the day after he graduated. Most of his classmates went on the customary mission, but he headed into a Navy flight program and Naomi went with him to Pensacola, Florida.

But back to her folks. After sizing things up, I explained to them how I was raised Catholic but married Janet who was Baptist and how religion never got in the way. Next day her father embarrassed hell out of Naomi, saying to me, well, now that your wife is dead are you turning back to Catholicism? Naomi started to jump down his throat, but I said, let me take this one, and I told the old guy that he was getting far afield, that Naomi and I had lived over a hundred years between us and neither of us were in a tizzy about it and furthermore we had no idea what lay ahead.

That made Naomi's mother clear her throat and say it's time for a little drink, so then I had to announce that I don't use the stuff. The two of them rattled ice cubes around and took the edge off while Naomi and I slugged down Seven-Up.

Naomi and I looked at each other and decided to cut the visit short a couple of days, so we went on up to Branson, Missouri which is only thirty miles from Harrison. I guess Branson is challenging Nashville as the country music capitol. It's a hoot. We saw some good entertainment, all the while wondering how so many tourists could get crammed into such a small burg. Jerome, every retiree with a pulse has an RV and travels to Branson. They see a couple of shows, then head for Florida or California, right turn signal blinking all the way.

I'm so busy and my mind is spinning about so many things that I forget how good life is.

So long for now,

Billy

P.S. Jimmie and I were driving home from the dinner at Naomi's and I told him how proud I would have been to pin his badge on had he become a cop. He looked surprised and I said, Jimmie, my eye sights a lot better these days. He said, that makes two of us, Dad.

• • •

August 15, 1991 – Thursday

Dear Jerome:

Sit yourself down in your old easy chair by the Victrola and take a pull on a cold bottle of Iron City because I have news. Your kid brother just put a first-and-last-month rent check in the mail for Mr. Lambeckie because I'm moving back to Youngstown. Mr. L. is giving me his place on Evanston which means I'll be able to pick up the scent when Mom is cooking a stuffed rib roast.

How did this all come about? Recently, Naomi reminded me of something that I think I told you, that after she lost her husband she survived by thinking of life as a day-by-day proposition. We were sitting on a bench in Balboa Park close enough to the Organ Pavilion to hear some classical.

After Naomi said the day-by-day thing she said, Billy, you and I have never really talked about your wife and my husband. Well, that jump-started us, so we spent hour after hour, me doing Janet-talk and Naomi telling me all about her pilot.

That led to examining relationships in general, a strength of someone like Naomi but certainly not a strength of mine. We agreed we loved each other, we loved spending time together with someone we trusted and didn't have to put on airs for, that we were great friends as well as lovers.

Naomi said, Billy, I feel silly about having been insecure about us when you were on your motorcycle trip, I want to go back to day-by-day which worked so beautifully for me during the years that I needed a formula.

I told her day-by-day sounded right to me, that maybe neither of us needed to hear the bells on the hill ringing, that just enjoying somebody and being able to count on them was enough.

Naomi said that for the last four months I'd talked a whole lot about Youngstown and she sensed I wanted to go home. I said, like go home on a visit again, and she said, no, like go home for good.

A few days later we were parked at Sunset Cliffs. Youngstown had been on my mind full time for seventy-two hours, and I told her I think I wanted to move there. She smiled and said, I think that would make you happy, Billy.

She was shading her eyes from the sun when I said why don't you go with me? I could tell it rattled her, so I said, don't fall apart, Naomi, I'm not proposing to you.

A week later we talked about memories that haunt us in San Diego. Naomi said every time she drives by the Naval air station and sees a jet land or take off her stomach knots.

Jerome, Naomi is coming to Youngstown with me. We decided we're not running away from anything in San Diego, rather looking at a new beginning.

Mom's first question will be, will they be married since they'll be living together under Mr. Lambecki's roof? The short answer is no, and let me handle explaining to Mom that Naomi and I don't know exactly what in hell we have, or what's down the road.

Oh, yeah, one more thing. Our kids! As we prepared to tell them Naomi and I convinced each other that we weren't really asking for their approval, but it was a little scary.

We needn't have worried. Her daughter broke into a mile-wide grin and hugged us, and Jimmie said what took you so long?

Well, Jerome, I guess I can quit buying stamps and you can quit looking for the mail, because with me and Naomi being two blocks away we can shout to one another. I'm looking forward to seeing the fall colors for the first time in forty years.

So I close with much love and with deep thanks for the kind of brother you are, and looking forward to playing catch among a thousand other things.

Billy

P.S. When I get home and get my bags unpacked I will definitely take your Victrola to an electronics shop and find somebody who can make it sing to you again.

ACKNOWLEDGMENTS

S TEVEN J. CASEY, wordsmith; Norm Stamper and the late Jon Blanton Standefer, who believed; and Mattie Catherine Sherman, my Forever Friend who made me get back to work.

ABOUT THE AUTHOR

Photo by Paul Scholtes

JACK MULLEN is a former Marine and retired San Diego Police Homicide sergeant. He earned a Bachelor of Science degree in Criminal Justice Administration from San Diego State University. He has published two previous novels: *In the Line of Duty* and *Behind the Shield.* Jack lives in Orange County, California.

www.CopWorldpress.com